My Side of the Story

Ian Rose Castro

Published in the United States by Every Rose Press.

Printed in the United States of America
ISBN 978-1-965839-00-3 (paperback)
Library of Congress Control Number: 2024921361

First U.S. Edition 2024

For my mom

All I can do is tell my side of the story and all you can do is tell yours. That's all anyone can really do.

Playlist

Track 1: "Astronaut" by Simple Plan

Track 2: "Everything is Alright" by Motion City Soundtrack

Track 3: "broken" by lovelytheband

Track 4: "Dance Dance Dance" by Astrid S

Track 5: "Hungover" by Kesha

Track 6: "Rumor Has It" by Adele

Track 7: "Way Less Sad" by AJR

Track 8: "Tonight, Tonight" by Hot Chelle Rae

Track 9: "Bad Blood" by Taylor Swift

Track 10: "Lost It All" by Black Veil Brides

Track 11: "Polygraph Eyes" by Yungblud

Track 12: "Human" by Christina Perri

Track 13: "If We Have Each Other" by Alec Benjamin

Track 14: "Forgive Me Friend" by Smith & Thell

Track 15: "Someone To You" by Banners

Track 16: "I Wanna Get Better" by Bleachers

Track 17: "The Story" by Conan Gray

Track 18: "Days" by the Kinks

Track 19: "Enemy" by Sandro Cavazza

Track 20: "You Won't Know Where You Stand" by Aquilo

Track 21: "Freaks" by Jordan Clarke

Track 22: "Bubbly" by Colbie Caillat

Track 23: "Maniac" by Conan Gray

Track 24: "i wanna be your girlfriend" by girl in red

Track 25: "Somewhere Else" by Razorlight

Track 26: "TALK ME DOWN" by Troye Sivan

Track 27: "Let Her Go" by Passenger

Track 28: "Older" by Sasha Alex Sloane

Track 29: "This Christmas (I'll Burn it to the Ground)" by Set It Off

Track 30: "Mess It Up" by Gracie Abrams

Track 31: "This Is The New Year" by A Great Big World

Track 32: "When You Love Someone" by James TW

Track 33: "Oh Well, Oh Well" by Mayday Parade

Track 34: "How Soon is Now?" by The Smiths

Track 35: "Whataya Want From Me" by Adam Lambert

Track 36: "I Like Me Better" by Lauv

Track 37: "It's My Party" by Lesley Gore

Track 38: "Introvert Party Club" by RODAN

Track 39: "Paradise" by Coldplay

Track 40: "All Good Things (Come To An End)" by Nelly Furtado

Track 41: "Speak Now" by Taylor Swift

Track 42: "Under Pressure" by David Bowie and Queen

Track 43: "Perfect" by Simple Plan

Track 44: "Go Your Own Way" by Fleetwood Mac

Track 45: "Ordinary World" by Duran Duran

Elena

1

Everything Will Be Okay

"I think you're going to really like it here, Elena. Woodview High is a very good school, right Jo?"

Jo doesn't respond. A few minutes earlier, she had slipped an AirPod into her ear and hidden it under her long, straight, blonde hair, so she probably hasn't heard a word her mom has said on this drive.

"There are a lot of extracurriculars too. I don't know what you're into, but I'm sure we can find something right up your alley." Mrs. Reilly rambles on and on, despite neither me nor Jo responding even once since we've gotten into the car. I know she means well, but I'm not up for small talk today (or maybe ever again).

"You have your class schedule, right? They're supposed to assign a student to show you around, but if you need anything else, just ask Jo. You'll help her out if she needs anything, won't you?"

Still no answer from either of us. You'd think she'd have caught on by now. Maybe she has and just prefers a one-sided conversation to a fully silent car ride.

We pull to a stop in front of a large brick building. Woodview High School. It doesn't look like anything special. Jo gets out of the car and slams the door, but I feel like I owe Mrs. Reilly a little more than that.

"Thank you for the ride, Mrs. Reilly," I say, as I unbuckle my seatbelt.

"It's no problem," she replies, "and please, call me Meg."

I nod, not quite ready for that level of familiarity yet. As I reach for the door handle, she speaks again.

"I know you're not psyched about moving here," she adds, "and rightfully so, of course. But if there's anything I can do to make things a little easier, just let me know."

I nod again. I probably should say something, but it seems like too much effort, so instead I give a half-hearted smile and exit the car.

Jo was far enough ahead of me that by the time I enter the school, she's nowhere to be found. Not that it really matters. She has already informed me that at school, we don't know each other. So contrary to her mother's belief, I'm on my own here.

The main office is easy enough to find, but somehow I doubt the rest of the day will go as smoothly. I approach the front desk where a secretary is sitting behind a name placard that reads *Ms. Goldberg.*

She hardly looks up from her computer as she asks, "Can I help you?"

"I'm supposed to get a tour or something," I say, feeling abnormally awkward. "I'm new here."

"Elena Flores?" a voice behind me calls. I turn around to see a boy who looks older than me, probably an upperclassman. He's got dark brown curls sticking out from under a backwards baseball cap and is at least a full head taller than me. I look up at him and he looks down at me. His eyes wander like he's examining every inch of my body. I involuntarily tighten.

"Yeah, that's me."

He extends his hand. "I'm Levi Haddad. I'm supposed to give you a tour of the school. "He's looking into my eyes now, and I realize I may have been examining him in the same way.

"Oh, right," I stammer, "nice to meet you."

"Should we get started?"

I nod slightly. "I guess so."

He leads me out of the office and down a long hallway. The walls are covered with plaques with photos of people whom I assume are former students. I wonder what they all did to be honored in this way and how there could possibly be so many alumni who've done noteworthy things.

"Your first period class is this way," he informs me as we turn the corner.

"You know my schedule?"

He nods. "They gave me a copy. I don't know why your Spanish class is being taught in the History wing this year, but that's the classroom right there."

I glance into the room that he's gesturing toward. The walls are decorated with maps of different regions of the world and there's a poster with the Preamble to the Constitution on it. It certainly looks more like a Social Studies classroom than a Spanish classroom.

"I had Señora Maldonado freshman year. She makes the class super easy."

I laugh at his comment, but when he looks at me with a raised brow, I realize how rude that must seem. "Sorry. I'm only laughing 'cause I don't really need an easy Spanish class," I explain, "or any Spanish class for that matter."

"Right. Flores. That makes sense."

We keep walking. He goes over which hallways are designated for which subjects. I try my best to pay attention, but, honestly, it's a struggle. I don't care where the library or the gym or the cafeteria is. My life has been turned completely upside down, and there's nothing I can do about it. It's hard to feel like anything else matters.

"Elena?"

I look up at him. We've stopped walking and he's staring at me like he's expecting me to answer a question I don't remember being asked.

He repeats himself slowly. "Do you have any questions?"

"I don't think so," I lie, knowing damn well I have no idea how to get around here. "Thank you."

"I feel like I did a real lousy job on this tour." He says it less to me and more just into the air. "Do you want me to walk you back to your first period class?"

"You don't have to."

"Do you have any idea how to get there on your own?"

I hesitate. I don't, but I don't want to admit it.

He starts to laugh. "There's my answer. C'mon, I'll show you." He starts to walk back in the direction we came from and I reluctantly follow. "So where are you from?"

"Miami," I answer, barely audible.

"Nice. Probably would've been easier if you moved over the summer rather than starting a month into the year."

"Well, what fun is it doing things the easy way?"

He smiles in a way so that only one side of his lips turn upwards. "Fair enough. So why'd you move here?"

I knew people would ask me this, but I was dreading it. I swallow and give my prepared answer, "My dad lives here." It's not a lie. It's just not the whole truth, exactly.

"That's cool. So you wanted to be closer to your dad?"

This question was a bit harder to navigate. I didn't exactly want to. I didn't have a choice. But I don't need to reveal all my baggage to a total stranger.

"What's with all the questions?" I snap.

"I'm just making small talk," he mutters. "I was under the impression that it was a normal thing to do."

I try not to roll my eyes. He's just trying to be nice. It's not his fault I don't want to be here. "Sorry, I'm just not in the mood to chat."

He shrugs. "Fine. We can walk in silence."

I want to feel bad. He's being perfectly nice, but I can't really bring myself to feel anything at all. I suppose it's better to stay silent. I really shouldn't use up all of my social battery before classes even start.

When we arrive back downstairs, Levi wishes me good luck and gives me a half-hearted smile before leaving me to face the school day on my own. I take a seat in the back row, hoping fewer people will look at me if I sit there. It doesn't exactly work. Nearly everyone stares at me as they enter the room. A few even whisper and glance back at me once they sit down. I try to ignore it.

"Buenos días clase." Señora Maldonado stands at the front of the class in a flowing, dark green dress. She has long, wavy, dark brown hair, which falls almost to her hips. It kind of reminds me of my mom's. "¿Quién quiere empezar hoy?"[1]

No one responds and she sighs, beginning to walk up and down the aisles. "I guess I'll just have to pick someone to start." In a singsongy voice, she asks, "Who should our first victim be?" She stops next to a slender boy with baby blue hair and slams her hand lightly on his desk. "Señor Hayashi, ¿quieres hablar?"[2]

The boy scrunches up his face but nods anyway.

"Muchas gracias!" She leans on his desk and flashes a smile. She seems young for a teacher. I can't imagine she's any older than her late twenties. She definitely seems to have the energy to support that theory. "Qué hicieron este fin de semana pasada?"[3]

He speaks softly and slowly. "El fin de semana pasada, yo fui al cine." It's clear he has prepared this

---

[1] She tells the class "good morning" and asks who would like to start today.
[2] She asks "Mr. Hayashi" if he would like to speak.
[3] She thanks him and asks him what he did last weekend.

answer in advance on the off chance that Señora Maldonado chose him to pick on today.[4]

"Qué divertido," she continues. "¿Con quién fuiste?"[5]

He blinks. She awaits his answer, but none comes. "¿Repita por favor?"[6]

This class is going to be torture. I could've answered these questions in Kindergarten, but these students clearly have no idea what's going on. Señora Maldonado seems to recognize this. Granted, she has a slight accent, but this is still pretty basic stuff.

Señora Maldonado decides to help him out. "¿Fuiste con amigos? ¿O con tu familia? ¿O con tu novia?"[7] A few students around the room snicker and she looks around unamused. "¿Qué es chistoso?"[8]

Most students take that as their cue to shut up, but the boy sitting in front of me decides it's his time to shine. "Ren no tener un novia," he starts to chuckle again as he speaks, "porque Ren está un ... how do you say *faggot* in Spanish?"[9]

The class laughs a little more. The blue-haired boy, who I now know is named Ren, puts his head down and his leg starts rapidly shaking. I get the feeling this isn't the first time someone's called him that word.

---

[4] He answers that he went to the movies last weekend.
[5] She says, "how fun" and asks him who he went with.
[6] He asks her to repeat the question.
[7] She asks him if he went with friends, family, or his girlfriend.
[8] She asks what's funny.
[9] He says (incorrectly) that Ren doesn't have a girlfriend because he's gay.

"There's no need for that kind of language here," Señora Maldonado scolds him, in English, suddenly losing her friendly demeanor.

"I'm only asking for educational purposes."

People continue laughing.

I don't know what comes over me. It is not something I'd usually do, and it's definitely not a good way to fly under the radar, but I speak up anyway.

"Maybe instead of trying to learn homophobic slurs, you should focus on learning the basics first." All eyes turn to me and I instantly regret saying anything, but I can't stop now. "It's not *tener*, it's *tiene*. It's not *un*, it's *una*. It's not *está*, it's *es*. And it's not funny to anyone except you, porque eres un idiota."[10]

A bunch of students chuckle again, but now it's directed toward the homophobic bully, instead of the blue-haired boy. They may not have understood all of it, but they can at least recognize *idiota*.

Our teacher looks oddly pleased and it makes me smile. "That's right, Señorita. Muy bien. Moving on."[11]

She returns to the front of the room and the boy in front of me glances over his shoulder. I glare at him until he turns around and then I hear him very quietly whisper, "Bitch."

I can't help but smile. This definitely isn't the way to make a good first impression, but it was worth it. I

---

[10] She corrects his mistakes and calls him an idiot.
[11] She says, "That's right, miss. Very good."

meet eyes with Ren for a second, but he quickly looks away.

I wonder how often this kind of stuff happens here.

2

Fake It Till You Make It

I walk home alone. Mrs. Reilly—or Meg, I guess—apologized about a billion times this morning for being unable to pick me up after school, but I assured her that it was fine. Except now, I'm only about a block away from the school and I realize I have no idea how to get back to the house. Jo had to stay after school for some rich white people shit called "color guard," so I'm by myself and every street in the suburbs looks the same. I pull out my phone and type the address into my GPS.

"Hey! Hey you!" It doesn't register that this voice is calling out to me until I feel a tap on my shoulder. I fling my head over my shoulder to see Ren, the blue-haired boy from Spanish class. "Sorry," he says, "didn't mean to startle you or anything. I just wanted to thank you for earlier, you know?"

"No problem." I look back down at my phone.

"Did you just transfer into that class? I don't think I've seen you before."

"I'm new to Woodview," I explain. "Just moved here."

"Oh wow! Welcome then."

"Thanks." I press start on the GPS and my phone shouts out the first direction. I quickly turn off the sound, but he's already heard.

"I'm heading that way too. Wanna walk together?"

"I guess so?" It's more of a question than an answer, but he looks happy. We start walking and he speaks a mile a minute, barely giving me a chance to respond, but I don't have much to contribute anyway.

We turn onto my block and I say, "Well, this is my street." He gives me a funny look.

"We live on the same block. Small world."

"Small town," I reply.

He laughs, although I don't think I've actually said anything funny. This *is* a small town.

"Woodview is a perfectly average-sized town, thank you very much. Are you from the city?"

"Miami."

"Damn, why would you come here?"

"Oh, I just decided that one month into my sophomore year was the best time to completely uproot my life and move to another state where I don't know anybody."

"Yikes," he says. "How difficult are you making your parents' lives in protest?"

I laugh. "Trust me, just my presence is complete torture."

"I'm sure that's not true."

He has no idea. Overnight, Kevin Reilly learned that he had a teenage daughter who needed to move in with him and his family. My father (if you could even call him that) definitely isn't pleased by me being here and I'm sure his wife, Meg, feels even worse. After all, what woman would want physical proof that her husband slept with another woman living in her house?

"This is me." He gestures to a gray house. Why are so many houses painted gray? Can't we as a society be a little more creative?

"You're kidding." I point to the house next door. "We're neighbors."

"Are you serious? I had no idea someone new moved in next door. That's awesome." He grins and crosses his arms over his chest. "We might as well be friends now, you know. It just makes sense."

I tilt my head. "Are you automatically friends with all your neighbors?"

"Of course not. That would be crazy. I'm only friends with the cool neighbors," he explains and shoots me finger guns. "The girl who lived there before you was definitely not my friend."

"Was that girl Joanne Reilly?" I ask.

He blinks repeatedly. "How did you know that?"

"'Cause she still lives here," I explain. "I'm staying with her family for a while."

"Shit. Don't tell her I said that."

I wink. "Your secret's safe with me."

♫

It's about three hours until anyone else gets home. The door to my new bedroom swings open suddenly and Jo storms in, throwing her bag on her bed and then flopping down beside it. I go back to my homework.

A few minutes later, she breaks the silence. "You wouldn't happen to have Spanish first period, would you?"

I look up at her. "Yeah, I do." I think I already know where this conversation is headed.

"I figured," she sighs. "My friend Nico told me some girl he's never seen before said all sorts of bitchy things to him in class today. Of course it was you."

"Did your friend tell you he was being a homophobic bully to our next-door neighbor Ren?"

She sits up and looks at me. "Nico is a family friend," she states firmly. "His mom and my mom have known each other since high school. They come over all the time. You really don't wanna make an enemy out of him."

"Then maybe he shouldn't be such a homophobic bully."

She rolls her eyes. I understand why Ren doesn't like her.

A knock on the door interrupts the awkwardness and Meg peeks her head in. I hadn't even heard her get home. "Hey, girls. I'm about to start dinner unless either of you needs a snack first?"

"No thanks," we say in near-perfect unison.

Meg smiles. "Alright then. I'll just call you down when it's ready."

She leaves the door cracked when she walks away and I can see that it frustrates Jo. She glares at me, as if somehow I control which doors Meg does or doesn't close. I roll my eyes, bothered just to be in the same room as Jo. I get up and leave, slamming the door behind me.

I don't exactly have a plan past that, so I go downstairs and into the kitchen.

"Do you need any help with dinner?" I offer Meg. I figure if I'm going to be this big burden in her life, I might as well pull my own weight where I can.

"Oh, thank you!" She puts her palm against her chest, as if she's taken aback by my simple offer.

"That's so sweet. Sure! Why don't you watch this pot while I grab some stuff out of the fridge?"

It's probably the easiest task she could've given me. I stand and watch water that hasn't started to boil yet.

"Do you want to tell me about your first day at Woodview?"

I don't, but there isn't a non-rude way to say no to this question. "It was fine, I guess."

"Were your teachers nice? What about your classmates? Did you make any friends?" She returns to the stove and looks me right in the eye. I look away, fiddling with my fingernails.

"You don't have to pretend to be interested," I say, hoping to put us both out of our misery.

"Don't be silly, of course I'm interested! I want to know how you're adjusting."

I look back at her and she's still smiling at me. She's very pretty. Her blonde hair has been pulled into a messy ponytail and she's wearing a stained apron over work clothes and yet she still looks beautiful. I can't imagine why my father would ever cheat on her. But then again, I can't imagine why he would cheat on my mother either. Or why any man would do that to any woman for that matter.

My father's been mostly quiet since I arrived in Woodview. It's hard to tell if it's guilt, disdain, or just disinterest, but he can never seem to figure out what to say to me. Either that or he simply doesn't want to try.

"I spoke to one guy who seemed nice," I tell Meg. "Turns out he lives next door, actually. Name's Ren Hayashi."

"Oh, that's Harry's son. He's a nice kid, one grade below you and Jo. We went to high school with his dad. Your father and I used to be good friends with him."

Her eyes begin to water, but I quickly realize this is probably due to the onion she's chopping and not because of our conversation. Still, her tone sounds a bit off, so I have to wonder if there's more to this story.

"Used to be?" I ask.

She lets out a sound that's somewhere between a laugh and a cry and shakes her head. "People grow apart," she laments. "It happens to everyone."

I lean against the windowsill and peer outside. There's a maple tree towering over almost the entire backyard. Some branches even hang into Ren's yard.

"How do you grow apart when he's right next door?"

She laughs again, and this one sounds more like a laugh, although I'm not sure I'm in on the joke. "You'll understand when you're older." She sighs. "Real life isn't as simple as high school."

Is high school supposed to be simple? I'm only a sophomore, but my life feels like it's already fallen into complete and utter chaos. But I don't say any of that. Maybe she's right. Maybe at some point, I'll look back fondly on these days. I wonder how long it'll take for that to happen.

♫

A little while later, we're seated around the table, eating silently. My father's absence does not go unnoticed. About twenty minutes ago, he called to let us know he'd be working late and told Meg not to wait up for him. Meg hasn't spoken more than two words at a time since she hung up the phone.

Her fork keeps scraping across her plate and the excruciating sound it makes causes me to flinch each time. I can tell Jo's feeling the same way. We eye each other from across the table, but we don't speak.

Suddenly, Meg slams her silverware onto the table, takes a deep breath in, and flashes a big grin. It's like someone flipped a switch inside her and made everything perfectly fine again.

"We should do something fun this weekend! As a family! Something to really welcome Elena to Woodview!"

Jo and I look at each other. She rolls her eyes before correcting her mother, "Just calling us a family doesn't make it true."

Meg looks down at her plate. "It is true. You're sisters."

"She's a total stranger," Jo insists. "There's more to family than DNA. We didn't become sisters overnight."

"Joanne, stop it."

"No, she's right," I interject, earning stares from both of them. "This whole situation is fucked. Neither of you need to pretend it isn't. Not for my sake, at least."

Jo's lip twitches into a smile. Meg quietly chuckles and then starts to gradually laugh louder. Jo looks at me with a raised eyebrow.

"You're right," Meg exclaims, her laughs slowly starting to sound more like cries, "this is completely fucked."

"It's so fucked," Jo agrees.

She and I are both smiling now. And at that moment, smiling hurts, but somehow I can't stop. My life was torn apart, and Jo and Meg are suffering because of it. It's so easy to feel like I'm their enemy, but maybe we're actually all on the same side.

3

Honesty Is The Best Policy

I walk home with Ren the next day and then again the day after that. Jo and I haven't quite reached a point where we talk to each other at school, but I see her around often. Sometimes she's with Nico, the boy from Spanish class. Right now, she's across the field, practicing some kind of dance routine with a red-headed girl and a pretty brunette.

I start to think about my friends from back home and what they're doing right now. My best friend Lana and I used to speak every day, but neither of us really knows what to say anymore. Words aren't coming as easily as they used to.

"Earth to Elena." Ren shakes his hand in front of my face, snapping me back to reality.

"Sorry," I mumble, "I think I zoned out for a minute."

"Yeah, you zoned out staring at Jo Reilly," he informs me. "I'm starting to think you're obsessed with her."

"Shut up."

"What's your relation to her anyway?"

"What?"

"You're living with her and her family," he says. "How come? Who are they to you?"

"Her dad knew my mom." It's not a lie. It's just not the full truth either.

"Knew?" he asks. "Past tense?"

"What are you writing a book or something?"

He puts his hands up in defense. "I'm just trying to get to know you." He sighs. "Although, a new girl who comes to town with a mysterious past and a chip on her shoulder? You do sound like a main character. Maybe your story is worth writing."

I roll my eyes. "If I'm the main character, what does that make you?"

"I don't know." He shrugs. "I could be your manic pixie dream boy."

"Is that even a thing?"

"It should be." He chuckles. "Or maybe I'm the leading man. The love interest. The knight in shining armor who rescues our dear damsel in distress from the horrors of suburbia."

"Who says I'm a damsel in distress?"

"Your face does." He laughs. "There's clearly a lot going on in your head that you aren't sharing."

"Why would I share the mess inside my head?"

"So that the leading man can fall in love with even the *darkest* parts of you," he says dramatically.

He stares into my eyes, so I try to stare back with the most serious look on my face that I can muster up, but after only a few seconds I burst into laughter. "You sound like such a douchebag."

"Maybe I am a douchebag." He laughs. "A manic pixie douchebag. We don't actually know very much about each other though, do we?"

"I guess not." Everything about me feels so sad lately. What am I even supposed to tell him? Although it might feel good to talk to *someone*. "How about a question for a question. We can go back and forth asking and answering."

"And we have to be honest?" He raises an eyebrow, causing his winged eyeliner to lift a little higher. It doesn't seem like such a bad request. If he asks me anything too serious, my answer will probably scare him into never asking me anything again.

"Yeah," I agree. "You go first."

"Where are your parents?" he asks with no hesitation, staring directly into my eyes while he waits for me to answer.

"W-what?" I stammer.

"You're staying with the Reillys," he says, "but where's your real family?"

"My mom passed away," I whisper, no longer meeting his gaze.

"Shit. I'm sorry."

I look up to see that his entire demeanor has changed, but I don't want his pity. "My turn," I declare "What's the deal with you and that jerk in our Spanish class?"

He squints at me. "What do you mean?"

"Is he like that to everyone or is it ... personal?"

Ren gulps. His eyes dart around like he's expecting the words to be written somewhere on a tree or telephone pole. "He's not as bad as he seems. Nico is a good person deep down."

I raise a brow, unconvinced.

His posture deflates, as he makes himself as small as humanly possible. "We used to be friends," he explains, "but then something happened and everything sort of fell apart." His voice breaks a little more with every word, but he keeps going. "It was right before he started high school, so it was sort of inevitable. I guess he didn't want to still be friends with an eighth grader."

"Whatever happened, you don't deserve to be treated like that."

He shakes his head. "It doesn't matter." His eyes are getting teary, so he dabs at the edges with his fingers, only slightly smudging his makeup. "It's my turn to ask a question. Tell me something about your mom."

"Where do I start?" I take in a breath. "She was an English teacher. Everyone loved her."

♫

I call Lana when I get home. I have the house to myself again and it feels too quiet.

She answers after three rings. "Hey." She sounds entirely drained of energy.

"Hey." I try my best to sound upbeat. "How was today?"

"More of the same," she replies. "I heard they're adding metal detectors to the school, but too little too late, right?"

"I guess it's still a good idea?" I didn't mean for that to sound so much like a question. "I mean, if it stops this kind of thing from happening again..."

"It's terrifying," Lana whispers so quietly that I'm not even sure I'm meant to hear. I think she's starting to cry, but I can't be sure. "I'm sorry," she stammers, "I shouldn't get so upset when I'm talking to you."

"It's upsetting," I remind her. "Be upset." Lana's always been emotional, even about little things. And I can tell each time we speak that she's expecting me to break down, so she tries as hard as she can not to fall apart first. Even after I give her permission to let it all out, she still does her best to hold it in.

I would never tell her that she can't cry just because someone else has it worse—because it could always be worse—but if I'm being honest, I wish she could pull herself together. I don't want to be a bad friend, but I'm too numb to comfort her.

She calms down after only a few minutes. We stay on the phone for almost an hour, but I don't say much. She must notice, but she just keeps filling in the gaps of conversation herself. I love her for that. She proceeds to give me a fairly thorough update on each of our friends. Rosa's parents are considering putting her in private school. They think she'll be safer there. She keeps going back and forth on whether or not she agrees with them, but it's probably happening no matter what she wants. Pilar's older brother came home from the hospital today. The doctors think that, with enough physical therapy, he'll be able to walk again. Tina's psychiatrist prescribed her medication to help with her panic attacks, but she still can't make it through the night due to the nightmares.

Lana moves on to catching me up on other current events. It sounds like the whole student body is broken and I can't help but feel like I should be there, recovering with everyone else. Instead I'm in another school, another town, another state, surrounded by people who don't even know what happened. I've never felt so alone.

After at least ten straight minutes of Lana talking without a single reply from me, she tells me she has to go. As much as I don't want to stop hearing her voice, I let her. I say goodbye and she promises she'll call me in a few days. When I moved, we told each other we'd still talk every day, but really it's been more like once a week.

I lie in bed with the covers pulled up over my head and music playing, so I can pretend to disappear. I think I'm only halfway through the first song when I realize I'm crying.

Even though I knew she would understand and want to help me, I couldn't cry with Lana listening. I don't think I could cry with anyone listening.

I'm not sure how much time passes before the tears finally stop. I don't think there is anything left in me. My face and my pillow are both soaked, but I can't find a way to care. I feel myself drifting off, when the music suddenly stops. I pull the blanket off my face to see Jo standing in our room.

"Oh sorry," she says. "I thought you were asleep."

"It's fine." I take my phone from her. I reach for my earbuds.

"You can keep listening out loud if you want," she offers. "I actually like that song."

I shrug, press play, and toss my phone to the side. Jo leans back on her bed. "Are you okay? No offense, but you kind of look like crap."

"Thanks," I reply. "I was going for a 'my life is falling apart' look."

"Well, in that case, you have succeeded." She laughs. I don't, so she quickly stops. "You can, like … talk to me. If you need to, I guess?"

"I don't really feel like talking."

"Right, of course." She taps her fingers against the bed frame, creating a click-clack sound from her perfectly manicured pink nails. "Hey, I don't know if this is weird…" she stops short, as if she's debating whether her sentence should end. "Do you want to come to a party this weekend?"

I roll over to look at her, positive I must've heard wrong. "What?"

"One of the marching band guys is throwing a party and a bunch of my friends are going," she explains. "I thought maybe it'd be fun. You could get to know some people from school. I don't know."

I roll back over to face the wall. "I'm not sure I'll get along with your friends. It doesn't really seem like we run in the same circles."

"Okay, never mind," she mumbles. "It was a stupid idea."

I shrug. "It's not so stupid. Are you sure you want me to come?"

"Yeah?"

"Okay, then I'll come." Why not? What's the worst that can happen?

4

What's The Worst That Can Happen?

Jo dug through every piece of clothing I had before she declared that I should wear a black spaghetti strap tank top, a flowy light pink sweater with silver buttons, and a pair of dark skinny jeans. I don't know why I let her make this choice. She and I don't seem to have quite the same style, but she knows the crowd for tonight much better than I do, so it seemed safe to let her guide me a bit. It's also easier not to think about it and just let her make the decision for me.

Picking out clothes for a party kind of feels like something real sisters would do. We are temporarily playing the roles of two girls who grew up together in the same house, with shared memories of family vacations, Christmas mornings, and long boring car rides to Grandma's house. It isn't real, but it is nice to pretend, just for a moment.

I had a good childhood. I'd never deny or even question that. I almost feel guilty for imagining it being any different. But Jo had a good childhood too. In a parallel universe, if time had shifted just slightly, I could've had her life. Is it really so horrible to think of that?

"Rachel just texted me," Jo says. "They're almost here."

"Whose party is this again?"

"It's Alex Dancey's birthday," she replies, "so his friends are throwing this whole big thing."

"Cool."

"It's kinda exciting because he's a senior and one of his friends specifically invited me and Rachel and Casey, even though we're only sophomores." She speaks quickly, lifting her voice for the last word of her sentences as if asking a question. "I mean, I know it's just 'cause they invited everyone in the marching band and color guard, but it's still nice, 'cause he didn't have to, you know?"

"Yeah, that's great. I guess?" She seems pretty excited for a marching band party. Is marching band cool in the suburbs?

"Plus, Casey has a huge crush on the host, but don't tell her I told you that."

I'm barely even listening, so I just mutter a quiet "sure" and move on. Jo stands up suddenly and grabs her coat, so I follow suit, and we go outside.

Rachel's older sister, Rebecca, picks us up in a blue minivan, which I assume belongs to their parents because it doesn't seem like a common car choice for a nineteen-year-old girl. I recognize Rachel and Casey from school but have never spoken to them.

Rachel is easily the friendlier of the pair. She is doe-eyed and energetic. She laughs with her whole body, causing her dark brown curls to bounce around. She excitedly asks me a series of questions the moment I get in the car, barely giving me any time to actually answer them.

Casey doesn't acknowledge me at all during the entire ride, except to squint at me with her emerald green eyes, staring me down as though she's silently calculating whether I am worth her time. It seems she has decided that I am not.

I learn that we are going to meet two more of their friends, Tyler and Nico, at the party. Apparently, Nico is Rachel's boyfriend and I wonder if he will recognize me as the "bitch" who called him out in Spanish class. Maybe I'm not important enough to have left a lasting memory in his brain.

We arrive at a packed house which is blasting music with a heavy bass. My first thought is that the house is massive. I thought my father's house was big, but this Alex Dancey kid must be loaded. The first floor is bigger than my entire apartment in Miami and it's got two more stories. Who even needs this kind of space?

The party is already in full throttle when we arrive, so no one pays us much attention as we push through the crowd. I follow the girls to the kitchen, where Nico and another boy, who I assume is Tyler, are leaning against the wall, side by side, with red solo cups in their hands.

I didn't realize how tall Nico is until now because I've never seen him standing up before. Honestly, I've barely even looked at him until now. He has brown hair, light tan skin, and classic Roman features. He would almost be cute if he wasn't such a jerk.

I don't know why it surprises me that Tyler is Black. Maybe it was the name, because "Tyler" sounds like such a white boy name. Or maybe it was because most of the people I've met at Woodview so far have been white. For a moment I'm comforted to know I'm not the only person of color in Jo's life, but then I remember that Tyler is also friends with Nico, so he might not exactly be the ally I'm hoping for.

Nico and Tyler have the same athletic build. I suspect that they're not in the marching band like the majority of the guests here.

"Spanish class girl," Nico exclaims as I approach. He says it like a term of endearment, which I guess is a good thing, although I'm still not sure I want to be on friendly terms with this guy.

"That's me," I reply, with a forced smile.

"No hard feelings, by the way."

I fake a laugh. Does he really think that he's the one with the right to have hard feelings? The audacity of teenage boys.

"Elena?" I turn around and find Levi standing behind me. "What are you doing here?"

"Oh, hey Levi," I stammer. "I came here with my uh … friends." It feels weird to call Jo, Rachel, and Casey my friends, but it's easier than explaining who they actually are to me.

"Hi, Levi." Casey pushes her way in front of me to stand between us. "Great party."

"Oh, thanks. Kelsey, right?"

She pushes a strand of red hair behind her ear and crinkles her freckled nose. "Casey."

"Right, right. Sorry." He completely looks past her and turns back to me. "I guess you made friends around here pretty fast, Miss Popularity."

"Not exactly," I say, deadpan.

"We'll see about that. Why don't you come with me? I'll introduce you to some of the guys."

"Oh, um," I start to look to Jo for permission, but then decide I don't actually need permission to talk to people.

"C'mon," he says, "you'll like them." He takes my hand and the next thing I know I'm in the living room, or what I think is the living room but could be a ballroom based on its size. A bunch of strangers, some already more intoxicated than others, are sitting on a huge couch together. Levi gives a less-than-thorough introduction, quickly rattling off a series of names that I definitely won't remember.

"You're so pretty," a drunk brunette who I think he said is named Danielle exclaims, reaching out to run her fingers through my hair. She starts to laugh. It's unclear what's so funny.

"Do you think maybe you should drink some water?" Levi suggests to her.

She slides off the lap of the large guy she was seated upon and sinks onto the carpet. We have our answer.

"I'm on it," the guy says, scooping her off the floor and carrying her away to get hydrated.

Levi takes his seat and shifts over just enough so that someone else can *almost* fit. He gestures for me to join him and I guess it beats standing awkwardly in front of everyone.

A boy with jet-black hair leans over the arm of the couch beside us. He's as close to me as he can be without getting out of his seat.

"You a freshman? I don't think I've seen you around before."

"Sophomore."

"Color guard girl?"

"No, I just came with a … friend," I explain. "She does color guard. Jo Reilly."

"Which one is she?" asks a guy sitting across from us. He looks toward a beautiful girl with deep brown skin and a glittery top.

"Sophomore, tall, blonde," the girl describes Jo. "She's pretty talented but always following around that pushy redhead."

"You know," the boy with the jet-black hair interjects, "the chubby one!" He laughs.

The other guy nods. "Oh yeah, I know who you're talking about."

I squirm a little in my seat. Jo isn't exactly thin, but I wouldn't call her chubby either. She's pretty average. I look around at the other girls in the room. Most are stick skinny. I suppose in this crowd Jo *is* chubby by comparison. But then, if I'm being honest, so am I.

A sudden crash in the next room makes Levi groan. "It sounds like I'm needed elsewhere," he sighs. "Nobody corrupt the new girl while I'm gone." I think I see him exchange a look with the girl in the glittery top, but I can't be sure.

"Don't worry, she's in good hands." The boy with jet-black hair leans closer to me and whispers, "You want something to drink?"

"No thanks. I'm good."

"Oh c'mon." He grins. "Let loose a little. I won't tell anyone."

"She doesn't have to drink if she doesn't want to," the girl in the glittery top defends me, rolling her eyes.

"I just wanna show her a good time," he claims, throwing his hands up in defense.

The girl grabs me by the hand and says, "Let's go dance." I let her guide me into another room. "So are you and Levi...?" She doesn't complete the question.

I stare at her, but she just stares back with wide eyes. I finally understand what she means.

"Oh. No, of course not. Isn't he a senior?"

"Just checking. Levi's a good guy, but you don't need to be worrying about senior boys."

I nod slowly. I'm only fifteen. It would be weird for one of those senior boys to want to get together with me. Wouldn't it?

"I need a refill," she says. I look around and don't see Levi or any of Jo's crew. I decide to stick with this girl, whose name I can't even remember, something with a P maybe? It seems better than standing awkwardly at a party alone. I follow her through the house like a lost puppy.

I don't quite remember when a drink lands in my hand, or when one drink becomes two, or two becomes four. I realize I haven't seen Jo in a while, so I decide to look around for her. The second floor of this house is as large and confusing as the ground floor. There's about a million doors and I'm scared to know what's happening behind most of them. I notice one door a few feet away that's slightly cracked open. Surely nothing too private can be happening in there if they didn't even bother to fully close the door.

I push it open slightly, but Jo's not there. A girl I don't recognize is lying on the bed, asleep maybe. She's dressed all in pink. Another girl, dressed all in black, sits behind her, furiously texting someone on her phone. The girl in black notices me suddenly.

"Sorry," I say quickly and start to shut the door.

"Wait!"

I push it open again.

She looks at her sleeping friend, then back at me. "Can you get Zeke?" she asks. "I don't want to leave her alone, but I can't get her out of here by myself."

"Uh, yeah, of course," I stammer, "but, uh, who's Zeke?"

"You can't miss him. He's freakishly tall, blonde hair in one of those stupid man-buns. He's downstairs somewhere, probably dancing, and looking like a lanky piece of spaghetti with no rhythm."

I laugh slightly but try not to, as this girl is clearly worried. I vaguely remember seeing a very tall boy on the dance floor earlier tonight, so I nod and head back downstairs. I'm immediately reminded of the heat radiating off the crowd. I desperately want to avoid the sweaty masses, but I'm a girl on a mission.

I don't see the boy right away, so I try calling out his name as I maneuver through the crowd. It's not long until someone notices and points me in the right direction. He does kind of look like a lanky piece of spaghetti.

"Zeke?" I call out as I approach him.

"Yeah?" He looks at me sideways, like he's trying to figure out who I am and how I know his name.

"There are these two girls upstairs who asked me to find you," I explain. "They need your help."

He sighs and rolls his eyes, so I assume he not only knows exactly who I'm talking about, but that this isn't the first time he's had to come to their rescue.

"Where are they?"

Soon we're back upstairs and the girl in black is holding the other one's hair back as she coughs over a trash can. I hover in the background, not because I'm still needed, but because I don't know where else to go.

"Should we call her dad?" she asks.

The drunk girl moans something that vaguely resembles the word "no."

"She'd never forgive us," Zeke answers.

"I don't understand. She barely even drank. I made sure of it."

"She must've had more than you thought." Zeke sighs. "We've gotta get her home."

She nods in agreement. Zeke scoops the girl in pink up in his arms, while the other girl grabs what I assume is her friend's pink purse. I move out of their way so they can pass through the door.

"Thank you for getting me," Zeke whispers as he passes me.

All I can do in return is nod. I watch them carefully carry her down the stairs until they disappear from my line of vision. The same hallway suddenly feels longer now. This is a big house and Jo could be anywhere. I have to find her, of course, but it seems impossible. I make my way back downstairs and walk straight into the boy with jet-black hair from earlier.

"Hey, new girl. You look like you could use another drink."

5

Playing The Part

The sun feels warm on my skin. I open my eyes and squint. The curtains are pulled open, allowing bright rays to shine through the wide window onto my face. Every morning that I wake up in Woodview, I expect to see my old room back in Miami. It always takes a minute to remember that I don't live there anymore. My eyes adjust to the brightness and I realize that I have no idea where I am. Nothing about this room looks familiar at all.

The walls are painted a pale shade of pink. The bed I slept in is still made, as I apparently spent the night on top of the comforter. Although it seems someone did cover me with a small knit blanket. Where am I? There's a pair of sliding mirrors, which open to a mostly empty closet, and a door, which leads to a small bathroom. I splash some water on my face and clean off some of my smudged makeup, realizing that I've probably gotten lipstick and mascara all over whoever's pillow I borrowed last night. I wish I had a toothbrush.

I struggle to remember details about the party from last night. What was the guy's name? Something Dancey? I can't recall if I ever actually met him. Does he know I'm still here? And what about Jo? She must be worried about me. Her parents are probably freaking out, thinking that I've gone missing. I have to figure out how to get home.

I stick my head out into the hallway, but I don't see anyone, so I tiptoe down the stairs. When I reach the bottom I see Levi sitting on a nearby couch eating a bowl of cereal. There's a soccer game on the television. He jolts to his feet upon noticing me.

"Hey! You're awake!" He flashes an adorably goofy grin. "Can I get you some breakfast? Water? Coffee? Aspirin?"

I shake my head. "I need to get home," I explain. My head is throbbing and my mouth is dry. "Actually, water would be great."

He grabs me a cold bottle from the fridge.

"Can I borrow a charger maybe?" My phone died and I don't know the way home without the GPS.

"Yeah, of course. There's one right over here." He leads me to the other end of the couch, where I plug my phone into the wall and wait for it to turn on. I take a seat next to it, and he sits across from me.

"What are you still doing here?" I wonder aloud.

He chuckles. "I could ask you the same question." He expects me to laugh, but I don't. "I live here," he explains.

"I thought this was some kid named Alex's house. Alex Dancey?"

"No, the party was for Alex's birthday," he corrects me, "but it's my house."

"Oh." I suddenly feel even more embarrassed. I hang my head slightly. "I'm sorry. I didn't mean to stay overnight. I guess I fell asleep?"

He laughs. "Don't worry. You're definitely not the first girl to pass out at a party."

If he thought that would be comforting, he was wrong. "Is there any chance Jo Reilly is passed out in another one of these rooms?"

"The blonde girl you were with? No, she left last night. Pretty early too. Couldn't have been here for more than like, an hour maybe."

"Are you serious?"

"I'm pretty sure." He shrugs. "She left with that redhead she's always with. I can never remember her name."

My phone buzzes beside me, so I reach for it as the screen turns on. There are nineteen missed calls from Meg and one text message from my father telling me to please answer Meg's calls. Nothing from Jo. I dial Meg's number and wait while it rings.

"Elena? Are you okay?"

"Yeah, I'm fine," I say. "My phone died. I'm sorry. I slept over at the party, but I'm coming home now."

"Oh, thank God," she sighs. "I've been calling you all morning. I'll come pick you up. What's the address?"

"It's um…" I look toward Levi, realizing I actually have no idea where I am. "What's your address?"

"37 Socasco Avenue, Woodview Harbor."

I relay the information and Meg tells me she's on her way. Just before she hangs up the phone I lower my voice and ask, "Did Jo make it home safe last night?"

"Yeah, of course," Meg replies. "I'll be there soon."

I place my phone on the table and lay my head back.

"You alright?" Levi asks.

I shrug.

"Family drama?"

I almost laugh. "You could say that."

"Are your parents pissed that you stayed out all night?"

"I think I've got a pretty good get-out-of-jail-free card this time."

He flashes another goofy grin. "Really? And what's that?"

"My dad just found out he's my dad," I confess. "So I'm hoping his fifteen years of absence will cancel out my one night. I can probably leverage that to get a more lenient punishment."

"Damn!" He laughs. "I mean, if you've got an ace, use it, I guess."

I half-heartedly smile. If my life is going to be this much of a disaster, I might as well learn to laugh at it. Of course, I probably shouldn't have shared any of that with him.

"Hey, don't tell anyone, okay?"

He laughs again. "Your secret is safe with me."

"You should share one of your own in return," I joke, "to make it even."

"Alright." He leans back on the sofa and kicks his feet onto the ottoman. "I know who both my parents are, so I'm not sure if I can match you, but..." He pauses to think. "...I throw these big parties all the time, but the truth is, I don't really like them. I don't even drink."

"So why do you do it then?" I ask.

His whole demeanor changes. He gets this focused look on his face, and I have a feeling he's been waiting for someone to ask him that for a long time, even if he didn't realize.

"I don't think anyone in my life actually knows me." His voice is quiet, softer than before. "Sometimes it feels like I'm playing a character, and I've been playing it for so long that I'm not even sure how to stop. But it isn't me. It's this fake persona that everyone—my friends, my family—everyone just *thinks* is me." He looks at me for a second but then quickly focuses his eyes on the wall across from him. "But that's not something I should say to a perfectly nice girl who I barely know, so I'll shut up now and we can call it even."

I'm thrown off. I didn't really expect him to tell me something genuine. I suspect he's wanted to say all this for a while now, but I don't feel like I'm the one who deserved to hear it.

A horn honks outside and my phone lights up with an incoming text from Meg. I jump to my feet and awkwardly stammer, "I uh, I think my ride's here. Thanks for the water."

Levi says something, but I don't hear it. I'm already out the door.

I get in the front seat of Meg's minivan. She came alone and I'm not sure why that surprises me. I guess I kind of thought my father would be with her, but I realize that wouldn't actually have made much sense. I can't expect him to drop everything for me.

"Elena, we were so worried!" Meg exclaims as I sit next to her. "You can't pull this kind of stuff. Your dad and I need to know where you are at all times."

"I know. I'm sorry." I do mean it. Meg has been perfectly nice to me since I've gotten here and I don't want to cause her stress. Overnight, she inherited a teenager. That's bad enough without me being a problem child. "It won't happen again. I promise."

She opens her mouth like she's going to respond, but she just exhales a breath and stays silent. Maybe she's just a really good actress, but she looks genuinely relieved that I'm okay. It's ironic in a way, because her life would probably be so much easier if I did just disappear.

She doesn't say much on the ride home, except that we'll talk more when my dad gets home from work. I wonder if I should ask what he does for a living that he works late every night and on Saturdays. It seems like the kind of thing someone should know about their own parents, but I couldn't really bring myself to care at first and too much time has passed to ask now.

We get to the house and I go straight to my room. Jo is there, lying on her bed and blasting music that I don't recognize. She glances at me as I enter but then quickly goes back to her phone. I expected at least some acknowledgement, if not an apology. I pass by silently and head to my own bed. It feels like hours pass before either of us says a word, but it was probably only a few minutes.

"I'm sorry," she whimpers, barely audible.

"Was it always your plan to leave me stranded? Or did you decide that in the moment?"

"Casey needed me," she states matter-of-factly. "And you ditched us first, remember?"

"I didn't ditch you. Levi wanted to introduce me to his friends," I defend myself, even though I shouldn't need to. "I'm new and I don't know anyone. He was being nice. What's so wrong with that?"

"Did you hook up with him?"

"Levi?" I scoff. "God! No! Why does everyone keep asking me that?"

"Because he was obviously hitting on you, Elena."

I roll my eyes. "No, he wasn't. And what do you even care? You got a crush on him or something?"

"Casey does!" she shouts. "He's the whole reason we went to the party in the first place and then you ran off with him the first chance you got."

"You told me she liked Alex."

"What? No, she likes Levi."

I sigh. Jo said Casey had a crush on the guy throwing the party. And although the party was for Alex, Levi threw it. The people in this town talk in code.

"I didn't know that's who you meant," I explain, "but either way nothing happened between us and it's still no excuse for ditching me."

Jo just stares straight ahead.

"I don't like Levi and Levi doesn't like me. So you can tell Casey to relax."

Jo leans back on her bed and begins picking at the skin around her fingernails. I wish she would make it less obvious that she is upset about something. Doesn't she know I'm still mad at her? I shouldn't have to worry about how she feels right now. Unfortunately, my empathy takes over.

"Are you okay?" I ask.

She nods even though she clearly isn't. "Casey and I got into a fight. A big one."

I don't care. At all. I couldn't possibly care less about the state of my sort-of-sister's friendship with a girl I barely know and honestly don't like very much. But I still try to be nice.

"Do you want to talk about it?"

"Not really."

"Okay, good." I lie down on the bed, but before my head even reaches the pillow, Jo contradicts herself.

"I don't know if she's ever going to speak to me again."

I sigh. "Isn't she one of your best friends?"

"I really screwed up."

"It's probably not as bad as you think."

"It is!"

"Okay, fine." I laugh. "You're a horrible person and Casey's going to hate you forever. Is that what you want to hear?"

"Oh, shut up."

"I'm sorry." I want to mean it, but I also can't stop laughing. "What do you want me to say? She'll probably be over it by Monday. Friends fight."

"What would you know anyway? You only have one friend."

"Well, apparently, so do you right now."

♫

I sit at the dining room table, with Meg across from me and my father to my right. It feels weird thinking about how I'm supposed to be part of this family. I don't look like I should be. Jo looks a lot like her mom and I can easily see some of our father's features passed down to her. They're a picture-perfect family. But I look like my mom. And I don't fit in here.

Neither Meg nor my father have met my eyes since we sat down, and they seem to be silently communicating with each other. My eyes dart back and forth between them until I just can't take it any longer.

"So what's the verdict?" I finally ask. "Am I grounded? Do I have to do extra chores for a month?

Are you sending me back to Florida? Putting me into foster care? Come on, the anticipation is killing me."

Meg looks to me, and then to my father. Her eyes are wide, like she's afraid I'm serious.

My father keeps his gaze focused on the table in front of him as he speaks with a slow, steady tone. "You have your mother's sense of humor."

My lip twitches and I inhale sharply. My whole life people have compared me to my mom, but it's never bothered me the way it does right now. He doesn't deserve to speak about her, not after abandoning her all those years ago.

"I don't know what she used to let you get away with," he continues, "but if you're going to live here, you can't pull another stunt like this."

"Leave my mother out of this."

"We're serious, Elena," he says. It takes all my self-control not to roll my eyes.

"Believe it or not," I blurt out, "I didn't come here to ruin your lives."

"We never said that," Meg chimes in.

"It's what you're thinking," I snap back her. "Isn't it?"

"Of course not," Meg assures me.

I twiddle my thumbs. I'm looking down at my lap, but I can feel both their eyes burning into me. No one speaks for a while. I think they're waiting for me to look at them again, but I never do.

"Elena, we're both really happy to have you here," Meg insists. "You're a part of this family now. That just means you have to follow our rules."

"I know," I say. "I will."

Meg smiles. It doesn't go unnoticed that my father does not say anything in agreement. He doesn't say anything else at all.

♫

On Sunday, I go next door to Ren's house, simply because there is nothing better to do. I'm glad I'm not grounded, not that being grounded would change my social life much anyway. We hang out in his room, with him lying on his bed, practically hanging off of it, and me in a swivel chair by his desk. He sets up music to play on his laptop, but neither of us pays too much attention as we mindlessly scroll on our phones.

"Oh damn," Ren exclaims out of nowhere. "Look what they posted on WoodNews." He reaches his phone out toward me.

I take it but also ask, "What the hell is WoodNews?"

"It's like the school gossip account," he explains. "They post anonymous stuff about people at Woodview High. Your old school didn't have anything like that?"

"No, that sounds awful."

"Of course it is, but everyone still follows."

I look down at his phone, which is open to the post in question. It's just a hot pink square with white text on it that reads:

idk how I'm supposed to be around Jo Reilly now that I know she's a lesbian

"What the hell?" I blurt out.

"Do you think it's true?" Ren asks.

"How would I know?"

"Well, you do live with her."

"We met like ten seconds ago," I remind him. "We haven't exactly gotten to the sharing secrets stage yet."

He shrugs. "I was just curious. Who do you think posted it?"

"Whoever runs the account, right?"

He shakes his head. "The account has a moderator, but anyone can send in a post submission."

"Well, someone really dumb sent this in." I sigh. "Who even cares if someone's a lesbian?"

He scoffs. "People here care. Trust me." I think back to the day he and I met, when Nico called him a slur in Spanish class.

I spin the chair from side to side with my foot. "Aren't people in New York supposed to be progressive or whatever?"

"That's New York City, hon." He sighs. "This is Long Island. It's like apples and oranges."

"That's dumb."

There's a sudden bang on the door, and before Ren can say a word, it bursts open. A boy with jet-black hair, who looks eerily familiar, stands in the doorway.

"Where's your dad?" the boy barks.

"At work," Ren replies.

"On a Sunday?"

"There's a track meet."

"Ugh." The boy groans, glances at me, and then looks away.

I suddenly make the connection. This is Levi's friend from the party. What the hell is he doing in Ren's house?

"Mom wanted me to grab some of Mei's stuff." He turns to exit. "Just let him know I was here," he calls out as he leaves.

Ren's leg starts to shake, rapidly. He stands to close the door and then turns back to me. "Sorry about him," he says. "That's my older brother. Half-brother."

A chill rolls down my spine, although I'm not sure why. "Don't worry about it," I mumble, half-heartedly.

"Do you wanna get some food?" Ren shifts his weight from one foot to the other.

I almost say yes, but out of nowhere, I feel this weight come over me and I just want to go home. Not to the Reilly's, to my real home. I know, of course, that

I can't do that, so burying myself in my new bed will have to suffice. I excuse myself and Ren looks deflated. I feel bad, but I'm not up to it. I need to be alone.

♫

Since I now share a bedroom for the first time in my life, I do not get to be alone as I so desperately want, because Jo is home. But she is curled up under the covers with her AirPods in, so it's almost like she's not here. I pull my blanket over my head and try my best to breathe. Fragments of last night have started appearing in my mind and it feels like I am falling, completely out of control of my own body.

I plug in my earbuds. Music usually does wonders to calm me, but today it just isn't doing the trick. I can't figure out why. There's nothing to be stressed about. Is there?

The room feels too bright, so I tightly shut my eyes. Suddenly I'm back at the party. The room is spinning and the boy with jet-black hair is guiding me up the stairs. I feel unsteady on my feet, so I wrap my arms around his neck to keep my balance. He kisses me and I think I kiss him back. Next thing I know, I'm lying in a dark room and can barely keep my eyes open. I feel someone start to unbutton my sweater. I force open my eyes, just for a moment and I remember his face so close to mine. I remember his grin. The smell of alcohol on his breath. Then everything goes black.

6

Just Be Yourself

On Monday, Meg drives me and Jo to school. Jo hasn't spoken a word all morning and she barely left our room yesterday. She must have seen the post by now, if everyone really does follow WoodNews like Ren said. I wonder if maybe I should bring it up and see if she's okay, but it doesn't feel like something she'd want to talk to me about.

I do my best to ignore both Ren and Nico in Spanish class but for very different reasons. Ren keeps looking at me during class, but I won't meet his eyes. Even though they don't look anything alike, thinking of him makes me think of his half-brother, and I don't want to think about that right now. I avoid Nico because I don't have the energy to even begin to comprehend the kind of terms we're on. Part of me wants to go through the rest of high school completely ignoring Jo and all of her friends, but another part of me kind of hopes we can find some common ground and learn to be real sisters. I doubt that'll ever happen, but it's nice to think about.

I go through most of the morning without interacting with anyone. I almost don't even realize it when someone tries to talk to me in the cafeteria. I'm standing in the lunch line, absentmindedly scrolling through the social media accounts of all my friends back home when someone suddenly starts talking.

"Hey, it's you." I don't assume they mean me until they add, "You helped us out at the party the other day."

I look up and standing before me is a pretty Asian girl dressed all in black. It's the girl who had been taking care of her drunk friend at the party.

"Oh, hey," I reply, awkwardly.

"Thanks so much for that by the way. I don't think we ever exchanged names in all the chaos. I'm Marisol. My pronouns are they/them."

"I'm Elena." Marisol stares at me for a second without blinking. "She … her?"

"Nice to meet you!"

"You too." I nod. "How's your friend?"

"Oh, Brooke? She's fine," they say.

"Glad to hear it."

"I'm so happy I got a chance to thank you," they continue. "I wasn't sure you even went to this school. I've never seen you before."

"I'm new."

"Oh, wow!" they exclaim. "Welcome!"

I smile. "Thanks."

"Come sit with me and my friends."

I stammer, "Oh, um, yeah, sure." I don't know why this invitation takes me aback as much as it does.

"Awesome!"

Marisol is very perky. It doesn't match their appearance at all. They're wearing ripped skinny jeans, massive combat boots, and a tank top that reads "what the hell" in silver writing. This is paired with black lipstick and extremely heavy black eyeliner. Their long black hair is tied into two loose buns, just like it had been at the party. It's like they have the personality of a cheerleader in the body of a vampire.

We get our food and head toward a table at the far end of the cafeteria. The tall boy, Zeke, is already there with two more people who don't quite look like they should all be friends. There's a large, beefy guy who looks like he could snap any of us in half with little effort and a tiny girl wearing a hoodie a few sizes too big for her.

"Hey guys," Marisol says as they sit down. "This is Elena. She's the one who helped us take care of Brooke at that party the other day."

The large boy reaches his hand across the table, knocking over a bottle of iced tea in the process. "Nice to meet you," he says, flashing a toothy smile. "I'm Ollie." Zeke picks up the bottle and I take Ollie's hand. He shakes it vigorously, knocking over the same bottle again.

"He's a dumbass," Marisol teases, as if that's a normal thing to call someone, right in front of them, "but we love him anyway. And we keep him around 'cause he gives great hugs."

"It's true." He nods, causing his light brown hair to fall slightly in front of his eyes.

"And that's Violet," Marisol continues, pointing to the girl next to Ollie. "She's probably going to take over the world one day, so you better be nice to her."

Violet smiles slightly and waves but doesn't say anything. Most people might interpret that as being rude, but I think she's probably just a woman of few words, which is perfectly fine by me.

"And I'm Zeke. We technically met, but you probably don't remember me."

"Of course I remember you." I instantly want to implode after realizing what an awkward thing that was to say.

He smiles, but I think it's just because he feels uncomfortable and can probably see that I'm uncomfortable too.

"Thanks for coming to get me that night," he says. "That was really nice of you."

"No problem."

"Where is Brooke anyway?" Marisol asks.

Ollie starts to laugh. "Where do you think?"

Marisol makes an overly dramatic act of rolling their eyes. "You know, I really never expected Brooke to be the kind of girl who gets a boyfriend and then abandons all her friends."

"I totally expected her to be that kind of girl," Violet says, deadpan.

Zeke shoves her slightly on the arm. "Hey, if he makes her happy, then I'm happy."

Everyone looks at me and I realize I accidentally said "oh" out loud and now they're expecting an explanation. "I just assumed *you* were her boyfriend," I admit, nodding in Zeke's direction, "'cause you seemed to care so much about her at the party."

The table erupts with laughter and I feel myself shrinking. Maybe Zeke notices this because he quickly stops laughing.

"Brooke's my sister," he explains. "Stepsister, technically. I can see the gears in your head working overtime."

I feel my face turn red. My brain did a double take just now and I instantly feel bad about it. I never would have guessed they were related since Brooke and Zeke look so different. Brooke is at least six shades darker than Zeke's white-as-snow skin. Of course, considering that I have an equally white sister, I should know better than to assume.

"Don't worry about it," Zeke reassures me, making me think everyone must be able to read my thoughts simply by looking at my face. "You're not the first person to be confused by our family and you certainly won't be the last."

His reassurance doesn't stop me from feeling weird about my assumptions, but I let it go. I try to stay quiet the rest of the time at lunch. I laugh along when everyone else laughs but never say anything myself.

♫

The day I got to New York, Meg gave me a journal. She said that when people go through a traumatic experience, it can help to have an outlet. I've tried to keep up with writing in it every day, but I'm not convinced it's doing anything for me. But Meg is a children's therapist, so I feel like I should trust her expertise and give this a chance.

When I get home today, I feel overwhelmed. My mind keeps wandering back to the night of the party, to the face of the boy with jet-black hair. The details are still fuzzy, but I know something happened. I know he was there. I know he did ... something. But what?

I write everything down that I can remember, starting with when I arrived at the party, all the way until my conversation with Levi the next morning. I write about meeting Levi's friends, dancing, and looking for Jo. I write about finding Brooke and Marisol in the bedroom and helping them find Zeke. I write about getting drunk, stumbling up the stairs with the boy with jet-black hair, and lying in the dark room. I don't want to write this part down, but I push myself to recall as many details as possible until I reach a point where I just can't remember anything else. I realize I'm crying.

That's when Jo walks in. I shove the journal under my pillow and hurry to dry my eyes. I'm sure she can tell I've been crying, but she doesn't mention it as she walks to her own bed.

"What are you looking at?" she barks at me.

I jerk my head away. I hadn't realized I'd been staring at her. "Sorry."

"It's not true, you know? That stupid post. It's just a dumb rumor."

"You don't have to defend yourself to me. I believe you, whatever you say."

She picks at her fingernails. "Thank you."

"And I don't actually care either way. There's nothing wrong with being a lesbian, but I do think that whole account is ridiculous."

"Yeah, I guess it is," she sighs.

"Do you know who posted it?"

She shakes her head, but I suspect she does.

"I'm sorry," I say.

"Whatever." She shrugs, although I'm not buying her carefree attitude. "I'm sure something else will happen soon enough and everyone will move on to talking about that instead."

"Have people been talking about it?"

"All day." Her voice breaks slightly, but she tries to cover it with a cough. "So if you don't mind I'd really like to drop it now."

"You brought it up."

♫

I sit with Marisol's friends at lunch again the next day. Aside from Brooke, they are all juniors, which means they are allowed to leave campus during their free periods, a privilege we underclassmen don't have. Since Ollie and Marisol didn't feel like cafeteria food today, the crew left me and Brooke alone but promised to bring us back something. It is awkward at first because Brooke is the only member of this little group I hadn't officially met until now. However, it doesn't take long for me to feel like I've known her for years. By the time everyone returns, Brooke and I are both hysterically laughing.

"Damn." Marisol sits down beside me. "What did we miss?"

"Elena is replacing you as my best friend," Brooke says with a shrug.

"Harsh."

"I got you a slice of pizza." Ollie slides a paper plate in front of me. "I figured you'd like it since you're Italian."

I blink. "What makes you think I'm Italian?"

"'Cause your name is Elena."

"I'm Puerto Rican."

Ollie's face falls. "Oh no, really? Should I have gotten you tacos instead?"

"Tacos are Mexican, dumbass," says Violet.

"What should I have gotten?"

"This is fine." I laugh. "I like pizza."

"Everyone likes pizza, Ollie," Marisol reassures him.

His big goofy grin returns. He greatly resembles a golden retriever puppy.

"Guess what! Donna Mariston is leaving school," Marisol announces through a mouthful of food. "That means she won't be on production staff anymore, so now the drama club is short one prop manager."

"Is that a big problem?" Violet asks.

They shrug. "Well, it's good because Donna is awful and I hated having to work with her, but it's also bad because now I have to do the work of two people by myself."

"Yikes," Brooke says. "Do you know why she's leaving?"

"Yeah, I heard she got knocked up, so her parents are, like, sending her to live with nuns or whatever."

"Jesus!" Brooke gasps. "That's awful!"

"Really?" Ollie asks. "I heard she was going to rehab."

"Both equally plausible scenarios," Violet adds under her breath.

"She should definitely finish rehab before she has that baby," says Ollie. "Drugs are probably bad for the little guy."

"Guys, don't spread rumors," Zeke scolds them, sighing, "especially not ones like that."

"Who cares? People have definitely said way worse about all of us." Marisol laughs. "Plus Donna deserves it. She sucks."

"According to WoodNews, she's pregnant," Brooke chimes in, scrolling on her phone.

Zeke rolls his eyes. "Yes, because WoodNews is the most reliable of all news sources."

"Hmm." Brooke continues to scroll through her phone. "It also says that Mike Giordano gave someone mono and Jo Reilly is a lesbian."

"Who's Jo Reilly?" Violet asks.

"She's in my grade," Brooke explains. "Kind of a bitch to be honest."

"She still doesn't deserve to be outed," Marisol says.

Zeke scoffs. "Oh, but it's okay to spread the rumor that Donna is pregnant and in rehab?"

"Well, getting pregnant and doing drugs is stupid. Being a lesbian isn't a choice."

"So, what's a prop manager?" I ask, kind of feeling some sort of responsibility to steer the conversation away from Jo.

"It just means being in charge of all the props used in the school play," Marisol explains. "I'm mainly in charge of the costumes, but with Donna gone, it means I'll have to handle all the props too."

"That's cool," I say. "Are you all in the drama club?"

"Yep." Ollie grins. "I build the sets, Zeke is a sound assistant, Violet does lights, and Brooke's in the cast."

I nod. "Wow."

"Do you like theatre?" Zeke asks.

"I don't know, I've never tried it."

"It's fun." Brooke smiles. "Maybe you can join in the spring."

"You should be a prop manager!" Ollie exclaims, overly excited. "We need another one now that Donna's gone."

"That's actually a really good idea," Marisol says. "Would you be interested?"

"Oh, um, I guess so? I don't really know anything about it."

"Neither did Donna!"

"Okay, I'll try."

"Awesome," they chirp, in that perky voice that still doesn't match their appearance. "Come with me after school and we'll talk to Mr. Brunner about getting you on board. I can't see why he'd say no."

"Um ... great." I guess I'm joining the Woodview High School Drama Club.

7

Good Things Come To Those Who Wait

It turns out Brooke and I have the same History teacher, and since I'm over a month behind, she graciously volunteered to help me study for our upcoming test.

We sit on her bed with her notes in her perfect handwriting sprawled out between us, trying to comprehend the philosophies of different thinkers of the Enlightenment.

Brooke groans and folds herself onto the bed. "In what logical situation would we ever need to know any of this?"

"We won't," I declare. "The only things certain in life are death, taxes, and the lack of real-world uses for most of what we learn in high school."

That at least gets a chuckle out of her. "I'm sure it sucks to transfer schools in the middle of the semester," she says, "but I'm really glad you moved here."

Zeke bursts into the room without knocking. Before he has a chance to speak, Brooke throws a pillow at him, but he catches it with ease and tosses it back to her. This just leads to her throwing it at him again, this time even harder.

"I'm just here to find out if Elena is staying for dinner," he shouts. "God!"

"Oh, no, I don't want to impose."

"It's no problem," Brooke assures me. "You're welcome to stay."

"This is a Jewish household," Zeke adds. "It's actually much more of a problem for you to refuse our food. My mom may never forgive you."

I shrug. "Alright then, I guess I'll stay."

"Fantastic." Zeke grins and leaves without shutting the door.

When I look back over at Brooke, she is deeply engrossed in her phone. Something tells me we aren't going to get much more studying done today.

"Anything good?" I lean over, pretending to look but not enough to actually see her screen. Still, she gets nervous and pulls her phone closer to her chest.

"Sorry," she mumbles, blushing. "My boyfriend Dylan just texted me, and he doesn't like it when I leave him waiting too long without a response."

"Sounds clingy." I chuckle. She kicks me lightly. "I'm just kidding! Tell me about him."

Her whole face lights up with a bright smile. "Well, we've only been dating officially for like a month now, but it's going really great and we're perfect for each other."

"That's awesome!"

She returns to her phone but doesn't stop talking or smiling. "He's in the school play too," she explains. "He's actually the male lead."

"Wow, I guess I'll meet him at rehearsal."

"Oh yeah!" she practically squeals. "Are you excited to start?"

"I think so," I admit, scrunching up my nose a little. "I don't have any experience with theatre, but it seems like it's gonna be fun."

"It will be."

"Oh, Elena!" Zeke sings my name as he returns to the doorway, dramatically leaning against the wall.

"Leave us alone," Brooke groans, flopping down on her back but laughing once she gets there.

"My mom wants to know if you have allergies or veganism or whatever."

"If she *has* veganism?" Brooke laughs. "Try learning English."

"Ugh! You know what I meant." He yells like he's angry, but he's smiling the whole time. He's such a weirdo. It's kind of adorable.

"I don't have any allergies," I say, "or veganism."

Brooke rolls her eyes. "Please. Don't encourage him."

♪

Later, I sit next to Brooke at the table with Zeke across from me. Their parents sit at opposite ends of the table. Mrs. Kaminsky isn't a very good cook, or at the very least, the meal she made tonight is not her specialty. I politely eat my baked chicken and potatoes but secretly wonder how this family is so okay with eating bland cardboard. Haven't they ever heard of spices?

"So, Elena," Mrs. Kaminsky says, "Brooke tells me you're new to Woodview."

I nod. "I moved here a few weeks ago."

"Where are you from originally?" Mr. Kaminsky asks.

"Miami."

"Wow!" Mrs. Kaminsky exclaims. "Must be a big change moving all the way here. You must miss the beach."

"We live twenty minutes from a beach," Zeke reminds her.

"But it's too cold to enjoy it most of the year," she corrects him. "In Florida, it's always beach weather. Right, Elena?"

"Uh, yeah?" I stammer, "I guess."

"You'll have to forgive my wife," Mr. Kaminsky interjects. "She never quite let go of her dream of living in a beach house year-round. She wanted to move to Hollywood right out of high school and become a big star."

She certainly looks like she could've made it in Hollywood if she wanted to. She's tall, thin, and blonde, with a pretty face. I don't know her exact age, but she looks a lot younger than Brooke's dad. She looks nowhere old enough to have a teenage son.

"That's enough about me." She gives her husband a death glare. "Elena, how are you liking Woodview?"

"It's uh, it's fine, I guess," I stammer. "A lot better now that I know Brooke and Zeke."

"I'm so glad to hear that," Mrs. Kaminsky continues. "We'd love to have your parents over for dinner sometime to welcome them to the neighborhood."

My leg starts to shake. I probably should've prepared for my parents to come up in conversation eventually. "I'm living with relatives actually," I half-explain. It's technically not a lie. "They've lived here for a while."

"Why don't you live with your parents?" Zeke asks, with a mouth full of food. "Are they like in jail or something?"

"Zeke." His mother sighs. "What have I said about personal questions?"

"Sorry."

Brooke gasps slightly and covers her mouth with her hand. "Were they deported?" she whispers.

"What? No." I can't help but laugh at their guesses. "Where would they even be deported to? I'm Puerto Rican."

"That's right." Brooke nods. "I knew that."

"So then where are they?"

"Zeke!" His mother scolds again.

He throws his hands up in defense and drops his jaw. "Brooke asked a personal question too!"

Mrs. Kaminsky shakes her head before looking back over to me. "I don't know what's gotten into them today," she mutters. "They're usually not this rude."

Brooke shrugs. "Zeke's always this rude."

"Hey!" Zeke shouts.

It's nice to be part of a real family dinner for a change. Every meal at my father's house feels like eating in a room full of strangers.

"So, who are you staying with?" Mr. Kaminsky asks. "This town's not so big. We might know them."

"Kevin and Meg Reilly," I reply.

Brooke cocks her head. "Reilly? Like Joanne Reilly's parents?"

I nod.

"Isn't that the lesbian in your grade?" Zeke asks. "The one you think is a bitch."

"Language, Zeke. Please," his mother scolds him.

"Lesbian isn't a bad word, mom!"

"I meant the other word, Zeke."

"I was just quoting Brooke," Zeke defends himself.

"Sorry, I didn't mean to call her a bitch," Brooke says quickly. "I didn't realize you two were like, related or whatever."

"That's okay." I shrug. "Jo is kind of a bitch."

This makes both Brooke and Zeke laugh, but their parents seem unamused. Oh well.

♫

Marisol and Ollie meet me at my locker after school the next day. I'm still putting my books away when Marisol wraps their arm around me.

"Are you excited? 'Cause I'm excited," they squeal. "This job is gonna be way more fun now that I actually like the person I'm working with!"

"You still haven't told me what I'm going to be doing," I remind them while shutting my locker, "so I'm not sure if I should be excited."

"Oh, you know, we're just gonna do some blood rituals, sacrifice baby animals, summon a demon," Marisol lists off, "maybe we'll throw a virgin into a volcano if we can find one. Do you know of any?"

"Virgins or volcanoes?" I ask.

"They're kidding," Ollie reassures me.

I look from Ollie to Marisol, who is trying very hard not to laugh, and then back at Ollie. "Thank you," I say, "I got that."

"Don't worry," Marisol continues, "today's actually gonna be an easy day because the cast is rehearsing separately from the crew. It's probably the best day for you to start 'cause you don't need to deal with any *actors*." They throw their head back at the end of their sentence as if it physically pains them to mention the actors.

"Isn't Brooke one of the actors?" I start to laugh.

"Yeah," Marisol sighs. "And we love her to death, but God, she can be a drama queen backstage."

We arrive at the theater. I had passed by this door pretty much every day since I started at Woodview High, but I always assumed it was a supply closet. I feel a little bit like I'm entering Narnia when I see the large room the door actually leads to. There are not many people here, but those that are, are bursting with energy. Everyone moves with purpose.

As soon as we enter, a thin brunette girl calls from across the room, "Ollie!" She is petite, with pink streaks in her hair, and an exasperated look on her face. "Get over here," she yells, gesturing to the stage she's standing on. "I need you!"

"Gotta jet." Ollie salutes us and jogs across the room. The girl immediately starts barking orders at him, which is a bit of a funny sight. Ollie could easily football-chuck her across the room if he so pleased, but after even one conversation with the boy, it is clear that he would never hurt a fly.

Marisol drops their backpack in the corner, so I do the same. They bend down to dig through it, eventually pulling out a small black binder.

"We've got much to do, my dear," they declare in a distinguished British accent. I raise an eyebrow and they sigh. "We've gotta find little ways to have fun in this world, Elena. Sometimes that requires a stupid accent."

I laugh. "Whatever you say."

With that, they make a beeline to a small door at the back of the room. I follow them into a tiny closet filled to the brim with the most random objects imaginable. I'm afraid if I touch anything we'll be crushed to death in an avalanche.

Marisol walks me through what needs to be done and before I know it, I'm squeezed behind a rack of clothes on my hands and knees because Marisol is *sure* there's a period-appropriate sewing kit in here somewhere. Eventually, I poke my head out of a small gap between potential costumes to report that I absolutely cannot find it.

When I emerge from the pile of clothes, I see Marisol attempting to duct tape a step back onto a wooden ladder.

"That doesn't seem safe," I warn them.

"Well, I can't reach the top shelf without it. We need Zeke," they mumble, collapsing onto the floor.

"Shouldn't Zeke be here?" I ask. "He's part of the crew, no?"

"Lights and sound don't join us until closer to the actual show," they explain.

"The drama club is a lot more segregated than I imagined it would be."

Marisol laughs. "Yes, but that's for our benefit," they say, slipping a black and red feather boa around my shoulders. They grab a pair of pink heart-shaped sunglasses from a nearby box and put them on. I think the prop closet is beginning to make them delirious.

"I did think I was gonna meet Brooke's boyfriend," I mention.

Marisol groans. "Sorry, that was dramatic."

"I take it you don't like him?"

They shrug. "He's fine, I guess. I just get bad vibes."

"Yikes."

"He hasn't actually done anything wrong that I know of," they clarify. "I just feel weird whenever he's around. You'll see what I'm talking about at the Halloween party."

"What Halloween party?"

"Brooke didn't tell you?" Marisol's eyes widen as they place a fedora on my head. I immediately remove it.

"I haven't seen her today," I explain. Marisol replaces the fedora with a blue cowboy hat, which I also immediately take off.

"Some of her boyfriend's friends throw this huge Halloween party every year. We're all going. You'll love it."

"Sounds fun."

Ollie suddenly peeks his head through the doorway. "What the heck happened here? It looks like a tornado hit. Mr. Brunner's gonna kill you."

I look at Marisol with wide eyes. They shrug. "He won't kill us," they say. "Probably.

8

All Together Now

"I need advice."

I look up from my laptop where I was scrolling through a listicle titled "27 Super Easy Halloween Costumes Using Items You Already Have In Your Closet." I wonder if the writers actually believe that the average person does, in fact, have a Catholic schoolgirl uniform in their closet.

"What's wrong?" I ask.

Jo sits up from her place on the bed and pouts. "I'm supposed to go to a Halloween party with my friends."

"And that's a problem because...?"

"Because my friends aren't talking to me!" she shouts. "God, Elena, keep up!"

"Sorry?" I laugh.

"This isn't funny."

"Sorry," I say, more seriously this time, but eventually I start to laugh again.

"So, do I still go to the party?"

"If you want to."

"But will they be mad that I'm there?" She leans back on her elbows. "Or will they be madder if I'm not there? The group costume idea doesn't work as well without me. Or does it?"

"How would I know how to answer that?"

"Or will they not want me in the group costume since we aren't talking?" she continues, completely ignoring the fact that I am missing many details. "What if they changed the group costume and didn't tell me? Do I need to find a new costume? How am I supposed to do that?"

"Do you have a Catholic schoolgirl uniform?" I ask.

"What?"

"Nothing."

She flops back on her bed so hard that I'm not sure how she didn't hurt her neck. "Maybe I should stay home," she sighs.

"You could always come to a party with me and my friends," I offer.

She leans up. "You're going to a party?"

"You don't have to sound so surprised."

"Is it a good party?"

"I don't know." I laugh. "What qualifies as a good party?"

"Will seniors be there?"

"I have no idea."

"Well, who's throwing it?"

"My friend's boyfriend. Or maybe his friend." I pause to think. "I don't completely know."

"Is there any chance your friend is dating someone popular?"

"I don't know," I explain. "I haven't met him."

"Do you know anything? Anything at all?"

"I guess not."

"Well, then thank you for being completely and totally useless." She groans and throws a blanket over her head.

I roll my eyes and return to my laptop.

After a while, she pulls the blanket downward, just enough so that her face peeks out. "Are you sure it's okay if I come?"

"I'm sure it is, but I will confirm it with my friends if that makes you feel better," I say. "We're also meeting a little early to pregame."

"Okay, so maybe you're not *totally* useless."

♪

Jo eventually figured out a way to salvage her original Halloween costume idea and found a corresponding one for me. I don't know why we needed to match, but it seemed pretty important to her, and it's not like I had any ideas of my own. She scolded me that a homemade costume was not good enough for a Woodview party, so she forced me to take a last-minute trip to the costume shop with her and Meg. Meg even insisted on paying for my costume. I think she was just happy that Jo and I were doing something together.

Jo's original plan with Casey was to go as Supergirl and Batgirl, while Rachel and Nico would dress as Harley Quinn and the Joker. She decided that Supergirl and Wonder Woman would be even better than Supergirl and Batgirl. Although I was apprehensive about the idea of wearing something so revealing, I gave in.

Jo nervously fidgets with her clothing during the entire walk over to Ollie's house. When we arrive, I ring the doorbell, as Jo smoothes down her skirt one last time.

Ollie opens the door wearing a giant white bedsheet as a toga. He immediately hugs me tight, picking me up off the ground and shaking me slightly.

"You look great!" Ollie says enthusiastically. He turns to Jo and puts out one of his hands. "I'm Ollie. Nice to meet you. Come on in!"

Ollie's house is somewhat similar to Jo's in size and architectural style but is decorated vastly differently. I kind of feel like I'm walking into a fairy tale cottage that has been invaded by hippies. It doesn't match him at all and makes me wonder about his parents. He leads us down to the basement, where everyone else is already scattered across the floor and couches.

"Elena!" Brooke squeals as she jumps up to run over and hug me, almost knocking me over with her excited energy. "You look so good!"

"You too!" I reply.

She does a little twirl to show off her Dorothy costume, complete with a little wicker basket and a stuffed dog. Only then, does she seem to notice Jo standing next to me.

She backs into herself, clasping her hands behind her back. "Hi," she says quietly, no longer making eye contact.

"Hey," Jo replies awkwardly.

Zeke swoops in next to his sister, cutting the tension ever so slightly. He's dressed as Where's Waldo in a red and white striped shirt with a matching hat.

"Nice to meet you. Want something to drink?"

"Uh … sure?" Jo hesitates, looking at me for permission.

"C'mon, I'll show you what we got." He takes her hand and leads her away, leaving me and Brooke by ourselves.

I lean in and softly say, "You said it was okay for me to bring her."

"I know what I said," Brooke mumbles. "It's fine. Whatever."

"Something's obviously wrong."

She shakes her head. "It's nothing. Don't worry about me."

"Are you sure?"

"C'mon." She leads me back to the couch and we sit down next to Ollie. Violet is cross-legged on a swivel chair across from us. She is dressed in a dinosaur onesie, which looks more like children's pajamas than an actual costume. It might actually be children's pajamas. She's certainly small enough. Marisol is sprawled out on the floor like they're in the movie *Titanic*, waiting for Jack to paint them like one of his French girls.

"Aw yeah, the gang's all here," they announce as I sit down. "Drink?"

I think back to Alex Dancey's birthday. I got drunk far quicker than I thought I would and it hadn't turned out so well. I was determined not to let the same thing happen tonight.

"No thanks," I reply, shaking my head. "I think I'll wait a bit longer."

"A responsible queen." They smile. They've clearly already had a few.

It takes me a second to realize Marisol is even wearing a costume, since they're dressed about the same way they normally are, with combat boots, black skinny jeans, and a leather jacket. The only thing separating this outfit from their regular day look is the bits of fake blood on their face and the fangs visible when they speak.

"When should we head over?" Violet asks, as she twists her swivel chair back and forth.

"What? You're just dying to get out of my house?" Ollie teases.

"So what if I am?"

"Then maybe I should throw you out." He shoots out of his seat and scoops Violet up in his arms. He starts running around the room with her, as if she's a toy he's just stolen from another kid.

She shouts, "Put me down!"

He plops her down on the couch next to me. She brushes her dark brown hair out of her face.

"You're so annoying," Violet sighs, but then she laughs.

"You know you love me," Ollie retorts, putting his arm around her.

"How long have you two been dating?" Jo asks.

Everyone, including me, laughs. She looks around confused, and I realize she must feel just like I did when I thought Brooke and Zeke were dating. It feels nice to not be the one on the outside anymore.

"Ew," Ollie says.

Violet whacks him softly on the arm.

"I don't mean *ew*," he explains, "you're just so … you're like … one of the boys. I can't think of you that way."

Zeke looks around the room with his hand on his brow. "Who are these *boys* you speak of?"

Everyone laughs again, and after a bit, even Jo joins in.

9

Look On The Bright Side

We walk to the party, and Jo does not bother to hide her annoyance at this, but she quiets down and gets a weird look on her face once we round the corner and our destination comes into view. We're back in the part of town where people live in pseudo-mansions, much like Levi's or Brooke and Zeke's houses. I've been in this town long enough to understand that somewhere along our walk, we entered Woodview Harbor, where the rich people are next level.

We go inside, where the vibe is identical to that of Alex Dancey's party, but I figure all Long Island high school parties must be more or less the same. It's only when I notice Levi across the room that I become suspicious.

"Whose house is this?" Jo asks suddenly. I think she must've seen Levi too.

"Dylan Strickland's," Brooke says. "He's a senior in the play, so you might not know him."

Jo's groan tells me she knows exactly who he is. "Elena, you idiot!"

"What did I do?"

"*This* is the party Casey and Rachel are going to!"

I scoff, almost laughing. "Well, how was I supposed to know that?"

"This isn't funny! What am I gonna do?"

"Jo, you're already here." I sigh. "Just have fun. If your friends won't talk to you, you have us. And if they will, then congrats, you're friends again, and you can ditch me like you did last time."

She smooths down her skirt for the umpteenth time and breathes in and out quickly. "How do I look?"

"Like you're about to save the world," I joke.

"I'm serious!"

I roll my eyes. "You look great. Right, everyone?"

"Oh yeah, you're hot," Marisol says instantly. "Real Kryptonian-girl-next-door vibe."

♫

I learn that parties are a lot more fun when you actually have friends. Unfortunately, so does Jo. I catch her longingly staring at Casey at least four times, but Casey either hasn't noticed her or is choosing to ignore her. Probably the latter.

"Why don't you just go talk to her?"

Jo shakes her head. "She obviously doesn't want me to."

"Well, you're lousy company when you're this distracted," I inform her.

"Your friends are fun," Jo admits.

"Thanks."

"They're nice too."

"I know. That's why I'm friends with them."

She rolls her eyes. "Do you know where the bathroom here is?"

"No clue." I look around. "You're definitely gonna get lost in this house, aren't you?"

"Probably." She shrugs.

"I'll come with you. At least then we'll be lost together."

We did get partially lost but eventually found a bathroom on the second floor. I am waiting in the hallway for Jo when someone stumbles around the corner. It's the boy with the jet-black hair. He's wearing an "FBI" cap and a t-shirt that reads "Female Body Inspector." Why am I not surprised that his costume is as creepy as he is?

"I remember you," he says, slurring his words. He comes closer, leaning against the wall next to me. "You're Levi's girl."

I take in a deep breath. "I'm Levi's *friend*, maybe," I say. "I'm not anybody's girl."

He flashes a grin. "Does Levi know that?"

"I'm fifteen," I remind him. "Levi at least knows *that.*"

"You look older," he whispers as he leans closer. He smells like liquor.

I cross my arms over my chest, suddenly more self-conscious of the amount of skin this costume shows. He shifts to stand in front of me, placing one hand on each side of me, against the wall, so I'm trapped between his arms.

He moves his face closer until I can feel his stubble rubbing against my cheek. I glance around. There is no one here, but we are still too out in the open for him to try anything, right?

"Get off of me!" I shove him, only moving him slightly. He takes this opportunity to grab my forearm and pull me closer to him until our bodies are against each other. He's stronger than he looks. He moves his other hand downward and grips my ass.

Then the bathroom door opens and Jo exits back into the hallway. She looks from me to him and then back to me. He releases me and takes a step back.

"You should be more careful," he says snidely. "You're lucky I was here to catch you."

I back up, closing the gap between myself and the wall. I nod. He looks at Jo as if he's just noticed her arrival, though I know her presence is the only reason he let go of me.

"She almost fell over," he explains. "Think she mighta had a little too much."

"Right," Jo says, looking back at me, and then at him again.

He walks away and I slip past Jo into the bathroom, slamming the door. I turn the lock and sink to the ground. My breathing is rapid, but that just makes me angrier. This asshole shouldn't be able to make me feel like this so easily. He shouldn't have this power over me.

Jo waits for me, and then we go rejoin the rest of the party. She doesn't mention anything about our interaction with the boy with jet-black hair. I force the thoughts of him out of my mind. I am at a party and I am going to have fun.

I'm not sure where everyone else is, so I'm glad that Jo and I decided to stick together. We wander through the giant rooms until we land in the kitchen. She grabs a beer for each of us, and we gravitate toward a corner of the room. I take small sips, wondering how anyone can like the taste of this.

We chat for a few minutes as I scan the rest of the room. I recognize a lot of people from Alex Dancey's party, including the girl in the glittery top who, thanks to Jo, I now know is named Parvati and is the captain of the color guard. Then I notice Jo's eyes widening, clearly focused on something other than me. I glance over my shoulder and see Levi walking toward us. He's wearing a red puffy vest over a button-down shirt. It takes me a minute to realize he is dressed as Marty from *Back to the Future*.

"Hey," he greets us. "I didn't know you were coming." He puts his arm around me, causing me to unintentionally flinch. He precariously lifts it off of me and turns his attention to Jo. "You're in color guard, right? Josephine?"

"Joanne," she corrects. "Or just Jo, really."

"Right, right," he nods. "I like your costumes. Wonder Woman and Supergirl. That's cute. I saw Batgirl before too. Are you with her?"

"Um ... sort of?" Jo says.

"Not really," I clarify.

"It was that redhead. Cassie?"

"Casey," I correct him.

"Yes?"

I turn around to see Casey standing on the other side of the kitchen island.

"Hey!" Levi exclaims. "Look at you three. So cute!"

Casey glares at me. I glance over at Jo, but her eyes are planted on the floor.

"Yeah," I say. "You look great, Casey."

She purses her lips and puts one hand on her hip. "Nice outfit," she mutters. "I wish I had your confidence and could just wear anything without caring about how it made me look."

I cross my arms over my chest instinctively. I had never been particularly self-conscious about my body before. I mean, sure, there were always things I was insecure about. I am a teenage girl, after all. But ever since I've been in Woodview, it feels like everyone is always looking at me. And I can't help but think about what they see. Back in Miami, there were lots of girls who looked like me. Here, I stick out like a sore thumb. Boys have no qualms about staring at me, and I hate it.

"I, um, I'm gonna go find my friends," I say quietly. I glance at Jo, who still won't make eye contact with any of us. "You coming, Jo?"

She nods slowly. I try to read her face as we walk past Casey. She averts her eyes as we pass. Whatever happened between them must be worse than I thought.

We enter the next room. After a few minutes, Violet comes running toward us.

"Elena, hey. I was looking for you. We kind of need to leave soon, if you wanna walk back with us."

I look at Jo, who doesn't seem like she's completely recovered from seeing Casey. She nods, her voice almost breaking as she says, "Yeah, let's go home."

The three of us join the others outside, where Brooke sits on the front stoop, crying.

I bend down to join everyone else on the ground, surrounding her, and ask, "What happened?"

She shakes her head. "It's nothing," she insists. "It's so stupid."

I look to Zeke for some sort of explanation, but he just shakes his head. I nod in understanding. I don't need to know what's wrong right now. At this moment, what matters is Brooke and getting her out of here.

♫

At some point, our group splits into two. Those who live in Woodview Harbor leave us for their own homes, while Ollie, Marisol, Jo, and I continue toward the other side of town. We stay silent until everyone else is clearly out of earshot.

Then I finally speak. "What happened to her?"

Marisol lets out a deep sigh. "Dylan happened."

"She got in a fight with her boyfriend," Ollie explains. "She didn't really tell us more than that. I think she was too upset to talk."

"That sucks," I say.

Jo and I eventually get home and head inside. Meg is waiting in the living room, watching TV. She mutes it when we enter.

"Hey, how was the party?"

"Fine," Jo says, in a voice that makes it fairly obvious that she did not actually think it was fine.

"It was fun," I add, calming Meg's nervous look a little bit.

She probably knows we were drinking. She isn't stupid. But we clearly aren't drunk, so I guess she gives us a pass. It's not the kind of parenting decision my mom would've made. She's probably just relieved that we actually made it home together, unlike last time.

We head to our room, where I immediately strip out of my costume and throw on baggy pajama pants and an oversized hoodie instead. I sit on the bed, comforted by the fact that all my curves are covered and there's no one else to see me other than Jo.

Jo doesn't change. She doesn't even take off her shoes. She sits at her desk and inspects her face in the mirror, though I'm not sure what she's looking for.

"I wonder what Brooke and Dylan were fighting about," she says without looking away from the mirror.

I shrug. "It must've been pretty bad. She looked really upset."

"Do you think it had anything to do with you?"

"Why would it have anything to do with me?"

"You know."

"I don't understand. I don't even know Dylan."

She sighs, finally turning around to face me. "You two seemed pretty close in the hallway earlier."

I shake my head. "That was Ren's half-brother in the hallway."

"Yes, Ren's half-brother Dylan." She emphasizes each word slowly like she thinks I'm stupid. Maybe I am? "That was his house. The house we were just at."

I don't say anything, but I notice my breathing becoming shallow. The boy with the jet-black hair is the same guy that Brooke's dating, the same guy who made her cry tonight. And suddenly, I realize what it all means. Suddenly, I'm keeping a secret I didn't even know I had.

10

Nothing Is As Bad As You Think It Is

"So, this is why you've been avoiding me for the past few weeks, huh?"

I look up from my desk to see Ren standing above me. I glance at the clock and see there is still time before class starts, which means I won't be saved by the bell.

"I haven't been avoiding you," I lie, poorly.

"Yeah you have," he insists. "And I've been racking my brain trying to figure out what I did, and then this morning I'm scrolling online and it finally clicks."

"What are you talking about?" At this point, I'm genuinely confused. What does the Internet have to do with any of this?

"Oh, that's right," he says, pulling his phone out of his back pocket. "I forgot that you don't follow WoodNews." He places the phone on my desk and slides it toward me. It's open to a new post:

that new girl Elena has been here for like 10 seconds and she already hooked up with Dylan Strickland. what a SLUT

A lump forms in my throat. I don't know what to say.

"I realized you've been acting weird ever since you met my brother," Ren continues. "So I'm guessing that wasn't actually the first time you met him."

I'm suddenly hyper-aware of the people staring at me, whispering about me. Ren keeps his eyes planted on me, and I wish I could just disappear. I know I should respond, but I just can't. Apparently, my silence speaks volumes, because Ren swallows, nods, and backs away. With his head hung low, he returns to his desk and doesn't look at me for the rest of the period.

♫

Between third and fourth period, I see Brooke in the hallway. She notices me from across the hall and makes a beeline toward me. I try my best to duck away, as I've never been one for confrontation, but before I know it, she's right in front of me.

"Is it true?" Her eyes are red like she's been crying, yet she looks noticeably more angry than sad.

"I don't—" I say the words, but I'm not even convinced she hears me, my voice is so meek.

She shouts, "Did you sleep with my boyfriend or not?"

"No!" I shout back, but I know that isn't the full story. "Or … maybe," I timidly add. "I'm not sure. I don't know. I don't remember."

"Were you just pretending to be my friend?"

"We *are* friends," I insist. "I don't even know if anything happened."

She scoffs. "Do you think I'm stupid?"

I look around. Our argument has caused quite a scene and plenty of people have gathered around us to watch. I don't want to talk about it here. Why couldn't we do this in private? I can't explain what actually happened, not in front of all these people, not when I'm not even completely sure myself. I stare at her. I don't know what to say.

With all her force, she shoves me into the wall. "You're a slut, Elena."

I don't respond. What would be the point? I just watch her walk away, as tears begin to form in my eyes.

♪

I eat lunch by myself, in the bathroom. I saw Marisol on my way to the cafeteria, but it was clear from the way they looked at me that I was not welcome at their table today. It makes sense. They've all been friends with Brooke long before they were friends with me, so if Brooke hates me now, they probably all do too.

I am just about done eating when I hear someone else walk in. I'm glad, because the sound of vomiting that ensues would've made me lose my appetite anyway. Between retches, I can hear the quiet sound of sobs and I just feel like I need to do something.

"Are you okay?" I quietly call out.

"Yeah," she sniffles. "Sorry, I didn't know anyone was in here."

"You don't sound okay."

"I'm fine!" she yells in a voice I recognize.

I exit my stall. Something tells me I shouldn't leave, even though she clearly wants to be alone.

I walk closer to the stall and whisper, "Jo?"

The sniffling abruptly stops. "Who's there?"

"It's Elena," I say softly. "Can you open the door?"

There's hesitation, but then I hear the toilet flush and the door unlatches. Jo is seated on the floor with her knees at her chest. Her face is wet with tears and her eyes are bloodshot. I perch down to get on an even level with her, but she looks away from me.

"What's going on?" I ask. "Are you sick?"

She nods. "Probably something I ate." More likely it's nerves, but I don't correct her.

"Should I take you to the nurse so you can go home?"

She shakes her head. "No, I can't miss class. Plus there's no one who can come pick me up since Mom and Dad are both at work."

"I really don't think you should stay at school like this."

"It's fine, Elena. You don't always have to put your nose in my business."

"Jesus, I'm trying to help."

"I don't need your help!" She sighs and deflates slightly. "I'm sorry. I'm just stressed today."

"I mean..." I start to laugh. "...I'd ask if you wanna talk about it, but I don't want to put my nose in your business."

Jo chuckles too. "Shut up."

I wait a moment before continuing. "*Do* you want to talk about it?"

She hesitates, picking at her fingernails like she always does when she's nervous. "I did something bad, and I know I shouldn't have done it, but I really didn't think it was going to be such a big deal."

I nod slowly. "Is this about your fight with Casey?"

"No," she shakes her head. "Well, kind of, I guess."

"I don't understand," I admit. "You've gotta give me a little more than that."

She looks toward the ground and speaks low. "I asked Casey if she could ever forgive me," she swallows as if choking on her own words, "and she said maybe, but first I had to do something in return." A tear rolls down her cheek, which she quickly wipes away. "And so I did it, even though I knew it was wrong. And now Casey still won't talk to me and I—" She stops suddenly. Her eyes are filling up and they look like they're about to burst. "I messed up, Elena. I didn't know she would twist it like that."

"What did you do, Jo?" I'm a little scared to know the answer, if it's really as bad as she's making it seem, but I want to help her. "You can tell me. I won't tell anyone."

She shakes her head. "I can't."

I nod slowly. "Okay," I say. "You don't have to tell me. But whatever it is, it's going to be alright. I promise."

She shakes her head harder this time. She's no longer trying to stop the tears from falling. "It won't."

♫

Jo insists she's okay to walk home after school, and I know there's no point in arguing with her. I decide to look for the silver lining of us both losing all of our friends at the same time and just enjoy the fact that we're walking home together. Not that long ago, Jo wouldn't even allow anyone at school to see us together, but these days, knowing me doesn't seem like her biggest problem anymore.

We get about a block and a half before I hear someone call my name. I turn around to see Levi, with his head sticking out of the driver's side window of the car pulled up beside us.

"Do you want a ride?"

I look at Jo, remembering how much of a problem my talking to Levi caused her at the first party. "No thanks. We're good."

"But … can we just talk?"

I hesitate. He gives a half-hearted smile.

Jo scoffs. "Elena," she whispers, "when a cute senior boy offers you a ride, you take it." Even at her lowest, she still has her priorities in order.

"But what about Casey? Won't she be mad?"

Jo shrugs. "She hates me now anyway."

I laugh but immediately feel bad and stop. I turn back to Levi. "Can you drive Jo too? We're going in the same direction."

I get in the passenger seat and Jo gets in the back. I can feel her eyeing me, but I refuse to give her the satisfaction of turning around.

"Where do you live, Jo?" Levi asks. "I'll drop you off first."

Suddenly, I realize how much we did not think this through. Jo made it very clear when I moved here that, as far as anyone else was concerned, we weren't sisters. I don't blame her for the secrecy. If people knew, they'd want an explanation, and then she'd have to tell people that her dad had a secret daughter. In a small town like this, that was going to be big news. I mean, all I did was maybe hook up with a guy, and everyone is talking about me. I can't imagine what they'd be saying if they knew everything else.

To my surprise, Jo doesn't hesitate when she recites our address. I wonder if this means she'll be expecting me to give him a fake drop-off location for myself. I hope not. I can't remember the names of any streets near us.

"Cool, I think I know where that is," he nods. "And Elena, what's yours?"

I try to get a look at Jo's face in my peripheral vision. I'm hoping to get some clue as to what she's thinking right now.

"Same one," she answers for me. "We live together."

Levi looks at me, a little confused, but he doesn't ask any additional questions. "Okay." He smiles. "Less work for me."

I exhale.

Aside from the blasting radio, we ride in complete silence on the drive home. It's only when we pull in front of the house that Levi puts his hand on my forearm and says, "So, can we talk for a minute?"

I look toward Jo in the backseat. She seems concerned when I prompt her to go inside without me; nevertheless, she agrees.

Levi turns off the radio, so now it's just me and him sitting in an eerily silent car.

"I just wanted to check if you were okay."

I stare at him. "Why wouldn't I be okay? Just because the whole school thinks I'm a whore and all my friends hate me? Nah, I can't let that get me down."

"Jo doesn't seem to hate you."

"Jo isn't exactly my friend."

He looks toward the house and then back at me. "So are you and her...?" he trails off like he's afraid he'll guess wrong.

"Half-sisters," I answer. "Same dad. Different moms."

"The dad who just found out he's your dad?"

I chuckle awkwardly. "Yep. That's the one."

"Damn." He pauses. "I don't hate you. We're friends, right?"

"I guess so."

"You could sound a little happier about it."

My body tenses. I think about how Casey and Jo were so sure that Levi was flirting with me. Apparently, sophomores dating seniors isn't as weird as I thought, since Brooke is dating Dylan. Plus, now that Levi thinks I hooked up with a senior, maybe he's hoping I would do it again. Is that why he offered me a ride home? Is that why he's been so nice to me this whole time? Levi must sense my change in demeanor because he suddenly leans away from me and focuses his stare on the steering wheel.

"Anyway," he says, almost stammering, "I heard you really went at it with Dylan's girlfriend today."

I drop my head into my hands. "So people are talking about that too?"

He gulps. "Someone told me they thought they heard you say that you didn't know if... That you didn't remember and I just..." he hesitates, shutting his eyes closed tight. "Do you actually not remember what happened that night?"

Our eyes meet, but I can't speak at first. "I don't know," I admit. "A lot of it is fuzzy."

He nods and sucks in his lips. "I feel like I owe it to you to put your mind at ease. Nothing happened between you and Dylan. I mean, not nothing, I guess. I know you kissed, but I made sure nothing else happened after that."

I let out an exhausted sigh. It would be great to just accept this and be happy, but I can't. "You made sure?"

"I, um," he swallows, nearly choking on his words, "I was there."

"Yeah, it was your house."

He grips the steering wheel tightly. "No, I mean, I was *there*. I saw him. I saw him trying to..." he trails off, looking out the window. "I saw him take you into the bedroom. You were totally out of it. He started to unbutton your sweater, but I stopped him, and I promise, nothing else happened after that."

"But if you hadn't?" I feel my face heating up. I should be relieved to hear nothing more happened, but instead, I'm angry. "You've known for weeks what he tried to do and you didn't think to say anything?"

"Because nothing happened. I came in. I stopped him."

"And that makes it okay? I've been going crazy trying to remember, and you knew all along."

He doesn't answer. It kind of looks like he wants to, but he doesn't. He just watches me, silently, for far longer than I'm comfortable with. So I open the door and get out.

Before it fully closes, he leans over the seat and holds it open. "I'm sorry," he says, like he's breathless and desperately gasping for air.

I just walk away.

11

It Could Always Be Worse

The doorbell rings around noon on Saturday. I'm in my room reading a book for English class that I cannot bring myself to care about, so I let someone else get the door. With Brooke and Ren both mad at me, and me mad at Levi, and pretty much everyone else just ignoring me, I've been stressed. I need a well-deserved break this weekend, and I figure someone else can deal with whoever is at the door. But my luck is not about to allow that.

"Elena!" Meg calls from downstairs. "Someone's at the door for you!"

I groan, rolling myself into a pretzel. Unless Lana has somehow managed to fly in from Miami and surprise me, I don't want to see whoever is at the door.

Against my best efforts, I give in and drag myself out of bed and down the stairs. The moment I see Ren standing in the doorway, I start to turn around and head back upstairs.

"Elena, please," he calls out. "I just wanna talk to you. Can we take a walk or something?"

I turn back around to face him, but my expression doesn't change. "What for?"

He kicks a pebble off the stoop. "I want to apologize."

"You don't have anything to apologize for."

He sighs. "I'm sure that this week really sucked for you, and I should've been your friend instead of getting mad at you for my own selfish reasons."

I glance at him and then at Meg in my peripheral vision. Her eyes widen, but I don't have the energy to tell her what's been going on.

"Let's go for a walk."

We get a few blocks away before either of us actually says anything. I know the ball's in my court, but what am I supposed to do? Tell the truth? That'll open up a whole can of worms that I don't think I could deal with. So maybe I just wait, and let Ren forgive me for something I never did.

He finally breaks the silence. "I just was surprised, I guess."

I look at him. His hands are shoved in his pockets, and his face is aimed toward the ground. He hasn't looked at me since we started walking, not even when he spoke.

"Surprised?" I ask.

He nods. "I guess I shouldn't have been. Everyone likes Dylan. Of course, you like him too." His lips curve, and I almost think he's going to laugh, but he doesn't. "I know I can't actually be mad at you. You're allowed to do whatever you want, with whoever you want. I can't even be mad at him, I guess. I'm just … mad at the world."

I laugh, and he finally looks up from the ground.

"What?"

"Nothing, I just…" I laugh again. "Mad at the world. I get it."

"I'm glad my misery is amusing to you." His tone sounds like he's mad, but when I look at him, he's smiling. And things feel like they did before I knew who Dylan was, so now I know everything's going to be okay.

"I'm sorry for avoiding you," I say, "I just freaked out when I realized he was your brother. I didn't know how to face you."

"I just wish you had told me."

"There was nothing to tell."

"For a while there, I kinda thought you just didn't want to be my friend."

"That's not it at all," I promise.

He nods but doesn't look convinced. I try to think about what this might look like to him. I ignored him while I got to know Brooke, Marisol, and all my other new friends. But now that they want nothing to do with me, I claim I still want to be friends with him. There are holes in my story, and he knows it. He just doesn't know what those holes are. I realize I owe him the truth; the full truth, no matter what that means.

"I didn't sleep with Dylan." I fiddle with my thumbs. I can feel his eyes on me, but I won't look at him until I'm done. "I thought I might have, but I didn't."

"I don't understand."

I swallow hard. "I couldn't remember what happened that night," I explain. "I still don't. Not fully."

"What? Like you blacked out?"

"Maybe?" I shake my head. God, what am I doing? "The details are fuzzy. I passed out..."

He stops in his tracks, so I stop walking too, but I still won't face him. "Elena, what are you saying?" I don't answer, so he continues, "What happened?"

I swallow again. My throat feels so tight. "Nothing," I finally let myself breathe. "Someone stopped him before anything happened. I'm fine. He didn't... He didn't."

I finally turn to face him. Ren's cheeks are flushed. He blinks rapidly and pants slowly. Before I know it, his arms are wrapped around me.

"You don't have to be fine just because he didn't do *that*. He's still an asshole for trying anything at all."

I don't even realize that I'm crying until my tears are already soaking into Ren's shirt.

"It's okay," he whispers over and over in my ear as he strokes my hair. "It's okay."

Once I finally stop crying, Ren tells me that he has an idea. He holds my hand as we walk, but he won't tell me where we're going. Eventually, we arrive at a train station.

"Are we going on a trip?" I ask. "Or … killing ourselves?"

He laughs. "No."

"Then what are we doing here?"

He walks along the platform and up a long set of stairs until we're standing in the middle of a bridge that connects the two platforms.

"Are you sure we're not killing ourselves?"

He shakes his head. "My mom used to work in the city when I was a kid," he says. "Sometimes my dad would walk us over, so we could be here when she arrived."

"That's sweet."

He nods. "My sister used to beg my dad to let us wait for her on the footbridge. I don't know why. I guess she thought it'd be cool to be up this high." He almost laughs toward the end of his sentence, but it isn't a happy laugh. Something about this story is hard for him to tell.

"I didn't know you had a sister."

He nods again. "Mei. She was always super determined. Once she decided she wanted something, she would never stop until she got it. She kept bugging our dad about the footbridge. I remember the day he finally let us go up here." He looks out into the distance, over the tracks, and just stares for a while. "Right as the train was about to come, she pulled my sleeve and whispered in my ear, 'Scream.' I have no idea why I listened to her, but I did. We screamed as hard as we could. Really freaked out my dad, but no one else could hear us over the train. I don't know if that had been her reason for wanting to come up here all along or if it was just something she thought of on the spot. It was oddly … freeing, I guess?"

He taps his fingers on the railing and smiles ever so slightly. "I come up here when things feel overwhelming," he explains. "There's something cathartic about screaming when no one can hear you. And there's not too many places around here where you can do that."

I smile and reach my hand out to place it on top of his. He interlocks our fingers and smiles back at me.

"So, we're here to scream?"

He nods. "If you want to."

I smile. "I do."

The bells begin to ring, signaling that the train is coming.

"Thank you," I quickly say.

"For what?"

"For being my friend."

And then the train rumbles on the track beneath us. And we scream.

♫

When it starts to get dark out, we each go home. As soon as I step inside, I hear voices coming from upstairs. Meg and my father are yelling, and the closer I get, the angrier they sound.

I enter my bedroom to see Jo sitting on her bed. She tries to hide her eyes when she sees me, but I can still see them. They're blood red.

I sit down on my bed because going to hers seems too strange. I pat the seat next to me, offering it to her. She looks at me with her eyebrow slightly raised, as if trying to decipher the hidden message in my gesture, like I'm trying to trick her into agreeing to some sort of unspoken fine print.

"They've never fought like this before," she says. "At least not when I could hear them."

"I'm sorry." I pause for a moment. "I can't really think of anything more useful than that."

This gets her to laugh slightly. "It probably seems so dumb to you. Getting this upset just 'cause my parents are fighting. It could be so much worse."

I lie back so that I can see the ceiling. There are a bunch of stick-on stars scattered across it. Jo probably put them there when she was a kid, back when her life was more simple.

I think about Lana and how hesitant she always is about opening up to me. She's been through something traumatic and she should be able to talk to me about that without feeling guilty that I've been through something worse.

Then I think about Ren and what he said to me today. We don't have to be fine, just because things aren't worse. We can be grateful for what goes right while still feeling the pain of what's gone wrong. Those feelings don't have to contradict each other. Why do we all act like they do?

"It's not dumb," I say. "It could always be worse, but that doesn't mean it hurts any less."

She shakes her head. "I've been so mad at him since we found out about..." she trails off, but I know what she's thinking.

"About me," I finish her sentence.

She slides off her bed and crouches on the floor with her knees to her chest and her arms wrapped around her legs. "Do you think he really didn't know?"

"What do you mean?"

"He said he had no idea your mom was pregnant," she explains. "Do you think that's true?"

I shrug. "Probably. My mom told me he left before *she* even knew she was pregnant. I don't think she would've lied about that."

"Crazy," she sighs. "Do you ever wonder what would've happened if he had known?"

"Of course I do," I admit. "I try not to, but I can't help thinking about what it would've been like if I had known him growing up. If we'd known each other growing up, that would've probably been pretty cool, right?"

She shakes her head. "I don't think he would've ever let us know each other. Even if he knew about us both, he probably would've still kept us apart."

"Where is this coming from?" I ask, sitting up so I can make eye contact with her.

"It's just something I've been thinking about lately." She sighs. "If Dad found out that your mom was pregnant before he found out mine was, then I would've been the one who got abandoned, right? Our whole lives would've been switched, and it's just so completely random that things happened one way instead of the other. It's completely random."

"But our lives weren't switched," I remind her. "Maybe it's random, but it's what happened. Nothing can change that."

Her lip begins to quiver, and soon enough, her eyes fill with tears that she's clearly trying to hold back. I slide onto the floor to sit across from her.

"Hey, it's okay," I whisper.

She shakes her head, and suddenly, she's crying for real. "I'm a terrible person, Elena."

"That's not true."

"It is!" She desperately tries to dry her face, but the tears are falling too quickly. "It's my fault, okay? That stupid post; it's my fault."

"What are you talking about?"

"The post about you on WoodNews! Casey submitted it because I told her about you and Dylan."

I blink repeatedly. "There is no me and Dylan. Nothing really happened."

"I saw you two outside the bathroom," she explains, avoiding eye contact. "I knew something was up. I told Casey so she would stop being so uptight about you and Levi. I didn't know she was gonna post anything online."

"What did you think she was gonna do with that information?" I scoff. "Why would you tell her anything?"

"'Cause she's my best friend!" She drops her face into her palms. "She was so mad at me after the party.

I was just trying to earn her forgiveness. She figured if Levi thought you had hooked up with Dylan, he would stop liking you. I didn't think she would tell the entire school!"

"Levi?" I don't know when I started shouting, but I'm loud enough that our dad and Meg can probably hear me. But I don't care. I'm angry. "All of this was because of Levi? I told you I'm not even interested in him."

"Well, Casey thinks you like him," Jo says in an exasperated tone, "or at least she thinks he likes you."

"Nothing would have even happened with Dylan if you hadn't left me at the party," I snap at her. "This is all your fault."

"Nobody made you hook up with him."

"I didn't hook up with him!" I shout. "But because of you, everyone thinks I did, and my friends hate me, and the whole school is talking about how much of a slut I am when this whole thing isn't even my fault!"

"Look, I'm sorry, okay? I just wanted Casey to forgive me," she explains desperately. "I can't lose her."

"Well then, I hope it was worth it."

I leave. I don't know where I'm going, but I know that I want to get out of here. My father and Meg have stopped fighting (probably because they heard me and Jo shouting at each other) but they haven't left their room to check on us. I race down the stairs and out the front door before they have a chance.

I run. I have no destination in mind or even any direction, but I run as fast as I can. I don't know how much time has passed, but when I finally stop running, the sun has set. I stand alone in the dark, not recognizing any of my surroundings.

I take out my phone to check the time and notice a missed call and voicemail notification. I hold it to my ear to listen to a faint, trembling voice.

"Hey Elena, it's Violet. Um, I know that you and Brooke aren't really talking right now, but, uh, I also know that she's still your friend, so I guess I thought you'd still want to know." She takes a breath in and out before continuing. "Brooke was in a car accident. She's in the hospital right now and we're waiting for more information. That's... I don't know. I just thought you'd want to know."

12

What Doesn't Kill You Makes You Stronger

I don't know how long I sat on the sidewalk. I tried calling back Violet, but she didn't answer. Neither did Ollie or Marisol, and I didn't exactly want to bother Zeke. I can't go back to the house yet, but I don't have anywhere else to go either. So I sit.

Jo and Meg both call, but I don't answer. I know I should answer them soon, just to let them know I'm not dead in a ditch somewhere, but I don't want to talk to either of them right now. There's only one person I'd really like to talk to right now, but I can't talk to her. I'll never get to talk to her again.

The tears that have been building in my eyes begin to fall and I let them. I'm too weak to do anything to stop it. I cradle my legs into my chest, as tight as I possibly can, and just stare out into the light of a lamppost across the street.

I want my mom. I need my mom. She's supposed to be here. I'm too young to not have a mom. It isn't fair that she's dead. It isn't fair that some psycho decided he had to bring a gun to school. It isn't fair that he shot her. It isn't fair that he's alive and she isn't. Bad things aren't supposed to happen to good people. That's what I always believed. That's what my mom always told me.

I try to imagine what she would do if she were here. She would hug me, that's for sure. And she'd probably tell me that everything would be alright. She'd tell me that everything always works out in the end. She's told me that so many times, and normally, it would make me feel better. But not now. It doesn't feel like the truth anymore. Nothing has been working out lately, at least not for the people who deserve it. Sometimes bad things happen to good people, and sometimes good things happen to bad people, and it doesn't matter if they deserve it or not because life is random. There's no master plan, there's no guarantee that things will work out, and there's no reason that things happen the way they do. It's all just random.

"Hey! Are you alright?"

I look up, but I can barely make out the figure down the street as it walks toward me. It's a person ... and a dog, I think, but that's all I see.

"I'm fine," I call out, but my voice betrays me by cracking.

"You don't seem fine."

As the person gets closer to me, he steps into the light, and I can finally see his face. I sigh. What are the odds? I look around and realize I'm in his neighborhood. I hadn't even been paying attention to which way I ran, but somehow, I still ended up here.

"Leave me alone, Levi." I sigh. "I'm having a bad enough day as it is."

"Yeah, I can see that," he laughs softly. "You're sitting by yourself on the ground, but I know you live nowhere near here. I really don't think I should leave you alone."

"Oh, I forgot how much you like to save me," I mumble.

His dog reaches me and starts sniffing my arm. I pet it because, well, I'm not a psychopath. You always pet the cute dog. I think it's a golden retriever; big, fluffy, and extremely friendly.

Levi sits down on the sidewalk with his dog between us. "What are you doing out here?"

I shrug. "I went for a walk."

He raises an eyebrow. "All the way to Woodview Harbor?"

"I don't know. I just started walking. Or I guess I was running. I don't know my way around your stupid town."

He leans back. I kind of snapped at him, so I'm sure he's surprised. "Well, is someone coming to get you? I don't want you walking home alone in the dark."

"What is your obsession with protecting me?"

"We're friends."

His dog climbs into my lap, placing its paws on my chest so it can better reach my face to lick it.

"Down girl," Levi commands her.

"It's fine. She's sweet." I pet her some more.

"She was supposed to be a service dog, but she couldn't get through training," he says, smiling just a little. "You big dumb dog," he adds in a baby voice, lightly moving the dog off of my lap.

I start to laugh.

He smiles wider. "I'm sorry I didn't say anything about Dylan. I should've told you sooner."

I sigh. "It's okay. I'm sure it wasn't a conversation you wanted to have." We both stand up. "Thank you for stopping him before anything else happened."

He moves a bit closer and I look up at him. I have no idea what comes over me, but I lean in and kiss him.

He pushes me away, shocking both me and his dog, who lets out a little bark.

"Elena—" he starts, but I cut him off.

"I'm sorry. I don't know why I did that."

"I don't—"

"I know. That was stupid. I'm sorry." I turn away and try to cover as much of my face with my hair as I possibly can.

"Shit," he mutters under his breath, "I'm sorry."

"I should go home." But then, I realize I have no idea where I am.

"Let me drive you," he offers. "You shouldn't walk home alone at night."

"I'll be fine," I insist, but his hand is already wrapped around my wrist. I look into his eyes, and he lets go, slipping his hand into his pocket.

"I'm sorry," he repeats. "I wasn't trying to…"

"No, I'm sorry," I groan. "Jo's stupid friends just got in my head."

His eyes dart around. "What are you talking about?"

"They think you like me," I tell him. "And they're pissed about it too." I run my fingers through my hair and pull hard. "I'm so stupid, I'm sorry." My lip starts to quiver, so he reaches out to grasp my hands.

"Hey," he whispers, "I do like you … but we barely know each other. And you're young. And your head's not in a good place right now."

"It isn't," I finally admit. "I'm not okay."

♫

Levi and I walk quietly back to his house and then he drives me home. I crack the front door open slowly because I'm sure that I'm about to be screamed at. Jo comes running into view before I'm even completely through the door.

"What the hell is wrong with you?" she screams.

"Please, I'm not in the mood for any more of your BS, Jo." I try to push past her, but she blocks me.

"Mom and Dad were freaking out!" she shouts. "They're out looking for you right now! What the hell were you thinking?"

"I'm serious, Jo," I warn her, "leave me alone."

"No!" She pushes me toward the door and my back hits it.

"What the hell is your problem?" I yell at her. "I get it if you hate me, but I've tried being nice to you. Why can't you just let me be?"

"You don't get to run off and disappear just 'cause you're sad," she continues as if I haven't even said a thing. "You scared me. No one knew where you were or what you were doing or..." she trails off, her breathing suddenly rapid.

"What do you care?" My voice cracks and I realize I'm beginning to cry again. "You don't even like me. You'd probably love it if I just disappeared for real."

"What are you talking about?"

"Do you think I'm stupid?" My voice is breathless and desperate, but I force myself to keep going. "Your parents are fighting, your friends won't talk to you, and when did that all start? When I got here. I'm ruining your life. I'm ruining all your lives because I don't belong here! I'm not a part of this family. I'm not a part of this town. Everything would be so much better if I just wasn't here!"

"God, shut up, Elena. Can you stop playing the victim for ten seconds?"

My face is hot, my throat burns, and my vision is blurred with tears. I'm just so angry. I swing my hand across her face, momentarily comforted by the loud clap it makes when it hits her cheek.

She covers her face where I've hit her and looks at me with her mouth agape. I do feel sorry, but I also feel like she deserved that. The second feeling is stronger than the first.

"I'm not playing the victim," I insist, "but you know what? I have every right to."

"I didn't mean—"

"My mom *died*. Someone *killed* her. I thought we were having an emergency drill, but then I heard a gunshot. And all I knew was that someone in the school had a gun." I'm physically shaking, but somehow, my voice is steady. I stare at Jo. Her eyes fill with tears. "I'm huddled in the corner of a classroom, and I'm terrified. My teacher keeps telling me that we're safe, that it's gonna be okay, but it *wasn't*! It wasn't okay. It'll never be okay. Because *my mom is gone*!" I scream the last part.

Jo stops holding back her tears. She tries to scream back at me, but no sound comes out. I think she mouths *I'm sorry*, but I don't actually care what she's trying to say. I'm not finished yet and I can't stop now.

"And while I'm trying to deal with the worst thing that could've ever happened, suddenly I have to move to a new place where I don't know anyone. I have to join the family of a man who abandoned my mom while she was pregnant. A man who never even wanted me."

Jo is fully crying by now. She shakes her head as her lips quiver. She's trying to speak, but I keep going.

"And this man, my father, can barely even look at me. I feel more alone than I've ever felt and I can barely hold myself together, so when my fake sister invites me to a party, it feels like a flash of light in total darkness. It feels like just maybe I won't have to go through the impossible by myself. But then she just leaves me there." My voice finally betrays me. It cracks, and I can barely even get the next part out. "You left me there and the next thing I know, I'm passed out in a dark room with a guy I barely know. If Levi hadn't shown up and stopped him, he probably would have raped me!" I'm sobbing now. And I don't try to stop. I collapse onto the ground. I'm just too tired. Everything I've been holding in is out in the open now and I just cry.

"Elena—"

"The whole school is calling me a slut because of something I didn't even do. Brooke hates me and now she's in the hospital. I-I don't know if she's gonna be okay o-or how bad the accident even was because *no one* will pick up their phones!" My breaths are short, and I doubt my speech is even comprehensible anymore.

Jo joins me on the floor. She wraps her arms around me and pulls my head toward her chest. I can feel her heartbeat.

"What if she dies?"

"She won't."

"I don't want to lose anyone else," I cry. "I don't want to lose her. She can't die if the last conversation we had ended with her calling me a slut."

"She's not gonna die!"

"You don't know that!" I pull away from her so we're eye to eye, but I can barely even see her through the tears. I try my best to catch my breath until I can speak again. "You can't just say that things are gonna be fine and expect that to be true. Sometimes it isn't true."

13

Actions Speak Louder Than Words

I go to school on Monday with every intention of keeping my head down, but when I walk into Spanish class and see Ren's black eye and swollen cut lip, my instincts take over.

"What happened?" I run to his desk and brush the hair out of his face so I can see his eye better. "Are you okay?"

"It's nothing." He pushes my hand away so his hair falls back into place. "You should see the other guy."

"And the other guy is…?"

He looks up at me with a twisted smile. "Dylan."

"You didn't."

He smiles wider, laughing slightly. "He deserved it."

"You fought your brother?" I probably look like an idiot standing there with my jaw dropped, but I can't believe what I'm hearing.

"I wouldn't say I *fought* him." He shrugs. "It was more like I sucker punched him, and then he beat the crap out of me until our mom intervened. Luckily, she intervened quickly."

I blink. "But you said, 'You should see the other guy.'"

"Well, yeah." He laughs. "Isn't that what people always say in these situations?"

"You're an idiot."

"You should see the other guy … he looks a lot better than I do, but it was worth it."

We both laugh. People look at us, and some of them whisper things, but I don't care. They don't matter. We do.

After unloading on Jo, I've felt a lot better. So much had been building up for so long, and for the first time, I wasn't trying to deal with it all by myself.

She sat with me when Meg and our dad got home, and I told them how I'd been feeling. I said that it felt like he was angry at me for existing, and that I blamed myself for him and Meg fighting, and that sometimes I thought that maybe things would be better if I was gone. And then I told them about Dylan, Brooke, and even Casey.

My father got frustrated and went to bed early, which stung because it kind of confirmed everything I'd been feeling about him. He just doesn't want to deal with me and my problems. But Meg hugged me and promised that she was going to help me. She told me that I wasn't alone, and for the first time in a long time, that felt like it could be true.

Señora Maldonado clears her throat behind me, so I leave Ren's desk and sheepishly take my seat in the back of the room. She starts talking to an unsuspecting girl in the front row, who is clearly not prepared to respond in Spanish.

Nico leans back from his seat in front of me, turns around ever so slightly, and whispers, "Who did that to him?"

My eyes dart around, looking for an explanation because I'm sure he isn't talking to me, but then he turns around a little more and we make eye contact. He looks genuinely worried and I'm not sure what to make of that. His usual cocky demeanor is replaced by a meek helplessness.

"Is he okay?" He seems desperate for information, but, for whatever reason, I can't give it to him. Maybe it's my weird way of punishing him for how he always treats Ren. He doesn't deserve to know.

"None of your business."

He starts to talk again, but Señora Maldonado interrupts. "Señor Roma, ¿tienes algo que decirle a la clase?"[12]

He drops his shoulders and scowls at me before turning around. "No Señora. Lo siento."[13]

♫

From the cafeteria entrance, I see Marisol, Ollie, and Violet at their usual table. Zeke and Brooke aren't with them. I nervously tap my fingers together, unsure if I should approach them, but then I take a deep breath, and before I know it, I'm walking over intently.

"How is she?" I ask.

"She's gonna be okay," Violet responds. She had finally returned my calls Sunday morning but didn't have too much info at the time. I hoped everyone would have a better update by now. "She's got a concussion and a broken arm, but she'll be fine."

"Thank God." I let out the breath I was holding.

"We're all going to visit her after school," Ollie tells me, "if you wanna come with us."

I shift my weight from one foot to the other. "I probably shouldn't. I don't think Brooke wants to see me."

---

[12] She asks "Mr. Roma" if he has anything to say to the class.
[13] He says, "No ma'am. I'm sorry."

"Brooke doesn't know what she wants," Marisol fumes. "The first thing she asked for in the hospital was to talk to Dylan."

"Seriously? If she's this mad at me, I figured she'd be even more pissed at him."

"She should be pissed at him," Marisol says. "He's the one who cheated on her, not you." I don't bother to correct them. "Plus he's the reason she's in the hospital."

I slide into the seat next to Marisol, shaking my head. "What do you mean he's the reason?"

The three of them exchange glances. "Dylan was driving the car," Violet replies quietly, "when the crash happened."

"Oh."

"He's fine, of course," Ollie mumbles. "Because of course he'd be fine." His usual happy-go-lucky attitude has been replaced by complete exhaustion, and I realize that they all care about each other so much. I never really thought about it before, but I'm not sure if I've ever had friends who cared about each other the way they all do. Of course, I'd never want anything to happen to any of my friends back in Miami, but it's just … different. We were friends. These people are family.

"I just don't like that guy," Ollie continues. This is the first time I've ever heard him say a bad thing about anyone. "A while ago, I was over at Zeke's when Dylan showed up, insisting on seeing Brooke. He just wanted to hang out with her, but when she told him she had too much homework, he got really annoyed."

"Annoyed?" I ask.

"Yeah. He said a bunch of stuff about how he really wanted to spend time with her and how he came all the way to her house just to see her and, eventually, she agreed to go out." He looks up at me. "But it just seemed weird, you know? Like, why didn't he text her before coming all the way there? Why didn't he take no for an answer? She was busy, but he, like, pressured her until she gave in. Maybe I'm crazy."

"No, that's exactly the stuff I'm talking about," Marisol interjects. "He's never done anything *wrong*, he just gives me a bad vibe."

"Yeah, but Brooke swears she's happy," Violet points out. "Like you said, he's never actually done anything wrong. We're not gonna convince her of anything based just on a bad vibe."

"He tried to sleep with me," I chime in. "It didn't actually happen, you know, but that's still wrong, isn't it?"

"She said she forgives him because he was drunk, so he didn't know what he was doing." Marisol rolls their eyes.

"She claims he would never hurt her on purpose," says Violet, "because he's a good guy."

"Bullshit," I mumble under my breath. Marisol glances at me, and I realize I may have said that a little louder than I thought.

"You got something to add?"

I shake my head. "No, I just..." I trail off, thinking about that night and how much worse it could've been if Levi hadn't stopped him. I wonder if there'll be a next time and if there'll be someone there to stop him then. I wonder if there was a last time and if that girl was as lucky as me. I wonder if that girl was Brooke or if the next girl will be. And I hate that I have this little piece of information that no one else at this table has. I hate that they get to sit here with the ignorance of thinking Dylan has never done anything wrong.

As much as I don't want to say anything, they need to know the truth. They need to know who he really is. And I guess I'm going to be the one to tell them.

14

The Truth Will Set You Free

One of Ollie's moms picks us all up and we pile into her minivan. I sit in the far back and stay silent while everyone else chats. I watch the town pass by through the window, as I wonder if I'm making a terrible mistake.

Woodview still doesn't feel like home to me, but I don't feel completely out of place anymore. I'm no longer a stranger passing through. I'm no longer the new girl experiencing everything for the first time. I'd thought that I could live here like a shadow. I thought I'd keep to myself, stay to the side, fit in, never draw attention to myself, and eventually fade into irrelevance, just counting the days until I could leave and press unpause on my life.

But life doesn't work like that. Everyone has an effect. The things we do matter. The things *I* do matter. I have an impact on the world around me. I have an impact on the people around me.

I can't exactly remember when I started forming roots here. All I know is that if I had to leave Woodview right now, there would be people I'd miss. There are people I care about here; people I won't allow myself to lose.

The chatter of my friends is just a buzzing sound to me right now. I'm too focused on rehearsing over and over again in my head exactly what I'm going to say to Brooke. Of course, it's no use. Her stepmother leads us upstairs into her bedroom. Zeke and his stepfather are apparently at the store, which feels like a relief for some reason. I don't think I could face both of them together. With five words, every thought disappears from my brain.

"What is *she* doing here?" Brooke's words cut like a knife. Everyone glances at me, but suddenly I can't speak. I shouldn't be here.

"Elena has something to tell you," Marisol states. They look so calm and collected that it just makes me feel humiliated. My ears are hot, my throat is tight, and I wish I could just disappear.

I had told Marisol, Violet, and Ollie everything about Dylan. I told them about how he acted creepy as soon as Levi walked away and how even Parvati seemed to understand that she shouldn't leave me alone with him. I told them about how all the drinks I had that night hit me like a truck out of nowhere and I couldn't even stand up or keep my eyes open. I told them how I remembered being led into a dark room by Dylan and then waking up at Levi's house the next morning. I told them how I couldn't remember what happened next. I told them that Levi had admitted he caught Dylan trying to unbutton my top and, luckily, stopped him before anything else happened. And I told them about the Halloween party and how he made me feel small and weak and then just acted like nothing had happened.

I told them everything so that this information would no longer be just my responsibility. It had been eating away at me, and I needed someone else to know so someone else could do something about it, so someone else could help Brooke. But Marisol said it had to come from me. So here I am, standing in Brooke's room, as her glare shoots daggers into me, trying to figure out how to tell her the truth about Dylan.

"I don't wanna hear it," Brooke snaps. "I don't wanna hear anything she has to say."

"Stop talking about her like she's not in the room," Violet insists, louder than I've ever heard her speak before. She takes a few steps toward me and clasps my hand within hers.

"We're worried about you," Marisol adds. "We're all worried about you."

"You don't have to be! I'm fine!"

The room breaks out into a heated argument, but I'm not listening. Brooke is yelling, begging for us to leave her be, but no one's backing down. It's like when an unstoppable force meets an immovable object. One of them has to give in eventually.

"Dylan tried to rape me." I don't even realize I've said it until the room falls silent and everyone looks at me. I stare at the ground. I just can't look up. I don't want to know what everyone is thinking. "It was at Alex Dancey's birthday party," I tell her. "I was practically unconscious. All I remember is him leading me into a dark room and getting on top of me, but luckily someone stopped him."

I still feel like I don't have the right to use that word. *Rape*. He didn't rape me. He was stopped. I'm one of the lucky ones. And I barely even remember what happened. And I can't even know for sure if that's what would've happened anyway. Maybe he would've stopped on his own. Maybe I had nothing to worry about all along. Maybe I shouldn't use that word.

"No," Brooke objects. "No. No way. He wouldn't do that."

I look at her eyes. There's a mix of pain, fear, anger, and something else I can't quite identify. And suddenly, I feel like I'm making a huge mistake. What am I even talking about?

"I'm sorry." The words escape in a single breath that I can't even control. "I'm sorry." Violet squeezes my hand.

"You don't have anything to be sorry for," Marisol assures me.

I feel like I might throw up. The room is spinning and I just wish I would disappear.

"You're wrong," Brooke continues. "He would never do that. I know him. You're just saying this because you feel bad about hooking up with him. You're trying to manipulate me into forgiving you."

"That's not what I'm doing. I swear." My eyes are welling up, my throat is on fire, and talking is starting to feel impossible.

"She's not lying," Violet defends me. "Someone else saw him."

"Well, then they're lying too!" Brooke insists. "None of you know what you're talking about. Just shut up!"

"No," Marisol says. Their voice is stern and powerful. I can't imagine being that strong and sure of myself. "You have to hear this," they continue, "because if he could do it to her, he could do it to anyone. He could do it to you."

"He loves me," Brooke sobs. "He would never hurt me."

It had always amazed me how strong my mom was. She never seemed to let anything get to her. She faced every challenge that ever came her way with her head held high and a big smile across her face. I used to think she was a superhero because she always seemed so invincible.

I've always believed that our loved ones can watch over us after they're gone, but I had never quite decided what I thought that meant. Are they watching us like we watch a movie? Are they shouting at the screen, begging us not to make the bad decisions we're clearly headed toward but unable to actually get through to us? Are they incapable of doing anything to help us or can they enact change? Maybe they're all around us, guiding us in the right direction without us even knowing it.

At this moment, that feels right. I have to believe that my mom is somehow here with me and she does whatever she can do from the great beyond, because suddenly, I feel strong, like I've never felt before. I have her energy, her strength, her wisdom, and just for a little while, the world seems so much clearer.

"Maybe you're right." The words don't even feel like they're mine. It feels like something's taken over and I'm just a vessel. "Maybe he'll never hurt you. Maybe I'm lying. Maybe I'm telling the truth. I can't prove it either way. All I can do is tell my side of the story and all you can do is tell yours. That's all anyone can really do. We can't force each other to believe anything. You don't have to forgive me. You don't have to be my friend. You don't have to listen to a thing I say. But I said it. And I know it's true. You can choose what to do with that. You can choose to do nothing. You can choose to hate me forever and trust that Dylan's a good guy. But with everything you know, deep down, do you really think you should?"

I feel a weight fall off my shoulders that was so heavy that I almost think I might start to float away. The room is so silent that I can hear my heart beating. You could drop a pin in the middle of the carpet and I think we'd all be able to hear it. Brooke stares at me and I stare at her and we both just stay there staring at each other until she finally speaks.

"Get out."

So I leave.

15

Where There's A Will, There's A Way

When I get home, I find Levi sitting on my front porch, his leg bopping up and down rapidly. He doesn't seem to notice my arrival until I'm right in front of him.

"You're pretty far from home," I say. He stands up as soon as I speak, but now he's towering over me, which I hate. "What are you doing here?"

"I needed to talk to you," he stammers. "I, um, I went to the police."

I blink. "What are you talking about?"

"I should've gone right away," he continues. "Dylan can't keep getting away with stuff like this."

I take a step closer to him. "Keep?" I ask. "So he has done this before?"

"I don't know," he admits. "I think so, but the only time I know for sure is with you."

I nod slowly. "That's why you followed us upstairs that night?"

He hangs his head low. He won't look me in the eyes anymore. "I had a pretty good idea. You were really out of it."

I sit down on the porch and he sits next to me. He looks down at the ground while my eyes remain focused on nothing in particular across the street.

"What are the police going to do?"

"Nothing," he explains. "They said I probably misunderstood the situation. And unless an actual victim comes forward, they won't know what really happened."

I swallow, understanding the implications of his words. "Did you tell them it was me?"

"No, of course not," he says. "That's your decision, not mine."

"But you think I should come forward?"

"I think you should do whatever you feel comfortable doing."

"That isn't helpful." I sigh.

He shrugs. "What do you want me to do?"

"I don't know." I slump down in my seat. "Do you think it even matters?"

"What do you mean?"

"Say I go to the police, what do I tell them? Dylan *didn't* rape me. Maybe he would have, but who's gonna care? Actual rapists get off because there's no proof. People don't believe women. And that's adults. Adult women. I'm fifteen and I was drunk and I barely even remember what happened that night. What do you think the police are gonna do? Why would they even listen to me?"

He's silent for a while. I listen to the sound of the wind rustling in the trees. There's the faint sound of a dog barking nearby and the fainter sound of a baby crying somewhere. The ambient noise of suburban life.

"They might not," Levi admits. "I don't know, really. But at least now, whatever you decide to do, there's someone backing you up." He stands, brushing the dirt off his jeans. He turns away from me before speaking again. "It was all I could think of to help, so it's what I did." He starts to walk away, and when he reaches the sidewalk, I stand up.

"Levi!" I call out. He turns around. "Thank you," I say, "for doing what you could."

He shrugs. "It's what anyone would've done."

"No." I shake my head. "It isn't."

I stand on the front porch and watch him get in his car and drive away, and I find myself smiling, though I'm not sure why.

Meg is sitting on the living room couch when I come inside. She glances back at me when she hears the door open.

"Elena," she says, "I scheduled an appointment for you with one of the other therapists in my office. It's next Monday after school. Does that sound alright?"

"Yeah, that's fine." I shrug. "Thanks, Meg." I head toward the staircase, but she speaks again before I get there.

"You know, I told your friend he could wait inside for you," she mentions, "but he didn't think you'd want him to."

I chuckle.

"He seems like a nice guy," she continues, obviously fishing for more, but there's nothing else for me to say.

"He's alright." I go upstairs. Even though it's a short conversation, and neither of us said much, it feels nice. It feels normal.

The bedroom is empty and the shades are drawn, letting in the rays of the sun on a day that's unseasonably nice out for late November. I lean against the windowsill and just enjoy the warmth on my face.

Directly across the driveway is another window that I can see right into without much effort. I recognize the pale lavender walls from the last time I was in that room. With a slight crane of my neck, I can see Ren sitting cross-legged on his bed. I tap on the window, softly at first, but when he doesn't move, I knock louder, until finally, he's standing at the window across from me with a confused expression on his face.

I wave. He smiles and then disappears momentarily, quickly returning with a sheet of paper he presses against the glass. In scribbled black writing it reads, *meet me downstairs in 5 mins?*

I chuckle, unsure why he didn't just text me, but I also nod. He holds a thumb up to the window and closes his curtains.

♫

We sit on my front lawn, each with one earbud in, while Ren explains that clouds are actually specifically designed to look like things, but most people just refuse to notice. He doesn't clarify who is designing them or why.

"Nico asked about you today," I mention, once the conversation lulls. I notice that he blushes as soon as he hears.

"Yeah? What'd he say?"

I raise my eyebrow, and he shrinks in on himself, embarrassed for caring.

"Never mind. It doesn't matter," he mumbles.

"He wanted to know about your black eye. He seemed worried."

"Oh," he says, "right." I'm not sure, but just for a second I think he's smiling, but he quickly turns his face, so if he is, he doesn't want me to see. "Is that Jo?"

I follow his gaze and can definitely see someone near the corner of the street. It looks like it could be Jo, but I can't know for sure until she gets a little closer.

I wave. We haven't really spoken since the night of the fight, so maybe it's my way of offering an olive branch. She doesn't wave back and I'm instantly annoyed. If either of us has the right to still be mad, it's me.

"Is she okay?" Ren asks.

I start to say something about how he should just ignore her, but, for some reason, I hesitate. I look back at her, a little closer this time, and notice the distressed look on her face. I stand and start walking toward her, squinting. I realize that tears are streaming down her cheeks. I guard my eyes from the sun with my hand.

"Jo," I call out, "what's going on?"

"Nothing!" She shouts back. She's walking faster now. I take more steps toward her, so she moves into the street to avoid facing me head-on. She does her best to cut around to the front door, but I'm not letting her pass me.

"Jo, what happened?"

"It's been the worst day," she sighs. "I just wanna go home." Her voice breaks as she speaks and I feel like I should press harder. But if she doesn't want to tell me, then who am I to force her?

"Fine. Whatever. Go home."

She pushes past me, purposefully smashing her shoulder against mine. She lets the screen door slam as she goes in.

I sit back down next to Ren. He won't stop staring at me. I lie back on the grass and he does the same. We lie in silence for a few minutes, but I can feel his eyes on me. Finally, I tell the truth I've been hiding for what feels like forever.

"We're half-sisters," I say quietly. "Kevin is my dad. That's why I'm living here with them."

Ren hesitates. "So when you said Jo's dad knew your mom..."

"Kevin and Meg dated in high school, but then they broke up," I explain. "He moved to Florida for school. He was getting his master's degree at the same time that my mom was doing her undergrad. All I knew growing up was that they fell in love, but he bailed on her before my mom could tell him she was pregnant. She never knew why he left and she never tried to find out."

Ren has stopped staring at me, maybe out of respect, or maybe he's feeling too awkward to look at me as I tell my story. Whatever the reason, I continue to talk, as we both face the sky.

"What I know now, is that he took a trip home and rekindled something with his high school sweetheart, Meg. But he never told my mom. Then one day he just packed up and left without so much as a goodbye. I guess he chose Meg." A tear rolls down my cheek that I furiously wipe away. I hate that I'm crying. "My mom found out she was pregnant with me a few weeks later."

Ren doesn't say anything for a while. He reaches out and wraps my hand in his.

"It feels like we've all been walking on eggshells since I've gotten here," I continue. "Meg keeps saying I'm part of the family, but this isn't how family is supposed to be."

"Sometimes family sucks."

I roll over on my side. He does the same, so our faces are inches from each other.

"I used to feel like I was missing out on something by having such a small family," I admit, "but maybe this is it. Maybe parents fight, and siblings don't get along, and kids feel alone. Maybe that's just reality."

"Maybe," he whispers. He shifts closer to me and our lips brush.

I pull away. "Ren."

"I'm sorry."

"What...?"

"I'm sorry!" He sits up.

I back away a bit. "I thought you were gay."

"I thought so, too." He looks back at me, but I scramble to my feet. "I'm sorry," he says again.

"It's fine, but I'm gonna go inside now."

"Elena, come on," he pleads. "That was stupid. I know."

"I can't do this right now." I sigh. "I just can't."

"Elena, I'm sorry."

"I'm not mad. I just have too much to deal with right now. I can't add one more thing. No offense. I'll see you tomorrow, okay?"

16

The End Justifies The Means

I flop onto the bed on my back, then turn just my head to look over at Jo. I notice an ice pack on her hand but don't really question it. She has stopped crying by now, but it's clear that she still isn't happy.

"Is it about Casey?" I ask.

"What?"

"You're upset," I say. "Is it about Casey?"

"Why do you care?"

I face the ceiling again. If it's true that family doesn't need to be friends, then I guess I don't need to care. But I do. Maybe it doesn't matter if we're sisters or half-sisters or nothing at all. Maybe I want to be Jo's friend, just because.

"I kissed Levi," I confess.

She sits up. "Are you serious?"

"It was when I ran away," I explain. "It was a big mistake though. Casey will be happy to know that it probably won't happen again."

"Screw Casey."

I laugh. "Okay, what the hell happened today?"

She lies back and breathes deeply. "She was never going to forgive me, no matter what I did." Her voice breaks a little, and I think she might cry again. "So I guess I screwed you over for nothing."

I shrug. "I get it. She's your best friend. I'm no one. Of course, your loyalty was with her."

"But you're not no one," she says, "you're my sister."

We smile at each other, but both look away as soon as our eyes meet.

"Ren kissed me."

She squints at me. "Ren from next door?"

I nod.

"Isn't he gay?"

"I guess not."

"Weird." I don't respond immediately. It gives her time to add, "You've been busy, haven't you?"

"Shut up."

We both laugh. I'm not sure either of us entirely knows why, but we don't stop for a few minutes.

"How's your friend Brooke?" Jo inquires once we're quiet again.

"She's okay," I say. "She's not my friend anymore, though."

"I'm sorry."

"She trusts her boyfriend more than me." I shrug. "Nothing I can do about that."

"Her boyfriend who tried to rape you?" Jo clarifies. "That's twisted."

"It's not my business."

"It literally is."

"Well, it isn't yours," I correct her. "That's for sure."

"Why don't you talk to my mom?" she suggests. "She's studied this kinda stuff. She knows about bad relationships."

"Brooke doesn't think she's in a bad relationship."

Jo scoffs. "She's dating a rapist."

"Well, she doesn't want my help."

"Sometimes we need things we don't want." She diverts her eyes almost instantly, lowering her voice to add, "I didn't want a sister."

I feel myself smiling, ever so slightly, although I try not to. "Yeah, I always wanted a little brother, not gonna lie."

She scoffs. "I hope you're joking because I'm way better than a little brother."

"Yeah, sure." I roll my eyes.

"Actually, if I'm being honest, I did always want a sibling," Jo admits. "I just always thought if I got one they'd be younger than me."

"I am younger than you."

"By two months? That doesn't count."

"Why not?" I laugh. "You ever hear twins brag about being like three minutes older?"

"That's different," she insists. "We're not twins."

"We're Irish twins."

"Are we?"

"I think so," I lean back and put my hands behind my head. "Unless there's a different term for half-siblings who are less than nine months apart."

"I don't think that happens often enough that there's a special term for it."

"There's a term for Siamese twins. How often does that happen?"

"The term is conjoined twins," Jo corrects me. "Siamese twins is racist. In fact, Irish twins is kind of racist too."

"Yeah, but we're Irish. Or at least I'm half-Irish. That means I can make Irish jokes now."

"No, you can't."

"But we're still Irish twins though!"

"You're not gonna spin this in any way to convince me that we're twins." She tosses a pillow at my head. "Twins share 100% of the same DNA. We don't even share 100% of the same parents."

We both laugh and she lies down. I tilt my head to look at her. She's giving me the side eye, but she's smiling. She even looks like she's trying to hold in laughter.

"I'm sorry you couldn't work things out with Casey," I offer. "For what it's worth, if she doesn't want to be your friend, that's her loss."

"Thanks, I guess," she mumbles. "What are you gonna do about Brooke?"

"What *can* I do?"

"I don't know," she admits, "but we've gotta do something."

"We?" I raise my eyebrow. "Since when are you a part of this?"

"Elena, this is bigger than both of us," she declares. "Dylan has to be stopped."

I don't respond, but I know she's right.

♫

The next day, I pull Ren aside in the hallway and he instantly starts rambling like an idiot.

"Elena!" His eyes practically bulge out of his head. "I'm so sorry about … yeah, you know. That was so stupid. It'll never happen again."

"It's fine."

"Like, I don't even know what I was thinking," he continues, rapid fire. "Or maybe that's the problem. I wasn't thinking. My brain was taken over by a crazy psycho who doesn't think before he acts."

"Ren!" I shout, finally getting him to slow down. "It's fine. That's not what I want to talk about."

"It isn't?" he confirms. "'Cause we should probably talk about that, no?"

I sigh. He's probably right, but I have bigger fish to fry right now. "What is there to talk about?" I ask. "I like you as a friend. I don't think I could handle any more than that from anyone right now."

"You're not mad that I kissed you?" He looks so worried. "You still want to be friends?"

"Of course I do," I say, almost laughing. "You're gonna have to try a lot harder than that to get rid of me."

A smile slowly creeps onto his face. "Good."

"So, friends?"

He nods. "Friends."

He extends his hand. I don't mean to roll my eyes, but I do, as I pull him into a hug.

"So what did you want to talk about?"

I take in a deep breath. I'd almost forgotten about this part. We release each other from the hug, and look into each other's eyes. I lower my eyes. A strand of hair falls in front of my face, but I don't move it. This feels easier if he can't see my entire face.

"I told Meg about what Dylan tried to do," I admit. "She took me to the station to talk to the police, and Levi backed up my story as a witness."

He nods. "That's good."

I tilt my head slightly to see his facial expression better.

"If that's what you want to do, that's good," he continues.

"I know he's your brother. I don't know what happens next. They said they'll open an investigation, but I don't know if it'll come to anything. It probably won't, but I just thought you should know."

"I'm proud of you, Elena."

"You're not angry?" I ask. "This is your family I'm messing with."

He shakes his head. "Dylan made his own bed," he explains. "Besides, my family's already messed up beyond repair."

I raise an eyebrow. "Why do you say that?"

He shrugs. "Doesn't matter."

♫

I'm barely in the cafeteria for more than ten seconds when Marisol plops down across from me.

"Hello."

"Hi?" I reply. I saw Brooke in the hallway earlier, so I know she is back in school today. I assumed that was the end of me having lunch with her friends. But then, Ollie and Violet join us.

"I'm so glad we have a long weekend coming up." Ollie takes the seat next to me. "It literally can't get here quick enough."

"Yeah, but it's not even going to be a real break 'cause we have to deal with our extended families the whole time," Violet adds.

Ollie frowns. "That's not a very thankful attitude, Violet."

"Thanksgiving is objectively the worst holiday," she continues.

"Worse than Columbus Day?" asks Marisol.

"You mean Indigenous People's Day," Ollie corrects them.

"Worse than Columbus Day?" Marisol repeats.

Violet laughs. "Who on earth celebrates Columbus Day?"

"I don't know, Italian people?" Ollie says. "Right, Elena?"

"Still not Italian," I remind him.

I let their conversation turn into white noise as I make eye contact with Jo across the room. She looks around hesitantly before quickly walking toward our table.

"Hey," she says, quietly under her breath, "can I sit here?"

"Yeah, of course." I smile.

"Sit down," Marisol encourages her.

Jo slowly and carefully takes a seat, like she's nervous we've somehow set a trap for her.

"I saw that video of you yesterday," they say. "It was badass."

Jo awkwardly ducks her head as she picks at her fingernails.

"What video?" I ask.

"Nothing," Jo quickly says, but Marisol instantly betrays her.

"You didn't see it?" They pull out their phone. "I don't know the whole context, but this red-headed girl was yelling at her and it escalated into a total cat fight. Just watch it." They slide the phone over to me.

I pick it up and press play.

"It's stupid," Jo interjects. "You really don't have to watch."

I instantly recognize Jo in the video, even though her back is to the camera. She's yelling something at Casey, but it's a little too loud in the cafeteria to fully make out what she's saying. I bring the speaker a little closer to my ear and I almost think I hear someone say my name.

"Watch it," Marisol tells me. "The audio is less important."

I move the phone away from my head in order to better see the screen, just in time to see Casey shove Jo backward. She stumbles but then regains her balance. And with the most force I've ever seen her have, Jo punches her right smack in the nose.

Casey immediately clutches her face, clearly choking back tears, but the fight's not over yet. She dives toward Jo and grabs a big clump of her hair. They exchange swings and tugs at each other until they're both on the ground and some other girls need to physically pull them apart.

"You crazy bitch!" Casey shouts. "You're gonna regret this!"

"Go to hell, Casey," Jo yells back, "and stay away from my sister!"

The video lasts about twenty seconds longer, but I'm not paying attention anymore. I stare at Jo from across the table. She won't meet my gaze.

"That was awesome." Marisol laughs. "That ginger seems like a total nightmare."

Jo shrugs.

"What did she do to you?" Ollie asks.

"Doesn't matter," Jo mumbles.

"Your sister is pretty lucky to have someone like you looking out for her," Violet adds.

Jo shakes her head. "Not really."

"No, I think so," I tell her. "And I bet she's really grateful."

Jo barely looks up, but when she finally does, I smile at her. She doesn't look up again, but I notice she's smiling too.

Ollie's face suddenly lights up. "Hey, do you have plans for dinner next Friday?"

Jo slowly turns to him. "Uh, um, I'm flattered but…"

"Don't worry, he's not asking you out," Marisol says.

"You should come to Friendsgiving!" He turns to Violet and adds, "It's okay to invite one more person, right?" He probably should have checked with her first.

"Yeah, of course." Violet smiles and turns to Jo. "The more, the merrier. It's a potluck, but you don't have to worry about bringing anything special. You and Elena can just bring something together if that's easier—"

"I didn't think I was still invited," I interrupt. "Isn't Brooke gonna be there?"

"Yeah, and?"

"I probably shouldn't go then," I explain. "She wasn't exactly happy the last time she saw me."

"Elena, you're our friend," Marisol says. "We want you to be there."

"But you were Brooke's friends first. I just wanna be respectful."

"It's my house, it's my rules," Violet assures me. "No pressure, but you're still welcome if you want to come. Brooke will just have to get over it."

"I'll think about it."

Jo looks hopefully at Violet.

"Don't worry Jo, you're still invited, even if Elena doesn't come..." She looks back at me and adds, "...but Elena should come."

17

Nobody's Perfect

I haven't seen Brooke or Zeke since they returned to school last week. I don't know where they've been eating lunch, but it wasn't in the cafeteria with us. It was somewhat of a relief because I still didn't know how to face either of them.

By Tuesday, everyone has moved on from the rumor about me and Dylan, and are talking about something new, but I don't have the mental energy for any more gossip. I still feel like everyone is always looking at me. During fifth period, I ask for the bathroom pass just so I can escape for a few minutes.

I splash some water on my face and take a few long breaths, in and out. Then I lean against the sink and let my head hang. I hear a stall door creak open, and some footsteps walk up beside me, but I don't care enough to move. Whoever's here will just have to witness my breakdown.

"You okay?"

I nod. I squeeze my eyes shut as I take a few more breaths and then finally add, "Yeah, I'm fine." I bring my head up and reopen my eyes, staring at my reflection in the mirror. Only then do I peer over at who's next to me.

Brooke stands there with bloodshot eyes. Her makeup is smeared and her hair is a mess, much different from the very put-together look she usually has.

"Brooke," I say, barely a whisper, "what happened?"

She shakes her head. "Dylan and I broke up," she replies softly. She turns on the sink and begins wiping her smudged eye makeup. "You're probably happy about that."

"I'm not happy about anything that makes you this sad."

"But you wanted us to break up, didn't you?"

I sigh. "Yes," I admit, "but only because I was worried about you."

"I didn't ask you to worry about me."

"I know."

"You think Dylan is this horrible monster, but you don't know anything about him." Her voice shakes as she speaks. "He was good to me. He cared about me."

"I'm sure he did," I say, even if I don't fully believe her. "But he also did … bad things. To me. Maybe to other girls. He's a dangerous guy. And you deserve better than that."

"No, I don't!" she shouts. "I don't deserve better! Can't you get that?"

"Brooke, what are you talking about?"

"I'm a mess, Elena. And I'm hard to deal with. And I'm not pretty like you, or cool like Marisol, or even funny like Violet. No one likes me. Why do you think I don't have any friends?"

"You have friends."

"They're all Zeke's friends," she corrects me. "They only hang out with me 'cause I'm his sister and they feel bad for me."

"Well, I'm your friend."

She scoffs. "You don't even know me."

"Of course I do."

"No, you don't," she almost sounds like she could start crying again. "You're just like every other person who becomes my friend for a few months but then gets scared off. Once you get too close to me, you'll realize that I'm too screwed up."

"You're not screwed up."

"Yes, I am." She sighs, getting more frustrated than sad. "I'm broken. And so is Dylan. That's why we worked."

"What are you even talking about?"

"You're friends with Ren, right?" she asks. "So he's told you about Mei?"

"His sister?" I shrug. "A little. He's mentioned her a few times, but I haven't actually, like, met her or anything."

Brooke blinks. "What? Of course you haven't met her." A wave of emotions I can't comprehend crosses her face until she whispers, "I'm sorry. I assumed he told you."

"Told me what?"

She doesn't answer. She crosses her feet, stepping hard on the toe of her shoe.

"Brooke, what are you talking about?"

She gulps but starts to talk slowly and deeply. "About two years ago, their younger sister Mei died." She swallows hard. "Some guy flew through a red light and hit her." She blinks back tears and I can tell this is hard for her to talk about, but I don't think I should stop her. A single tear escapes her eye. "She spent two weeks in a coma before..." More tears fall, and I don't need her to finish.

"That's horrible," I whisper. "I had no idea."

"None of them were the same afterward. Their parents even got divorced." Her speech is chopped up by short breaths. "Then Dylan and I got close through the drama club. He's not perfect, but he has his reasons."

"Brooke, a terrible thing happened to that family, but that's not an excuse for his behavior. You don't have to put up with him treating you badly."

"You don't get it."

"Maybe I don't," I admit, "but I know you're a great person. And I know that people see that. People are always gonna see that. You don't have to settle for Dylan just because you feel bad for him."

"That's the thing, I wasn't settling," she explains. "He's not a bad person. He's done bad things, but that's because he's hurt. Losing Mei did something to him. If I hate him for the mistakes he's made, I have to hate myself too."

I shake my head. "I don't know what mistakes you think you've made," I assure her, "but you can't compare yourself to him."

"You don't get it," she says.

♫

After school, I sit on a bench outside and scroll through social media on my phone. It's been a while since I've spoken to Lana, and I wonder how everyone back home is doing. I think about everything that's happened since I moved, and it feels crazy that so much has gone down in such a short amount of time. It's even crazier that my best friend doesn't know about any of it.

I start to text Lana to catch her up, but I don't even know where to start. I settle on a simple message. *Hi.*

"You wanna walk home?"

I look up to see Ren and his goofy smile.

"I'm waiting for Jo," I explain, "but if you wanna wait too, we can all walk together."

"Sure thing." He takes a seat next to me and pulls out his phone. I put mine down on my lap.

"Hey, remember that thing we did where we went back and forth asking questions, and we had to answer honestly?"

"Yeah, of course." He nods.

"Do you wanna do that again?"

"Sure." He shrugs.

"Why didn't you tell me about what happened to Mei?"

He instantly looks away.

"That's my question," I add, "so you have to answer."

He sighs and shakes his head, linking his fingers behind his neck. "I don't know." He shrugs. "I guess I've just been the kid with the dead sister for so long that it felt nice to just be Ren again." He kicks a pebble across the courtyard before adding, "Although to you, I ended up being the guy with the rapey brother, so I'm not sure if that's any better." He laughs slightly, but I can tell he's just trying to hide the pain of the situation.

"At least you're not the girl who grew up without a dad because he knocked up his ex and left your mom before she had the chance to tell him she was pregnant, but then your mom died, so you had to move in with said dad who has barely even acknowledged you since you came here."

His eyes widen.

"Or I guess I also could be the girl who was cyberbullied by her own sister and her friends after they took me to a party where I didn't know anybody and left me there to almost get raped."

"Jesus, Elena."

"You're not the only one with a dysfunctional family."

He smiles. "Maybe we should start a club."

Just then, Jo approaches us meekly. "Hey, are you ready to go?"

♫

Almost immediately after we walk through the door, Meg calls out from upstairs, "Girls, is that you?"

"Yeah," Jo shouts back, "what do you want?"

She appears at the top of the stairs and starts making her way down. "I was thinking, I have so much cooking to do the next two days, that tonight, I don't even wanna look at that kitchen. So what do you think about the three of us going out for dinner? Pizza maybe?"

"What about Dad?" Jo asks.

Meg sighs. "He called a few minutes ago. Working late again."

"Of course he is," Jo mumbles.

"That just means that we have some time for us girls," Meg continues, "so let's do something fun together."

"Pizza sounds good to me," I say.

"And maybe we'll get ice cream too! How's that sound?"

Jo shrugs. "Whatever."

Meg puts her hands on her hips. "Well, that's the highest level of excitement I ever expect from you, so okay! Great!"

♫

Jo sits on the passenger's side and I get in the backseat. She turns on the radio and some pop song I don't recognize starts to play. As Meg drives, I watch the leaves blow in the wind and the lookalike cartoon houses of the neighborhood pass by.

I feel like the main character in a music video, and that seems oddly comforting right now. What if I was just a character in a video and after three minutes I ceased to exist? What if the past and present didn't matter and everything about me could be seen right here and right now? That isn't how life works, of course. We're fully formed people with fully formed lives, but maybe we're just going through a series of three-minute music videos. Maybe you need to put them all together to get a full picture.

So much has happened. So much will happen. But right now, I'm in the backseat of a car, staring out the window at the peaceful suburbia that's slowly becoming my home. Right now, I'm in the backseat of a car, listening to my sister quietly sing along to the radio. Right now, I'm sad and happy and tired and confused and angry all at the same time. But right now, somehow, I know that I'll be okay. Because this isn't the end of my story; it's only the beginning. And something tells me, it's gonna be a wild ride.

18

Everything Happens For A Reason

Brooke and Zeke still don't eat lunch in the cafeteria with us on Wednesday, but when I pass Brooke in the hallway before eighth period, she almost smiles at me. Not quite a smile but almost. It's progress. Most classes today are pretty low-key. We've all mentally checked out for the long weekend and the teachers know it.

After school, Jo and I help Meg start Thanksgiving preparations in between cooking for the Friendsgiving potluck. Because it is Violet's year to host, she is providing all the beverages and two lasagnas, one with meat and one without, just in case Marisol is a vegetarian again this week. The rest of us are expected to contribute side dishes and desserts, so she emailed everyone a sign-up sheet.

"We don't want a repeat of what happened at Ollie's house," she said, referring to the year that they ended up with six pies and no actual dinner.

"Mmm." Ollie smiled, thinking back. "Piesgiving. That was a good time."

Jo bakes apple and sweet potato tartlets decorated with beautiful ornate designs. I had no idea she even knew how to do that. I decide to bring tostones with pique verde.[14] It was one of my mother's favorite dishes for us to make together. I haven't eaten it since before she died, but it feels right to be back in the kitchen cooking her recipe.

♫

When we arrive at Violet's house, everyone else is already there.

"It's like Piesgiving but tiny!" Ollie exclaims when he sees Jo's tartlets. "They're so pretty." She beams with pride. I can tell how much she wants to be accepted by this motley crew of misfits.

Brooke is quiet most of the night, but she laughs when Ollie offers to help feed her because of her broken arm.

---

[14] Puerto Rican tostones are crispy fried green plantains. Pique verde is green hot sauce.

"I'm left-handed," she reminds him. He stares at her. She gestures to her bright pink cast. "I broke my right arm." I notice that most of the group has signed her cast. I'm tempted to ask her if I can sign it too, but I chicken out. The fact that we've been able to sit at the same table all night is already a big deal and I'm not trying to push it. Baby steps.

Later in the evening, when Brooke is in the bathroom, Zeke leans over and whispers to me, "I've been meaning to thank you."

"For what?" I look up at him, confused.

"For always looking out for my sister."

I don't know what to say back to him, so I just nod.

He smiles. "Even the first night we met, that's what you were doing. She can be kind of stubborn, but she just needs time. I think we'll be back at the lunch table by Monday. You'll see." He gives me a friendly shove and I breathe a sigh of relief.

I look around the table and think about how so much has happened in such a short time. If I could change things and never meet my dad, never discover I have a half-sister, never move here, never become friends with these weirdos … yes, I would. If it meant I could have even one more moment with my mom, I would trade all of this. But I can't change things and I know that. I never wanted to move to Woodview and meet these people, but I did, and I realize that I'm glad I did.

I have a lot to be sad about and a lot to be angry about. I don't know when that sadness and anger will go away. It might not ever. It's hard to believe it is my first year celebrating Thanksgiving without my mother and even harder to believe that I could possibly have *anything* to feel thankful for. Yet somehow, despite all that has happened, I do.

19

Keep Calm And Carry On

I instinctively shut my eyes tight as I step on the scale, terrified of what number it will show. I slowly peel my left eye open and look down.

163. Up two pounds. Disgusting. I ate way too much on Thanksgiving. I just couldn't stop myself from having seconds. Something is seriously wrong with me.

"Jo! Are you ready yet?" Elena yells up from the bottom of the staircase. "Meg said we're leaving in five minutes, with or without you."

"I'll be down soon!" I call, gripping the sink tightly.

I look at my reflection in the mirror and try to breathe. In for four seconds, hold for two seconds, out for eight seconds, and repeat. It was the method my mom had drilled into my head when I was younger and I knew I could count on it to temporarily calm me down. I give my long blonde hair a few finishing brushes and head downstairs.

"Took you long enough," my mom says, chuckling to herself. "What were you doing up there?"

I flip my hair dramatically. "*This* does not happen naturally."

She rolls her eyes. "Yeah, yeah. It's high school, not a beauty pageant."

I get in the front seat and Elena sits in the back. I fiddle with the radio for a few blocks until my mom swats my hand away, claiming that it's distracting her.

She leaves a song playing that I don't recognize, but I still try my best to focus on it. I need to think about something other than the mess waiting for me at school.

I think I knew deep down that my friendship with Casey was over after that party at Levi Haddad's house about a month and a half ago. The way she looked at me that night, there was no coming back from that.

We had gone to that party for one reason, and one reason only: Casey wanted to get Levi's attention. She had told me back in July, that by the next summer we would *all* have boyfriends. I think it really bugged her that our friend Rachel got a boyfriend before she did. She always wanted to be first at everything. She was the first to have her own cell phone, the first to start wearing a bra, and the first to kiss a boy. When Rachel started dating Nico freshman year, it drove Casey crazy. So she set her sights on someone even better. Rachel may have been able to get the attention of a boy our age, but Casey was going to be the first one of us to date a *senior*. And she'd chosen Levi.

Unfortunately for her, that plan hasn't exactly been seamless. She believes this is, at least in part, my fault.

She had arrived at the party in an outfit perfectly selected to show off her best attributes, but Levi seemed to only notice Elena. Casey couldn't hide her frustration. Aside from one extremely awkward interaction where he called her "Kelsey," Levi didn't even look at Casey all night. It certainly wasn't due to her lack of trying. We'd only been at the party for an hour or so, and Casey was already devastated.

"This is so humiliating," Casey sighed dramatically, as she tugged at a piece of her long red hair.

"It's not that bad," I assured her. "He's hosting. He's busy running all over the place. You can't take it personally."

"He had time for the new girl," she mumbled. "I wish you hadn't brought her."

"I was just trying to be nice," I explained. I couldn't exactly tell her that Elena was my surprise half-sister. I didn't want anyone to know about that. "I just feel bad for her, you know?"

"Well, she seems to be doing fine now." Casey scoffed and pouted as she leaned her head on my shoulder. "Can we just go home?"

"Already? Look, just because the night's not going exactly as planned doesn't mean we can't still have fun."

"Please Jo," she begged and looked up at me with puppy dog eyes, "this party was a total fail and it's all your fault for inviting Elena. I just want to get out of here."

"Okay, fine. Let's go then." I glanced around the room. "Rachel said Nico's gonna take her home, so let me just find Elena and then we can go."

She groaned. "No, I don't wanna see her right now. She's the whole reason I want to leave. Let's go hang out," she pleaded, "just the two of us."

I bit my lip. "I can't just leave her here."

"She'll be fine," Casey insisted. "She basically threw herself at the host. She doesn't need you, but I do."

I nodded. "Okay. Let's go." I had no idea what a big mistake I was about to make.

She didn't want to be alone, so we went to her house. We sat on her bed and we talked for what felt like forever. It started to get later and later, as she kept going on and on about how I was her best friend and how we'd always be there for each other. Maybe I was a little drunk, or maybe I just got too wrapped up in being so close to the most beautiful girl I knew. I was staring into her emerald eyes and the next thing I knew, I had leaned in and kissed her.

"What the hell are you doing?" She pushed me away so hard that I almost fell off the bed. She stood up and backed up against the wall, getting as far away from me as possible.

"Shit," I stammered. "I'm sorry. That was—"

"What's wrong with you? Why would you kiss me?"

"I…" I didn't know what to say. What was I thinking?

"What are you, a *lesbian*?" The look of disgust on her face, the sound of hatred in her voice … it was everything I'd feared. What had I done?

"Of course not!" I shouted in desperation. "I just … that was stupid. I'm sorry."

"Can you get out of my room?"

"Casey, come on," I said, nervously laughing, "this doesn't have to be a big deal. We're best friends. You were just saying that."

"Get out, Jo!"

Ever since then, everything has been horrible, and it is all my fault. After all, there's no way you can kiss your best friend and expect things to stay the same.

When we finally pull up in front of the school, I feel myself sink lower into my seat. In for four seconds, hold for two seconds, out for eight seconds, and repeat. I breathe slowly and steadily, but it doesn't really help. The last month and a half have been bad, and I just know today won't be any better.

20

Another Day, Another Opportunity

First period, I sit in my usual seat, the fifth desk in the second row. Tyler is already there, one row behind me, with his long legs stretched out. These one-size-fits-all desks really don't fit all.

Rachel should be here soon to sit next to me like she always does. Or at least she always *used to* sit next to me. Ever since my fight with Casey, Rachel has been sitting across the room instead. I'm hoping she decided to forgive me over the long weekend.

"Hey Tyler." I turn to lean on his desk. "How was your Thanksgiving?"

"Great, how was yours?"

I blink a few times. "Yeah, it was, um, fine." It isn't exactly the truth, but I don't think you're supposed to answer these kinds of questions with anything worse than *fine*.

Rachel enters the classroom. She glances at me for a second but quickly turns away and heads to the opposite side of the room. As she takes a seat, she looks over at me again. I can't read her emotions at all. I have about a minute before the bell rings and I know I won't be able to focus on any lesson if I'm this distracted, so I stand up and cross the room as quickly as I can.

"Rachel, are you really still so mad that you can't even sit near me?" I ask.

"I don't want to talk about this." She sighs, shaking her head. "Class is gonna start soon. Just ... sit down."

"Look, I don't know what Casey told you, but it's not the whole story."

"How could I know your side of the story when you don't tell me anything?"

I tap my fingers together nervously. "That isn't fair."

"Why didn't you tell me you had a sister?" she asks. "You said Elena was a family friend. Why weren't you just honest?"

"I don't know," I admit, stammering. "It was new. I was freaked out. I don't know."

"Casey would never have posted that stuff about Elena if she knew she was your sister," Rachel explains. I'm pretty sure Casey still would have, but I don't tell her that.

"What she posted was horrible whether she's my sister or not."

"Oh come on. Don't act like we don't all do stuff like that all the time." She rolls her eyes. "Don't pretend you've never talked about someone behind their back or sent something to WoodNews that you probably shouldn't have. You don't get to retroactively decide that posting about Elena is any worse."

"Okay, well what about the post Casey submitted about *me*?" I remind her. "Sure, we gossip about other people, but when did it become okay to turn on *each other* like that?"

"Casey didn't post that," Rachel insists. She shakes her head, causing her brown curls to bounce around her shoulders. "It was completely unfair of you to accuse her of that."

"Casey's lying. Of course she posted it. Everyone thinks I'm a lesbian now because of her."

"She said she didn't and I believe her," Rachel states firmly. "What makes you so sure it was her anyway?"

I hesitate. There's no way to explain how I know, without admitting to the kiss. And there's no way to admit to the kiss without losing any chance I have of convincing people that what Casey said was false. "I just know, okay?" It is clear that I won't change her mind, so I just return to my seat.

"Under no circumstances do I want to get in the middle of," Tyler pauses and gestures to the air between me and Rachel, "*that*, but are you alright?"

I'm holding back tears, but I'm not about to break down during a high school English class, especially not one held at 7:30 in the morning.

"I'm fine, whatever."

He looks at me and shrugs. "I'm not gonna pry because the last thing I need is for something I say now to come back and bite me in the ass later when you're all friends again."

I look down at the floor. "I really don't think you have to worry about that happening."

He shrugs again. "Well, for what it's worth, I don't care if you're a lesbian." He pauses and smirks. "Girl-on-girl stuff is hot."

"Ew, Tyler, that's disgusting." I quickly add, "And I'm not a lesbian."

"Okay. Whatever you say."

♫

When I arrive at the cafeteria for lunch, Marisol is the only one at their usual table. I hesitate before walking over. I've never interacted with Elena's friends without her being there. I used to sit with Rachel and Casey, but obviously, I can't do that anymore. Then I ate lunch with a few other girls from color guard, but ever since the viral video, they all think I'm a psycho. Elena's friends seemed to think the video was great, but that doesn't mean they want me around. I'm about to duck out of the room when I see Marisol wave to me from across the cafeteria.

I wave back sheepishly and walk over. "Hey," I say, barely louder than a whisper.

Marisol flashes me a bright smile. "Hey, Jo! How was the rest of your weekend?"

"Pretty good," I shrug. "How about yours?"

"It was kind of annoying, actually. My uncles still haven't gotten the hang of they/them pronouns. Oh, well!" Their bubbly personality really doesn't match their goth appearance. They grin at me. "I hope you had fun at Friendsgiving."

I nod. "I did. It was ... a good time." I cringe at my inability to find more descriptive words. "I see why Elena likes you all so much."

"Speak of the devil." Marisol gestures behind me, to Elena, who has just arrived at the table. She takes a seat which makes me realize I have just been standing this whole time, so I quickly sit next to her. Why am I so horribly awkward?

"Did I hear my name?" Elena asks.

"Jo was just saying how much you both love me."

"That wasn't exactly—" I cut myself off. They're joking. I have to stop taking things so seriously, but it's so hard to stay cool and collected when I feel as on edge as I do right now. As I do all the time.

The rest of Elena's friends slowly join us, so I try to fade into the background. Even if I had the mental energy to talk to people right now, I doubt I could successfully insert myself into their conversations. They talk about things I've never heard of and use words I don't understand. I don't know if they notice how lost I am, so I stay silent almost the whole period. They're quite a weird bunch, if I'm being honest, but at least I don't have to sit alone.

I make the mistake of glancing over at Rachel and Casey, who are sitting at our usual table. They seem happy, which makes me sad. Did I really mess things up so much that they don't even care that I'm not there with them? Casey and I have been friends since we were seven. How could she just throw that all away?

21

Some Rules Are Meant To Be Broken

Color guard practice is definitely going to be the worst part of the day. Casey has always had more friends than me, but ever since our fight things feel even worse. Most of the girls look at me like I'm a total psycho. It probably wasn't a very smart idea to punch her in the face in front of so many people. And of course, anything that happens in front of that many people is bound to end up on the Internet. I didn't even know I was going to hit her until it was too late. My reflexes just took over.

I was just so angry at her for everything she had done. She made me leave Elena at the party where she almost got raped, she posted online that I was a lesbian, and she told everyone Elena had slept with Dylan, even though she hadn't. And then she had the nerve to be mad at *me* after all that. So when she shoved me, the punch came without even thinking.

I mentally prepare myself for an hour and a half of isolation as I walk toward the field. I can already see Casey and Rachel talking to a group of girls in our grade. I hope with every fiber of my being that they aren't talking about me.

I stand just far enough from all the little huddles of friends that I can't hear what anyone is saying and begin to stretch by myself. I might be the only one actually using this time to stretch. Technically, it's what we're supposed to do before our coach gets here, but everyone uses it to socialize. I don't have anyone to be social with right now.

I tense up as I notice three seniors walking toward me. It's not just any seniors; it's Parvati, Danielle, and Olivia. They are three of the most beautiful and popular girls on the team. And they're walking toward me. This can't possibly lead to anything good.

"Hey," Parvati says. "It's Joanne, right?"

"Um, yeah, hi," I stammer. "It's just Jo really."

"Well, 'Just Jo,'" Olivia banters with a big smile, as she pulls her long black hair into a ponytail, "I don't think we've ever gotten a chance to really talk before. We just wanted to say hello."

"Oh." I try to hide my surprise. "Hello."

Our coach arrives not long after, so we don't get a chance to chat any further. Throughout all of practice, I rack my brain trying to figure out what that whole interaction was about. Were they somehow making fun of me? Is this a big joke I'm not in on? Or did they actually just want to talk to me? They've never shown any interest in me before today. What changed?

Eventually, practice ends and I start gathering my things to leave. Suddenly, the three seniors are in front of me again.

"Do you want a ride home, Jo?" Danielle offers.

This has to be a prank. It's the only explanation. I look past them toward Casey, and I see that she is staring at us, but she quickly looks away once she notices me looking at her. She looks angry. If this is some sort of joke, she doesn't seem to be in on it either.

"That'd be great, thanks." I hope I'm not about to get humiliated in some way.

"Awesome." Parvati grabs my hand and leads me toward the parking lot. "Come with us."

I sneak one more glance at Casey over my shoulder. She looks so furious, smoke might as well be coming out of her ears. It almost makes me laugh.

I get in the backseat with Olivia. Danielle starts the car while Parvati plugs her phone into the console and starts playing some generic pop song.

"So that girl Elena..." Danielle peers at me in the rearview mirror. "She's your sister?"

"Half-sister," I clarify. "Why?"

"We met her a few weeks ago at Levi's house," Parvati tells me. "She's nice."

"It's really uncool that Casey made that post about her and Dylan," Danielle says. "You were totally right to call her out like that."

"Yeah, Casey doesn't know what she's talking about," Olivia mutters.

Parvati turns around in the passenger's seat to better face me. "A lot of people saw the video of your fight, but they don't know the full story. So if anyone on the team gives you a hard time, you let us know, okay?"

"Oh, um, yeah." I nod. "Okay. Thanks. I will."

♫

I hear voices and laughter coming from my room before I even make it all the way up the stairs. I open the door to find Elena hanging out with Ren Hayashi, like always. He lives next door so I guess it's convenient for him to come over so often, but it seems like lately they've been practically inseparable. I've been meaning to ask her if they're dating or something. I kind of thought he was gay.

"Hey, Jo," Elena says. "How was flag-twirling club?"

"It's called color guard and it's a serious sport," I correct her.

"A serious flag-twirling sport," she continues. She sure is throwing a lot of shade considering she's the *assistant* prop manager of the school play, but I roll my eyes and decide to let it go.

I throw my bag on my bed before sitting down at my desk. "Is Dad home yet?"

She scoffs. "What do you think?"

I sigh. "His job is suddenly so much more demanding than it used to be."

I don't know who he thinks he's fooling by pretending he has to work late so often. I can't remember a time that he ever worked this much. I guess nowadays he'll do anything to avoid his family.

I spin around in my seat to look at Ren and Elena. "What are you guys doing?"

"Homework. Or really, I should say that *I'm* doing homework. Ren isn't doing anything."

"'Cause homework is boring," he whines.

She hesitates but eventually admits he's right. "You got me there." She trades her pen for her cell phone. "What should I get Marisol for their birthday?"

"It's Marisol's birthday?" I ask.

"On Thursday," she says. "Oh wait, I forgot to give you the invitation to their surprise party this weekend." She begins digging through her bag, which will probably take a while. She's so disorganized. "Brooke's hosting it at her big fancy Woodview Harbor house."

"Really? I'm invited?"

"Don't feel too special," Ren interjects. "Even I'm invited. And I only kinda know Marisol from QSA and the Asian Cultural Society."

I didn't even know Woodview had an Asian Cultural Society. It can't have more than five or six members.

Elena finally fishes a small envelope with my name written across it in perfect calligraphy out of her backpack. "I know you don't know them that well yet, but I think Marisol will be happy if you come."

"They will?"

Elena passes me the envelope. I open it, pull out a note and read it to myself:

You are cordially invited to a dinner party to DIE for this Saturday at the Kaminsky residence. We will be investigating the death of Mr. Boddy while secretly celebrating the BIRTH of Marisol Castillo. (They haven't got a CLUE, so don't ruin the surprise.) Your identity is enclosed. Please dress accordingly.

"What the hell?"

"It's a murder mystery," Elena explains. "*Clue*-themed. There should be a card in the envelope with your character's name."

I peer inside and pull out a card that has "Yvette" written on it in cursive. "Who's Yvette?"

"Have you never seen *Clue*?" Elena's jaw practically drops to the floor. "She's the maid."

I groan. "So I have to dress like a maid?"

"I can't believe you've never seen the movie *Clue*," Elena says incredulously. "We have to watch it tonight."

I pull out my phone, search for *Yvette Clue*, and click on the first video I see. "Oh," I accidentally say out loud, "I could do this. I'll just need a French maid's outfit."

"I don't think you need to go too crazy with it. I'm just wearing a dress."

"It's fine. It's not hard to get a costume." I shrug as I start to search for one that will ship in time.

Elena raises an eyebrow. "You're gonna buy a costume just for this?"

"Not, like, an expensive one," I claim, not yet totally sure if that is the truth. "It'll be worth it. I'll wear it again." I know that's not the truth.

"Will you?" Elena begins to laugh. I shoot her a death glare, but she doesn't stop.

I continue searching online and feel a smile creeping onto my face. This sounds like it could be fun. I'm glad I was invited, even if it wasn't directly by Marisol.

Oh no. What am I gonna get them as a birthday gift?

22

The Opposite Of What You'd Expect

I wander around Brooke's house by myself. She had explained earlier that one of us was the "killer" and there were "clues" hidden around the house to help us figure out who it was. I'm not exactly sure what I'm supposed to be looking for, but I don't think I've found anything that could be a clue so far. To be honest, all I've really done is get lost. Brooke's house is unnecessarily large. I open a random door on the second floor, go inside, and start to look around a desk.

"Find anything?"

I jump at the sound of someone else's voice and look around.

Marisol peeks up from behind the bed, giggling. "Sorry," they say. "Didn't mean to scare you."

"I just didn't think anyone was in here," I explain, even though I don't really have to. They obviously already knew that.

They walk over and lean against the desk next to me. "Brooke must've spent forever planning all this."

"It's pretty cool. I've never been to a murder mystery party before."

"Neither have I, but I'm having a lot of fun."

"I don't think it's for me." I shrug. "I'm not very good at this."

"Well, that doesn't matter. You don't have to be good at something to enjoy it."

"I guess." I return my attention to the desk. I pick up a gold, heart-shaped locket lying on the table and admire it. It's not a clue, but it sure is pretty.

"What are you looking at?" Marisol is suddenly behind me, looking over my shoulder. It makes me jump again.

"Just a necklace," I reply, holding it up for them to see. "It's cute. Rachel has one like it. I was so jealous when Nico gave it to her."

"You could probably find a similar one that isn't too expensive."

I shake my head. "You can't buy heart-shaped jewelry for yourself."

"Why not?"

"Hearts represent love. So they should come from someone who loves you. Or at least someone who likes you. Someone who could love you someday."

"That's silly. Don't you love yourself?" I don't answer, so they continue, "I think if you want something, you should get it. You don't have to wait around for someone else to give it to you."

I shrug. "But it means more when it comes from someone you love. I know it's dumb but—"

"No, I get it. It actually sounds kind of sweet." Marisol brushes my hair to the side and puts the locket around my neck. "It looks good on you." I take a step away and admire it for a few seconds, before undoing the clasp and putting it back on the desk where I found it.

"What are we supposed to be looking for here?" I ask, desperate to change the subject.

"Clues."

I put my hands on my hips. "Yes, but what does a clue look like?"

Marisol doesn't answer. They begin canvasing the room and eventually enter the walk-in closet. I sit on the bed. If there's anything here, Marisol will be the one who finds it, not me.

Elena and Ren did make me watch *Clue*, although I fell asleep before it ended. It wasn't bad, but it was just so old that it didn't really hold my interest. Still, I stayed awake long enough to learn who all the important characters were. I understand that Marisol is dressed in a nice black suit to be Wadsworth, the butler and main character of the movie. I wonder if Brooke assigned us the characters at random or if she purposefully decided who should be whom. I wonder if I was chosen to be Yvette because I'm blonde or because she thinks I'm a ditz. Probably a little bit of both.

Brooke is dressed as Mrs. White in an impeccably tailored black dress, pearl necklace, and even a hat with a mesh veil. She not only looks perfect, but she also has memorized Mrs. White's monologue about flames on the side of her face and recites it periodically during the night.

Zeke, on the other hand, is dressed less accurately. He's wearing full head-to-toe yellow … a yellow tracksuit, yellow sneakers, he's even got his long blonde hair pulled back with a yellow headband. There's no way he had this much yellow in his wardrobe already, or at least I hope he didn't, he's really too pale for this color. I assume that he purchased yellow clothes specifically for this event. That's a lot of effort to put in to purposely *not* match the theme correctly, so he was probably just trying to piss off his sister. He was successful. I probably wouldn't have even realized who he was supposed to be if not for everyone else calling him Colonel Mustard, except for Ollie who mispronounces it as *Colonial* Mustard.

Ollie seems to have misunderstood the assignment because he arrived dressed in a giant peacock costume. Brooke was not pleased.

"I assigned you Professor Plum," she had scolded him.

"Yeah, but me and Violet swapped," he explained, as Violet chuckled softly. "Plum. Violet. They're both purple. It just makes more sense."

Honestly, I couldn't have pictured Violet dressed as Mrs. Peacock anyway. She's such a tomboy. She looks much more comfortable in her tiny blazer and bowtie than she probably would have been in a dress.

Ren and Elena are Mr. Green and Miss Scarlet, but neither went all out with their apparel. He just wore a simple suit jacket over a green shirt and she wore a red dress, although Ren did add some green to his previously blue hair. That was a nice touch.

I don't know how Brooke made sure Marisol would arrive at a surprise theme party dressed appropriately, but she pulled it off. Either way, I have to admit Marisol makes a good Wadsworth. They always wear all black, but today they've replaced their usual ripped jeans and leather jacket with a black suit and tie. Instead of their signature hairstyle of two loose buns, today their hair is slicked back into a single ponytail. They look incredible.

"I found something!" Marisol calls from the closet.

I stand and walk toward the closet to see Marisol struggling to untie a big rope from around a hanger. It looks more like a clue than anything I've seen so far, but I'm not sure if I understand what we're supposed to get from this.

"Rope?" Part of me hopes that Marisol knows what it means so I can finally figure out what the hell is going on. Another part of me hopes Marisol is as lost as I am because I don't want them to think I'm an idiot.

"Yeah," they explain, "it's one of the murder weapons. So this has to be a clue, right?"

"I guess so? What do you think it means?"

"I'm not sure," they admit. "I thought maybe if I could untie it I'd find something, but it's tight."

"Let me help." I walk over and begin picking at the knot. Marisol lets go of the rope but stays standing right next to me, a bit closer than necessary.

It's not easy, but eventually, I untie the knot and a small slip of paper falls onto the ground. At the same time, we both lean over to grab it, bumping heads on the way down.

"Sorry," Marisol says, laughing.

"No, it was my fault."

We both reach for the note and our fingertips brush against each other slightly. I pull my hand away.

Marisol looks up at me and smiles before grabbing the note and unfolding it. "This rope was last held by Colonel Mustard," they read aloud.

"So Colonel Mustard is the killer?" I ask. "That's Zeke, right?"

"Colonel Mustard *could* be the killer, but we don't know if the rope is the real murder weapon or not."

I deflate. "Well, how do we find that out?"

"I think we need to find more clues." They spring to their feet.

"How many clues do you think Brooke hid?"

"Knowing her … *a lot*." They extend their hand to me, so I take it and let them pull me up. They pull a bit harder than necessary, so I lose my balance upon standing and almost tip over. They reach out and grab my arms to help steady me.

"Whoa, are you okay there?"

I look into their deep brown eyes. Their smile is so friendly and genuine that it makes me smile too. In the short time I've known Marisol, I've learned it's pretty hard to feel sad around them. It's like their happiness is contagious, which is completely the opposite of what you'd expect from someone who dresses as dark as Marisol does.

"Yeah, I'm good," I say, stuttering slightly. "Thanks."

"No problem." They release me and I instantly miss their touch, which makes me suddenly feel self-conscious. "You wanna stick together? We make a pretty good team."

My smile gets wider, but I quickly force my face to go back to normal. "Okay," I respond as nonchalantly as I can, "that's fine with me."

Marisol smiles, and it looks like they want to laugh, but they don't. "Okay. Good."

As we leave Brooke's room, we bump into Elena and Zeke.

"Oh, hey," Elena says. Her lipstick is smudged.

"Solve the mystery yet?" Zeke asks, grinning.

"Not quite," I reply.

Marisol leans in and whispers to Elena, "You might want to fix your makeup."

Elena covers her mouth with her hand and scurries off toward the bathroom down the hall. Zeke follows her as Marisol chuckles.

♫

When it's time for cake and presents, we all sit around the table in Brooke and Zeke's giant dining room. I pass on the cake. I'm not a huge fan of frosting, so it's really not worth the calories. Ollie excitedly takes my slice.

I feel an odd mix of nervousness and excitement as Marisol starts to open their presents. I hope they like what I picked out.

They start with Zeke's gift, which isn't wrapped. It's a vinyl album still in the plastic bag from the record store. I've never heard of the band, but Marisol seems to be very excited about it. Next is Brooke's gift, accompanied by a long, thoughtful, handwritten note.

I involuntarily tense up when they grab the gift that I brought. After sifting through all the black tissue paper, they eventually pull out the charm bracelet that I spent hours picking out. I try to judge their facial expression, but I can't really read it. They examine the bracelet a little closer, looking at each individual charm: a skull and crossbones, a sword, a bat, and a pentagram. I think for a second that I notice Brooke roll her eyes, but Marisol looks up at me with a big smile across their face.

"This is awesome," they say. "Thank you, Jo."

I know there's a good chance they're just being nice because I've never actually seen them wear a bracelet that wasn't leather or spiked, but I still feel like I did okay. A smile slowly creeps onto my face.

♫

Ren's dad drives me and Elena home. As we all get out of the car and begin walking toward our respective houses, I silently pray they can't hear what I hear. It's embarrassing for strangers to know how screwed up our family has been lately. I guess they aren't really strangers. My parents have known Harry Hayashi since they were in high school, but they rarely socialize as adults. Still, I don't want anyone to know our private business.

I fumble with my key, distracted by the indistinct shouting coming from inside. I can see Elena's concerned expression in my peripheral vision, but I don't acknowledge it.

We open the door and go inside. After only a few seconds, the shouting abruptly stops. They must've heard us. It's probably the only thing that could've gotten them to stop fighting.

"Hi, girls." My mom enters the living room. Her face is flushed, but she smiles wide like nothing's wrong. "How was the party?"

"Good. Elena was the killer."

"Guilty," Elena says.

"Wow. I'm glad you both had fun."

"What are you wearing?" Dad gripes.

"We're *Clue* characters," Elena explains. "I'm Miss Scarlett and Jo's Yvette."

"That's quite a short skirt, don't you think?" He turns to my mom with his arms crossed. "Did you know she was wearing this?"

"Of course," she tells him. "She used my credit card to buy the costume."

He scoffs. "And you didn't think to run that by me first?"

"Well, I would have," her voice raises at least two pitches, "but you were busy *at work*, as usual." The way she stresses the words "at work" makes me wonder if she's implying he was actually somewhere else.

Dad twists his face. "In the future, I'd appreciate it if you checked with me about these things. She's my daughter too, you know."

"Oh, I am well aware of whose daughter is whose."

I look at Elena, and without thinking about it, I grab her hand. "We're gonna go upstairs." I pull her along with me. "See you later!"

I go as fast as I can and slam the door shut behind us. "Are you okay?"

"Yeah, whatever. I'm fine."

I nod, even though I'm sure she's lying.

"How are you?" she asks. "I know it kinda stresses you out when..." she trails off, but she doesn't need to finish for me to understand. I get freaked out when they fight because it's so new to me. Throughout my entire childhood, my parents seemed to love each other so much. Of course, they had disagreements and bickered about little things, but it's never been like this. Or at least, not to my knowledge.

Everything changed when we found out Dad had another daughter. Of course it did. How could it not?

My mom tries to pretend that everything is fine, but it isn't. We can't ignore the elephant in the room, especially since the elephant lives with us now.

I actually do like having a sister. Elena is great, but nothing has been the same since she got here. The second we learned she existed, my family started falling apart.

"I'm fine," I lie. "Don't worry about me."

She looks at me in that pitiful way that I hate, but I realize it's probably pretty similar to how I'm looking at her right now and she probably hates it as much as I do. I see her reach for her earbuds like she always does when things get tense, so I plaster a fake smile across my face and start a new topic before she can tune me out.

"Do you think there's any chance of us getting out of the Roma holiday party next weekend?" I ask. "I'm assuming you don't want to go any more than I do."

Elena shrugs. "It seems like it's important to Meg. We should probably go."

I sigh. I know she's right, but I don't want to accept it. I turn around to look at her. She's already changing out of her dress from the party and throwing on an oversized t-shirt and sweatpants. I guess I should probably change too.

"How much do you wanna bet Dad finds some excuse not to go?"

"Probably," she mumbles.

"If he doesn't have to go, I don't think we should either."

"Whatever," she sighs. "It'll probably be a more peaceful party without him there anyway."

My eyes dart to the ground. I don't like thinking about that. It's easier for her to write off our dad as some horrible ball of negativity. She's never known a time when he wasn't like that, but I remember what it was like before he learned he had another daughter.

23

If It Was Easy It Wouldn't Be Worth It

"Have you guys seen this?" Brooke slides into the seat beside Violet at our cafeteria table. She pushes her phone in Zeke's face and he takes it from her.

His whole expression changes. He turns to look at Elena but passes the phone to Marisol.

"Elena, did you post this?" Brooke demands.

Marisol hands the phone to Elena next and she looks at it. I notice a pained expression when she looks back up at Brooke.

"No, this wasn't me. I swear."

"What does it say?" I ask. Elena promptly gives me the phone. It's open to the WoodNews gossip page. There's a new post with a black background and white writing that reads:

Dylan Strickland is a piece of shit who tries to rape girls and gets away with it.

"Jesus," I say, passing the phone down the line to Ollie. "You didn't post this?"

"No. I mean, I did go to the police," Elena admits. "They basically said there's no way to prove he would have raped me if Levi hadn't interrupted him. But I wouldn't post something like this." She sighs and looks down. "What would be the point? I'm not trying to make any more enemies at this school, and I'm definitely not trying to antagonize the enemies I've already made."

"Well then, who posted it?" Brooke asks accusingly.

Elena shrugs. "I have no idea."

"Didn't Levi say he's done stuff like that to other girls?" I remind everyone. "Maybe one of them could've posted it."

"This is a serious accusation," Brooke scolds me. "You can't just post something like this online like it's no big deal."

"It's probably true, though," Zeke says matter-of-factly. "People don't usually lie about this stuff." He looks at Elena again.

Brooke takes a long breath in and out. "I wonder if he's seen it yet. I hope he's okay."

Marisol sighs. "Who cares, Brooke? He sucks."

"He's still a human being with feelings." I don't understand how Brooke can still defend him.

"Fuck his feelings," Violet mumbles.

"Whatever. I should've known you guys wouldn't understand."

I definitely don't understand. How can she still care about the feelings of a guy who dumped her and tried to rape her friend?

Marisol decides to change the subject. "Jo, are you going to come see the play?"

"Oh, um, maybe. When is it again?"

"Next week. There are shows on Thursday, Friday, and Saturday, so you have options," they explain. "You should try and see it if you can. You're the only one at the table who isn't in the drama club so we need *someone* to actually buy tickets."

"Yeah, okay." I grin. "I totally will."

Marisol lifts their hand to push a loose strand of hair out of their face and I realize that they're wearing the charm bracelet I got them. They smile at me.

♫

After color guard practice, I walk around to the front of the school to meet Elena. I see her sitting in a tight huddle with her friends, so I start walking faster, trying to get close enough to hear what they're talking about.

"Hey," I say as I approach, "what's going on?"

"Nothing," Elena quickly replies.

"It's not nothing." Zeke gives Elena's shoulder a little squeeze. "Dylan flipped out at rehearsal today."

"What do you mean he flipped out?"

"He saw that stupid post on WoodNews and started screaming at Elena," Violet explains, "calling her a psycho for posting it."

I look at Elena, but she looks down at the ground. "I tried telling him it wasn't me, but he wouldn't listen."

I shudder. "That's insane. What is wrong with him?"

"I don't think we have time to answer that," Marisol groans.

"It's a good thing Ollie wasn't there. He would've thrown Dylan across the room," Violet says. I can't imagine Ollie ever hurting a fly, but I do know how protective he is of his friends.

"What am I gonna do?" Elena sighs. "I can't keep going to rehearsals if he's gonna be there harassing me."

"I don't think you have to worry about him doing that again," Zeke reasons. "Everyone saw him threaten you today. Mr. Brunner won't let that happen again."

My ears perk up. "He threatened you?"

"Not really." She shakes her head. "He just said that if the post doesn't come down soon, I'll regret it."

"Sounds like a threat to me," Violet mutters under her breath.

"That's not fair," I grumble. "How are you supposed to take it down if you didn't post it? Maybe we can find out who actually submitted it and ask them to take it down."

"That's a good thought," Marisol says, "but how are we supposed to do that?"

I don't have an answer and I feel stupid for even bringing it up. "We'll figure something out," I say, just because everyone's looking at me and I have to say something. "I promise."

"Thanks," Elena sniffles, "but you really don't have to worry about me. I'll be fine."

"No, we've got your back," Marisol vows. "We always do."

♬

When I wake up the next morning, I see a text from Marisol.

Have you seen it?

I text back a question mark and start my morning routine. It's only a few minutes before I feel my phone buzz in my pocket.

The post about Dylan. It's got like a million new comments.

I open WoodNews and scroll through the comments. There's girl after girl talking about their own experiences with Dylan. I keep scrolling and there's just more and more people backing up the original post.

Another text from Marisol appears at the top of my screen.

Idk if Elena's seen it yet. She's probably gonna freak out when she does.

At first, I think that Marisol isn't giving Elena enough credit, but then I realize that freaking out right now would be totally justified. What is Dylan going to do when he sees this?

I try to gauge Elena's emotions on the way to school. Mom had to go to work early today and Dad is hardly ever around anymore, which means we are on our own. Any feelings she might be having about the post are masked by how annoyed she is at having to walk in the snow.

"It's so cold," she complains for the third time since we'd left.

"It doesn't tend to snow when it's hot." Sometimes I forget that she's used to Miami weather.

We spend most of the walk in silence, as I try to decide whether I should tell her about the comments or not. She's definitely going to freak out, but maybe it's better to let her know so she has time to prepare for whatever Dylan decides to do today.

"I assume you saw the comments," she eventually says. I guess the decision is made for me.

I nod.

"I'm torn," she continues. "On one hand, it's great that all these girls feel comfortable sharing what happened to them. But on the other hand, Dylan might actually kill me."

"I'm gonna message the account," I say. "Maybe they can tell me who submitted the post."

"Isn't anonymity the whole point of WoodNews?"

"Yeah, but maybe we can get them to make an exception."

Elena shakes her head. "So then we put a target on another girl's back? No."

I deflate. "I guess I hadn't thought about that. Maybe Ren can do something." I know I'm grasping at straws now because Ren hates his half-brother even more than Elena probably does. "We'll think of something."

"Thank you for trying, but it is what it is."

24

Now I Have You

Marisol comes over to my locker just before my free period. They appear so silently that I jump when I notice them standing there, which makes them laugh.

"Sorry."

"No, it's fine." I can feel my face blushing. "What's up? Did you want to talk about Elena?"

"No, we spoke earlier and she said not to worry about her. I'm just looking for something to do during this period and I saw you here."

"You have a free period now?"

"I'm not supposed to, but we're doing dissections in A.P. Bio today and I told my teacher it was against my religion to cause unnecessary harm to animals."

"Is it?"

"No," they admit, "but I still don't want to do it. Hence, an impromptu free period." They take a little bow, proud of their genius.

I laugh. "Fair enough."

"So if you're free this period too, we should hang out." They smile. "If you want to, of course."

"Oh, uh, yeah, sure."

"Okay." They take my hand. I think my heart skips a beat. As much as I want to keep holding their hand, I stick mine in my pocket as we start to walk, hoping that Marisol doesn't get offended.

We head to the school's common area and find an empty table. I sit down first, and then Marisol sits close enough that our legs touch. We're much closer than we need to be, but I don't complain.

"So, what do you usually do during your extra free?" Marisol asks.

I try to think of something interesting to say, but my mind goes blank, so instead I'm honest. "Homework mostly. Unless I don't have any. Then I usually just listen to music and go on my phone."

"We can do that." Marisol pulls out their phone and a pair of earbuds. They hand me one end and press *play* on a song I don't recognize.

We lean in toward each other so the earbuds can reach both of us. A few loose strands of Marisol's hair brush against my cheek. I know I should mention that I have wireless AirPods we could use instead, but I don't. I like being this close to them. I wish we were even closer.

"Do you know this one?" they ask.

"Never heard it before," I reply, shaking my head slightly, "but I like it."

They hum along very quietly to the music and tap their fingers on the table to the beat. It might be the most adorable sight I've ever seen. I can't imagine being as sure of myself as Marisol is; the kind of person who can just be happy. Marisol seems to have gotten it right. They know completely who they are at all times. It's incredible.

Suddenly, Marisol rips their earbud out and spins around in their seat. I hesitantly remove mine as well and turn around to see what the problem is. Dylan is sitting a couple of tables away from us, loudly complaining about how he hasn't done anything wrong.

"All those girls think they can tell lies about me just 'cause that dumb sophomore did first," he complains, "but she only said that 'cause she was upset I wouldn't hook up with her. I don't know why she's so obsessed with me."

A few guys are at the table listening to him. None of them seem to be questioning a thing he says. I look at Marisol. They're gritting their teeth and their hands are in tight fists. Just when I'm about to say something to them, Marisol stands.

"Why don't you shut the fuck up?" they shout across the room. "Everyone knows you're the only liar here."

He looks at his friends and then back at us. "I'm sorry, who are you?"

Marisol turns their attention to Dylan's friends, who seem more taken aback than anything. "Are you all seriously buying his bullshit? What's easier to believe? Twenty-plus people all got together to make up a fake rumor about your friend? Or he's a sleazy creep who preys on drunk girls?"

"Wait a second, you're friends with Elena," Dylan says, finally making the connection. "Of course, you're in on this. She's the one who started it all with that stupid post about me."

"Elena didn't write the post." The voice comes from the other side of the commons. Marisol and I both turn around and see Levi Haddad.

"I posted it," he admits. "For years I've seen you try to get girls drunk so you can take advantage of them. That's why *I* submitted that post to WoodNews. 'Cause I know this shit is real and I'm sick of it. The police might not want to do anything about it, but everyone else deserves to know who you really are."

"What is your fucking problem?" Dylan charges across the commons until he's face to face with Levi. "What, are you pissed that Elena likes me and not you?" He lunges forward, but Levi stops him and punches him right in the face. Dylan stumbles for a second, before regaining his balance. Now filled with rage, he swings back in retaliation.

The fight doesn't escalate too much further before two teachers run over and separate them, dragging them both in the direction of the main office.

"Well, that was a twist I didn't see coming." Marisol returns to their seat next to me. "Honestly, I kinda thought it *was* Elena who made the post."

I realize that I'm sitting here with my mouth open. I'm in shock at how easily they can return to this level of calm. "You were awesome just now," I marvel. I'm well aware of how much of a dork I must sound like, but I don't care. Marisol deserves the praise.

"That was nothing." They shrug. "He was being a dick. Someone had to say something."

"Elena's really lucky to have a friend like you."

They shake their head. "I was just doing what any decent person would do. Friends stick up for each other."

"I don't think Rachel and Casey would have ever done something like that for me," I admit, "even back when we were still talking."

"Well, they don't sound like they were very good friends then," Marisol counters, "but that's okay, 'cause now you have me."

They hold my hand under the table and give it a squeeze. This time I don't pull away.

♫

"You're not gonna believe this!" Elena bursts into our bedroom.

I've been enjoying having my room to myself more often due to all of Elena's late rehearsals. I've especially appreciated that most days she gets home too tired to really bother me much. It looks like today is not one of those days.

"What happened?" I close my laptop so she won't see that it was open to Marisol's profile.

"Dylan got kicked out of the drama club," she announces.

"Isn't the play, like, next week?"

"Yes!"

"So, how—"

"He has an understudy."

"Is this because he threatened you?"

"No, actually," she explains, taking a seat on her bed. "Well, kind of. Apparently, he also got into a fight with Levi." I nod. I guess she doesn't realize that I was there to see it all firsthand.

"So that means he can't be in the play?"

"Mr. Brunner has a zero-tolerance policy for violence," she explains. "He was already on warning after he threatened me, but a fistfight is *actual* violence. When Mr. Brunner found out what happened with Levi, he permanently banned him from the drama program."

"Wow."

"I think he's getting suspended, so he wouldn't have been able to do the play anyway. But now he can't do next semester's play either. Serves him right, no?"

"Yeah, totally," I say. "Is Levi getting suspended too?"

"Yes. As far as the school's concerned, he started the fight." From where I was sitting, Dylan started it, but I guess Levi did throw the first punch.

"I can't believe he's the one who sent the post to WoodNews."

"Yeah. I was kind of pissed, but he texted me and apologized. He didn't think that Dylan would take it out on me." It was pretty obvious to everyone else that he would, but I guess Levi didn't realize. Elena continues, "He said he just felt helpless that he couldn't do anything else to stop him. And I can't really be mad, 'cause in the end, it worked out good for me. He's the reason Dylan got suspended *and* kicked out of the play."

"And punched in the face," I add.

Elena chuckles.

"How did Brooke take it?"

"I think she finally realized that she was wrong about him. She apologized to me and everything."

"Oh, cool."

"Are you okay?" she asks. "You seem distracted."

"What? Yeah," I stammer, "I was just doing some homework when you came in."

"Oh, I'm sorry," she says, "I won't bother you anymore." She puts in her earbuds, lies down, and starts scrolling on her phone.

I pick up my laptop and move over to my bed, putting my back against the wall, so Elena can't see my screen. I put my AirPods in, reopen Marisol's profile, and click on another video. It's of them singing a cover of a song. I recognize it as the same one they played for me at school today. Marisol is very talented. They sing as they play ukulele and I'm mesmerized. I can't believe I'm lucky enough to even know them.

25

Tough Times Never Last, But Tough People Do

As predicted, my dad gave an excuse to skip the Roma family's holiday party, but Elena and I are still being forced to go, despite my many objections.

The good thing about your mom and her best friend both having kids the same age is that you grow up with an automatic friend at every annual gathering. The bad thing is, if he starts dating your other friend and then she stops talking to you, your moms will still force you to see each other at these stupid annual gatherings. Rachel has barely spoken to me since that day in English class and now I have to spend an evening at her boyfriend's house.

I assume it's awkward for Elena as well. This is the first big event she's had to go to since we stopped pretending she was just a family friend and openly admitted that she was really my half-sister. Honestly, it's gotta be kind of awkward for my mom too. She's here with her daughter and her husband's *other* daughter and he's not even here to support her. But at least her friends are here. I have no one.

I had hoped that having Elena here would at least make things a little better. She and Nico haven't gotten along very well since an incident on her first day at Woodview High. Apparently, he called Ren a slur or something. I don't fully believe that he would do that, but I don't know, I wasn't there. I had figured that with her at the party, I'd at least have someone to keep me company. It didn't occur to me that Ren would also want to take advantage of having Elena there. I guess I finally know how he felt at last year's party. It sucks.

Rachel barely even acknowledges me when we arrive. Nico only does because his mom makes him.

"Nico! Come here! Say hello to the Reillys."

He stands up from his seat on the couch next to Rachel and walks over to us, visibly annoyed. "Hi."

Almost an hour later and I haven't seen much of either of them since we got here. I'm sitting at a table receiving an unsolicited lecture about college from a man who apparently works with Nico's dad. I try to signal to Elena across the room that I need saving, but she hasn't looked in my direction in a while. She and Ren are deep in conversation.

Rachel comes into the room and clearly sees me, but she doesn't say anything. She passes by me to get to the drink table, where she grabs two iced teas.

As she passes again on her way back, she interrupts us. "We're all hanging out in the basement. You should come down."

I stare at her, unsure if I've heard right, but she just stares back at me. I politely excuse myself, stand, and follow her.

"That guy is so boring," she says once we're out of earshot. "He talked to me about stocks for, like, an hour earlier."

"Thanks for rescuing me." I'm not sure if I should laugh. This is the first conversation we've had in weeks. I don't think that one nice gesture automatically makes us friends again, but maybe this is her way of offering an olive branch.

"It's fine," she says flatly. "See you around." She heads down to the basement, closing the door behind her.

I'm left standing by myself in the hallway. I suppose I'm not actually welcome in the basement after all. Guess it wasn't much of an olive branch. I decide to go over to where Elena and Ren are chatting. Ren immediately stops speaking and tenses up as soon as he sees me. I don't know what they were talking about, but I thought I heard Nico's name. I wonder why Ren and Nico aren't friends anymore. It's probably nothing as dramatic as what happened with me and Casey.

"Oh hey Jo, sit with us," Elena offers. I feel like they don't actually want me there, but I sit anyway because it's better than the alternative.

"It's so unfair that Dad got out of this party, but we still had to come," I complain as I sit down.

"Poor Meg," Elena frets.

"Oh don't worry, I saw her talking to my dad before," Ren says. "She was laughing. She looked like she was having a ton of fun."

Nico's mother comes over to let us know that dinner is almost ready. She directs us to the "kids' table," which is actually all teenagers and one precocious eleven-year-old. I was especially dreading this part of the night. It's weird enough being here at all, but I can't imagine anything more awkward than eating dinner with my ex-friend, her boyfriend, his ex-friend, and my surprise new half-sister. Oh, and Tyler. This ought to be interesting.

Everyone sits quietly around the table because we all understand how weird it is to be together right now. That is, everyone except for Nico's little brother Gianni, who won't shut up.

"Ren, is that your girlfriend?" Gianni asks, pointing at Elena.

"Ren doesn't have girlfriends," Nico says snidely.

Ren rolls his eyes at Nico. "No, this is Elena. She's Jo's half-sister."

"Sister? But you don't even look alike."

"I'm half Puerto Rican," Elena explains.

"I don't remember you ever having a sister. Since when do you have a sister?"

"I've always had a sister," I lie, even though I didn't actually know about her until a few months ago. "She just lived in Miami with her mom. Now she lives here with us."

"Why don't you live with your mom?"

"She died," Elena says softly. Everyone is silent for a bit.

"Oh. How did she—" Nico shoves him so he switches gears and turns to Ren instead. "How come you and Nico don't hang out anymore?"

"What's with all the questions Gianni?" Nico snaps, as he puts his arm around Rachel.

"I don't know." Gianni shrugs. "Nobody ever tells me anything."

"Ren, I heard your brother got expelled," Tyler chimes in. "Is it because he fought that dude Levi or because he tried to rape a bunch of girls?"

"Jesus Christ, Tyler. You're worse than Gianni."

"Hey!" Gianni protests.

"He didn't get expelled. He just got suspended," Ren corrects him, "but he's not coming back to Woodview. His dad decided to send him to boarding school."

Elena looks down at the table again.

"Good riddance," I say. "I'm just glad there was finally something *true* on WoodNews." I look directly at Rachel.

"What's WoodNews?" Gianni asks.

Tyler starts to answer. "It's this page where—"

"Dude." Nico interrupts him.

"Eh, don't worry about it." Tyler quickly tries to change the subject. "So Gianni, you got a girlfriend yet?"

"Ew, gross." Gianni makes a face. "Do you?"

"Nah, I don't wanna be tied down." He grins, leaning back in his seat. "I like to keep my options open." He looks directly at me and winks.

Rachel doesn't say anything the entire meal.

♫

On the way home from the party, I continue to complain. "I still think it's unfair that we had to go, but Dad didn't."

"Yeah, it is pretty unfair," Mom huffs. "Your dad should've been there."

"It seems like you were having a nice time with Harry Hayashi," Elena chimes in from the backseat, probably trying to diffuse the situation.

"Jo, you know we go to this party every year," Mom scolds me, completely ignoring Elena's comment. "We can't revolve all our plans around you fighting with Rachel about nothing."

"It's not about nothing," I snap.

"Well, do you want to tell me what it's about?"

"No," I grumble.

"I thought the party was nice," Elena says.

"Shut up. No, you didn't."

Mom decides to change the subject. "Elena, what time is your play on Saturday again?" "Are you going to that?" I ask.

"Of course. I want to support Elena. You know, I was Ursula in *Bye Bye Birdie* when I was in high school."

"It's at 7:30," Elena answers. "By the way, is it okay if I go to the cast party after?"

"I thought you weren't going to the cast party," I say before Mom can answer.

"Yeah, but that was when it was at Dylan's house," she explains. "Now it's at Brooke and Zeke's."

"Isn't it usually at a senior's house?"

"Yeah, but Dylan got kicked out of the play and none of the other seniors could host last minute, so Brooke stepped up."

"Of course she did." I roll my eyes, even though Elena can't see my eyes from the backseat.

"So, is it okay if I go?"

"Of course, you can go," Mom says. "You can't miss the cast party. It's tradition." I can't believe Elena has a better social life than I do.

26

Too Much, Yet Not Enough

The play is just okay. Dylan's understudy is extremely mediocre. Dylan probably would've done a much better job, but I'm still glad he was replaced.

I'm not sure why Mom wanted to come to support Elena. She just moves the props around. We hardly even see her, and when we do, most of the lights are turned off. However, we still applaud extra loudly when she and Marisol take their bow.

Afterward, we wait for Elena by the backstage door. My mom gives her a big hug that seems to surprise her more than anything.

"That was great!" she exclaims.

"Thanks," Elena says sheepishly. "I didn't really do much though."

"Oh, don't be modest. That play would've fallen apart without props. Right, Jo?"

"Uh, yeah." I'm a little distracted. During the time that we've been talking to Elena, Marisol has emerged from backstage as well. They stand off to the side, talking animatedly to Violet, Ollie, and other crew members. They seem excited and happy.

"Do you want to go say hi to your friends?" my mom suggests, probably because she notices me staring.

Before I have a chance to answer, Marisol comes rushing over to me and gives me a big hug. "You came!" I wasn't expecting that reaction, so I instinctively pull away a little bit.

"Oh, you must be one of Jo and Elena's new friends! I'm Jo's mom." She extends her hand in Marisol's direction, adding, "Meg Reilly."

"Nice to meet you. I'm Marisol Castillo, my pronouns are they/them." They shake my mom's hand.

"Oh, so *you're* Marisol. I've heard a lot about you."

I feel my face blush as I look down at the ground, avoiding eye contact.

"Meg, could we possibly give Marisol a ride to the cast party?" Elena requests. "Their parents came to the show yesterday, so they're not here tonight."

"Of course, I'd be happy to."

"Jo, you should come to the party too!" Marisol says excitedly.

"Isn't it just for the cast and crew?" I ask.

"Yeah, technically, but Brooke and Zeke are doing everyone a huge favor by hosting at the last minute, so they can invite anybody they want. You can be my guest." Marisol grins. "Come on, it'll be fun."

"Oh, isn't that nice?" Mom muses. "Jo, you should go! Have fun! Who knows, maybe it'll inspire you to join the drama club next semester."

"But I'm not dressed for a party."

"You're dressed fine for this kind of party." Marisol chuckles.

"They're right," Elena adds. "You should come."

I look at each of them and then at my mom, who nods and smiles.

"Uh, okay. I'll come."

♫

I can't believe Brooke and Zeke's parents are okay with them having all these people over while they're in the house. Usually, when I go to parties like this, the parents are away and have no idea, but their parents are right upstairs on the third floor, pretending not to know what we're all doing down here. They must at least have some idea, though.

I grab a wine cooler from a bucket of ice and try to act normal. I feel so uncomfortable at this party. Brooke said it was fine that I tagged along, but I don't necessarily believe her. I feel like all the other cast members are staring at me because I don't belong here. I don't even see Elena most of the night. Every time I do, she's deep in conversation with Zeke. But Marisol never leaves my side.

After a little while, Marisol reaches for my hand. "Hey, come with me." They lead me upstairs to the second floor and into Brooke's bedroom. We sit down on the bed, and Marisol pulls out their phone and earbuds. "Help me pick a song to sing at the open mic next week?"

"Right now?"

Marisol shrugs. "You looked a little bit uncomfortable out there. Thought you could use a break."

I smile. "Thanks."

They smile back. "You're definitely gonna come see me perform, right?"

"Yeah, of course I will."

"Good. I'll feel more confident knowing you're in the audience."

I blush. I don't think Marisol actually needs any help with confidence, but the sentiment is nice.

"So what do you think? I've got it narrowed down to two choices." They hand me one earbud and open one of their videos. I've seen this one before, but I pretend that I'm seeing it for the first time. We lean our heads together and listen.

"They're both great," I say after I've heard the two choices, "but I think I like the first one best."

"I wanna be your girlfriend?"

"What?" I blink.

"That's the name of the song."

"Oh. Right. Yeah. That one. I really like the chorus."

"Oh yeah, which part?" they ask, as they lean in closer.

"The part about wanting to…" I trail off, distracted by how beautiful Marisol looks.

"…kiss," they finish my thought and start to sing the chorus, softly and slowly. They lean in even closer as they sing until we're just inches apart and I can smell their strawberry-scented shampoo. My heart is practically beating out of my chest.

Just then, the door to the bedroom bursts open. I jump back, away from Marisol.

"Oh sorry, I didn't know anyone was in here," Brooke says, barely looking up. "That idiot Kyle spilled his drink all over me, so I need to change."

"We'll get out of your way," I blurt out. Marisol reaches for my hand, but I stand up and walk toward the door before they can grab it.

They follow me out into the hallway. "Technically, Brooke did say her room was off limits tonight." Marisol laughs slightly.

"Yeah," I mumble, "um, I should go find Elena."

"I'll come with you."

"No, you should stay with Brooke," I say quickly. "She seems upset."

"It's just clothes."

"It's okay. I'll … see you around."

I hurry down the stairs, back to the crowd of the party, leaving Marisol looking confused in the hallway.

That was too much.

27

You Need To Kiss A Lot Of Frogs To Find Your Prince

When I go to school on Monday, I'm still replaying that moment with Marisol over and over again in my head. What was I thinking? Well, that was the problem, I wasn't thinking. I was about to make the same exact mistake I'd made with Casey a couple of months ago, and that didn't exactly work out great for me.

I look across the room at Rachel. She still won't sit near me in class or wave at me in the hallway or anything. Nothing good has come from any of this. I wish I could just rewind time to before I knew Marisol, before Rachel hated me, and before I kissed Casey. I wish I could go back to the person I was before I started letting my stupid impulses take over. I need to start using my head again.

Tyler comes into the classroom and takes his seat behind me. "Hey, Jo. Looking good." He looks me up and down and then winks.

My first instinct is to roll my eyes, but instead I turn around and giggle. "Thanks, Tyler." I give my hair a gentle flip. "Hey, do you have plans tomorrow night?"

He looks a little surprised because I usually ignore his flirtations. "I could check my calendar," he teases playfully. "Why? What's up?"

"We should hang out." I twirl a strand of hair around my finger. "Do you wanna come with me to the open mic?"

"Sure, sounds like fun, I guess."

"Great." I smile, giggling slightly. "It's a date." I try to wink, but I think it probably looks more like an awkward blink, so I just turn back around.

This is what a normal girl does. She flirts with boys, she goes on dates, she doesn't kiss her friends, she is normal.

♫

Tyler meets me at my house and we walk over to the school for the open mic together. We don't really talk much, other than a few typical niceties, but he does hold my hand as we walk. It feels a little bit like we're middle schoolers going on a date for the first time, but I decide that that's okay. At least it feels like something a normal girl would do. He holds the door open for me as we enter. I try to feel nervous or excited or anything really, as I walk inside.

I see Elena right away, sitting with Ren and her other friends, so we go over and join them. She gives me an odd look when she sees Tyler with me. I think I made the right decision not telling her I was coming with him. She probably would've asked me way too many questions that I wouldn't have been able to answer.

Marisol is sitting at the front with the other performers. I breathe a sigh of relief. I haven't seen them since the cast party and I'm grateful for some extra time before I finally have to face them. In the meantime, I try to flirt with Tyler. I'm trying to do all the normal things a normal girl would do on her normal date with a normal boy.

First up at the open mic is a girl I don't recognize reading an original poem that's actually quite good. She's followed by two boys rapping poorly, a band playing a cover of a pop-punk song that I don't recognize, and a girl singing a cappella just slightly off-key. Then finally there's Marisol.

Our friends cheer when they approach the microphone and even Tyler claps a little bit. I don't. Marisol begins strumming their ukulele and they look me directly in the eyes for the first time tonight. I lean in closer to Tyler, who takes this opportunity to put his arm around me. Marisol doesn't look at me anymore after that.

They sing their song and it's beautiful. They decided to go with the one I picked out at the party and I feel entranced by every line. I want to go right up onstage and kiss Marisol right now in front of everybody. I try to force that thought out of my mind, but it won't stop.

Tyler doesn't seem to notice any change in my demeanor, so hopefully I'm not being as obvious as I feel like I am. He bops his head slightly to the beat of Marisol's song. At least one of us is having a good time.

I lean in so I can whisper in his ear. "Do you wanna get out of here?"

His eyebrows perk up slightly. "Uh, sure," he nods.

I plaster on a fake smile. I don't actually want to leave, but I don't want to still be here when Marisol finally joins our table.

"Great," I say.

Elena gives me another look as we stand up, but I ignore her.

♫

Tyler and I walk quietly. We don't even hold hands this time and I wonder if somehow he knows about me and Marisol. I remind myself that there's no way he could, but that doesn't really settle my nerves.

"Do you wanna grab coffee?" he suggests, finally breaking the silence. "Or ice cream maybe?"

"Sure," I say. "Either."

He nods but doesn't respond for about half a block. "Ice cream shop is closer."

"Let's go there then."

He nods again. I wonder if other dates are as tense as this one. We might beat the record for the most awkward date of all time.

He orders a shake. I think for a second that he wants to do that thing in movies where a couple shares a drink with two straws, but then he asks me what I want. I panic and order a kid's cup with no toppings.

"You can order something better than that if you want," he offers. "It's my treat."

"No, it's fine."

He shrugs and pays. We take our ice cream outside and start walking around aimlessly. We didn't really think this through. It's a little too cold to be eating ice cream outside, but there wasn't anywhere to sit in the shop so I guess we have no choice.

Eventually, we take a seat on a bench. I shiver a little bit so he puts his arm around me again and I lean onto his chest.

"The show was better than I expected," he says. "How bad were those dudes rapping though?"

"They were awful," I agree.

"I'm offended on behalf of my entire race." He laughs. I don't know if I'm allowed to laugh at that or not, so I just smile. Tyler quiets down pretty quickly. "You seemed kinda off towards the end though."

"No, I had fun."

"Really?" he asks again. "'Cause you kinda seemed upset as soon as that goth girl got up there."

"Marisol is nonbinary," I correct him.

"What?"

"Nonbinary," I repeat. "They don't identify as a girl or a boy."

"Oh, okay." He nods slowly, clearly not understanding what I mean, but I drop it anyway.

We sit silently, surrounded by the mundane sounds of our suburban town. I think about one more normal thing that we haven't done yet on this normal date. We probably should...

I lean in and kiss him. It's ... weird, honestly. It feels forced and unnatural and his stubble scratches my face. I pull away after what feels like forever but was probably only a few seconds. He looks about as uncomfortable as I feel.

"Uh..." He hesitates. "That was..."

"Bad," I finish his sentence.

"I was gonna say *strange*," he explains, "but *bad* works too." He removes his arm from around me and sits back.

I lean forward with my elbows on my knees and my face in my hands.

Tyler leans forward to match me. "Can I ask you something?"

"I guess."

"Why did you ask me out tonight? I mean, don't get me wrong, I appreciate the invite, but it doesn't really seem like you were having a good time."

"Well, I couldn't have known we wouldn't have a good time," I mutter. "I can't see the future, can I?"

"No, but a good rule of thumb is, if you don't actually like the person you're going out with, you probably won't have a great time."

I blink. "Who says I don't actually like you?"

He laughs. "Just call it a hunch."

I bury my face in my hands again, humiliated. "I'm sorry."

"It's all good." I look up and he's smiling, though I'm not sure how real that is. "How about I walk you home now?"

28

All That Glitters Is Not Gold

I'm awake at 6:00 a.m. the morning of Christmas Eve because my dad said we were leaving for my grandparents' house at 7:00 sharp. I scramble to make sure I don't forget anything I might possibly need for the holidays and am ready, waiting at the door by 6:50. Of course, we don't actually end up leaving until 7:28, but that's absolutely no fault of mine.

Once we pile into the car with all our stuff, we set off on a horribly tense four-hour drive that none of us really want to be embarking on. But it is tradition that we always go to my grandparents' house for Christmas Eve, so that's what we are doing.

Elena's leg has been bouncing up and down since we got in the car and it's really starting to bug me. I guess I can't blame her though. I'd probably be pretty stressed if I was about to meet an entire extended family that didn't even know about me until a few months ago.

My mom doesn't say a word the entire drive and my dad only breaks the silence to shout at other drivers on the road. The drive feels a lot longer than four hours.

When we finally arrive, my grandmother gives me a big hug.

"Joanne!" she shouts as she squeezes me tight. "It's great to see you!" She shakes me by my shoulders and gives me a kiss on the cheek that is sure to leave a big lipstick stain.

"Hi, Mom." My dad gives her a one-armed hug and then he goes out to start unloading the car.

"And you must be *Elena*." She overenunciates her name, but I'm not sure why. "It's. Great. To. Meet. You." She is practically shouting, putting a pause between each word.

Elena gives me a weird look before returning her gaze to our grandmother. "Nice to meet you too."

She smiles. "Her English seems good," she says to my dad.

"English was her first language, Colleen," Meg corrects her, coldly.

"But those people don't always teach their kids properly," she says more softly, but not softly enough. "I wasn't sure what to expect."

"Where's Grandad?" I ask, hoping to cut the tension at least a little bit.

"Oh, he ran down to the store to grab some last-minute stuff for tonight. He'll be back soon. How was the drive up here? You must be hungry. Can I fix you something to eat?"

I say yes, of course. Anything to get out of this awkward conversation. And I'm also actually hungry. I'm always hungry.

Most of the extended family is already here waiting for us and that includes Kate. She's my favorite cousin because she's only seven months older than me, so we've been thrown together at family events ever since we were little. Growing up, she was the closest thing I had to a sister. When I walk into the living room she jumps straight out of her seat. I run over to her, almost knocking her down with a hug. We don't get to see each other very often anymore, ever since her family moved to Chicago, so I'm always happy when they fly out to visit. After the past few months I've had, seeing Kate is exactly what I need to get into the Christmas spirit.

"Jo!" she exclaims. "I missed you!"

"Not as much as I missed you!"

We squeal and jump up and down until my dad tells us to stop because we're being too loud.

"Let's go upstairs!" Kate suggests.

I nod and we run upstairs to the room that always serves as the "kids room" on holidays because it's the room with the most beds. She sits down on a bed and pats the spot next to her, so I sit down as well.

"How have you been?" I ask her. "I want to hear everything!"

She shrugs. "I'm fine. I mean, it's a city, so there's always something happening, but I want to hear about you first. A secret sister is way more interesting than anything I've done lately."

"Right." I'd anticipated a lot of the family having questions about Elena today, but I kind of assumed most of them would be directed at her or my dad. I didn't really think anyone would be interested in my take on the situation. "Elena's pretty cool actually," I admit. "We're starting to get along better." It's then that I realize I completely left her to the wolves downstairs. I'm sure she's fine.

"Did you have to give up half your room? The absolute best part about Louise going to college is that I finally have my own room."

"Yeah, it's annoying not having my own space anymore, but she's not a bad roommate, I guess."

"How did your mom take the news?" She leans forward with her eyes practically bulged. "I've been dying to know, but my parents won't tell me *anything*."

"She's taking it surprisingly well."

"That's crazy. I would be so pissed if I was her."

There's a knock on the door, and then it slowly opens to reveal Elena standing there awkwardly. "Hey. Meg told me I should come upstairs and see what you were doing."

"Oh yeah," I say. "Come in."

She nods and sits down on an adjacent bed, carefully, as if she's afraid she's going to break it.

"This is our cousin Kate."

"It's nice to meet you," Elena says timidly.

"You too. Your hair is gorgeous by the way."

They begin to chat and I just sort of sit back and watch it happen. I hope Elena is able to feel like she's part of the family this holiday. After all, she is.

♫

Grandma Colleen pulls out all the stops for Christmas Eve dinner. I sit in between Cousin Kate and Elena and cross my fingers that my parents' drama won't ruin the night for everyone else, but of course, it will. It's inevitable.

They barely speak to each other the entire dinner, and when they do, they bicker. Even something as simple as "pass the potatoes" sounds like it's dripping with disdain. Elena is clearly miserable. My dad barely acknowledges her, while my mom is trying almost too hard to prove she's part of the family. It's clear no one else really thinks she is, including Elena.

"Oh, you should've all seen the production of *Little Women*," my mom boasts. "Elena did such a good job with the props. It's a shame Kevin was too busy to come and support her."

"I had a work emergency," my dad responds, even though we all know he never actually works on Saturdays. "Somebody needs to put food on the table."

"Work sounds a little more important than watching her move around props, now doesn't it?" my grandma says. "Especially now that you have an extra mouth to feed." She gives Elena the side eye.

"I also work. I also help put food on the table. And I cook it. And I eat it with *your* daughters when you're *working late*." She uses air quotes on that last part.

"It's fine, really," Elena says softly. It's clear she does not like being the topic of conversation, even if it's just an excuse for them to criticize each other.

It's like that the entire night. Eventually, Meg suggests that Elena and I go upstairs to finish wrapping our presents, even though she knows we already finished days ago.

♫

I can't sleep. I'm lying on an uncomfortable air mattress because I lost the game of rock paper scissors with my cousins and didn't get to claim a real bed. I look around the room for anyone else who might be awake, but they all seem to be sound asleep. I reach for my phone and see that it's almost 4:00 a.m. It's technically Christmas morning, but I'm not feeling any Christmas cheer. Any ounce that hadn't already been destroyed by my parents' fighting at dinner vanished a few hours ago.

Earlier tonight, all the older cousins had been scattered around the kids' room, whispering about everything and nothing at the same time. We attempted to stifle our laughter, so as not to wake the younger cousins sleeping just a few feet away. I should've stayed with them, but my laughs turned into coughs, so I went downstairs to get a glass of water. Everything went downhill from there.

On my way back from the kitchen, I passed the guest room that my parents were staying in and could hear muffled voices coming from behind their closed door. I tried to ignore it as I tiptoed back to my room, but then I heard my own name. I froze. I didn't mean to eavesdrop, but I couldn't help myself.

"I can't take much more of this," Mom snapped.

"Let's just get through this trip and then we can tell the girls."

"Oh, don't act like you're doing this for their sake. You just don't want to admit to your parents that we're separating."

My heart stopped. I must have heard that wrong, right? My parents can't be separating. That's not what they're supposed to do. I guess I probably should've seen this coming, but at that moment, it felt like a slap in the face. It felt like my family was falling apart right in front of me.

I headed back to the kids' room, forcing away any tears that tried to form in my eyes. I lay down on the air mattress and pulled the covers up high.

"You alright?" Elena asked.

I shot her a glare before turning over, my back to her. This is her fault.

It's been hours now and I still can't sleep.

29

All's Fair In Love And War

My younger cousins wake us up bright and early on Christmas morning because our grandparents have a rule that no presents may be opened until everyone is downstairs. I wish I could be as excited as they are, but alas, I am no longer ten.

"Merry Christmas," my mom greets me. I roll my eyes at her fake smile. I'm sure neither of us are feeling very merry right now.

I take a seat on the couch and wait, while everyone else gets settled. My dad tries to hand me a gift, but I won't even look at him. He is completely ruining our family. How can he act like nothing's wrong?

"This one's for you Jo," he says. I snatch the gift out of his grip, still refusing to look him in the eye. "It's from me and your mother."

"Oh yeah, I'm sure you picked it out together," I mumble sarcastically under my breath.

"What's that?" my dad asks.

I glare at him. "I find it hard to believe that you and Mom went shopping together because we know that the only thing you two ever do together is fight!" I stare him down, waiting for his response, but he looks like he's at a loss for words. "I'm shocked you even had time to go shopping since you're always," I pause, putting down my gift so my hands are free for dramatic air quotes, "*at work*."

My mom tries to interject. "Jo, that's not—"

"You're gonna defend him after he's been lying to everyone this whole time," I snap, spinning my head around to face her. "I can't believe you've been going along with it. You both really think I'm so stupid and immature that I can't handle the truth?" I should probably realize that I'm not exactly proving myself to be mature, but I can't stop. My voice continues to get louder. "What, were you worried I'd cause a scene? Well, here you go!" I stand up and announce to the entire room, "Guess what, everybody! Wanna hear the big secret?" I lock eyes with my dad. "They're getting divorced."

The room goes silent.

"Why don't we all go play in the snow?" Aunt Nora suggests, awkwardly. I've officially ruined Christmas.

After everyone gets bundled up and goes outside, my parents sit us down at the kitchen table. I glare at my mom.

"Jo, would you please stop looking at me like that," she requests.

"Would you stop lying to me?" I snap back.

"We couldn't just have a normal family Christmas?" my dad grumbles.

"Nothing about our family has been normal lately."

"She has a point." Elena gives me an understanding look.

"You know what, fine." My dad turns to my mom. "There's no use hiding it anymore." He turns back to us. "Your mother and I are separating."

My mom sighs.

"Does this mean you're getting a divorce?" I ask.

"Not necessarily," my mom answers at the exact same time that my dad says, "Probably." They truly can't agree on anything anymore.

"Kevin!"

"You said you wanted us to be honest."

"Oh my God. You can't even stop fighting long enough to tell us?" I yell. "You know what? Screw this. Screw both of you."

I get up and storm out, but my mom chases after me. Elena just sits and stares at the table.

"Jo, please talk to me," my mom begs as I run upstairs to the kids' room.

"No."

She sits down on the bed next to me.

"Joanne, I'm sorry."

"How can you throw away sixteen years of marriage?"

"It's a complicated situation." She looks down.

"Is it just the affair? That was years ago. Can't you forgive him?"

"There's more to the story than you realize."

"Then why are you breaking up?"

"Marriage is hard. You'll understand when you're older."

"I wish you'd stop acting like I'm a little kid. I'm almost sixteen, Mom. You don't need to hide stuff from me."

She hesitates before replying. Finally, she looks up and asks me, "What do you want to know?"

"Do you think it's really over?"

"There's no easy answer for that."

"Yes or no. That's as easy as it gets."

She hesitates again. "I've made peace with your father's actions."

"Then what's the problem? Why can't you stay together?"

She puts her arm around me and pulls me toward her. "Sometimes people just aren't meant for each other, no matter how hard they try."

♫

The ride home from my grandparents' house manages to be even worse than the ride there. Obviously, I am somewhat to blame this time, but I absolutely refuse to accept total fault. My parents are the ones who are ruining everything.

No one speaks a word or even makes eye contact the entire drive. After a while my mom turns the radio on, I think trying to cut the tension, but it doesn't really work. Eventually, my dad turns it off.

When we get home, I go straight to my room and slam the door, even though I know Elena's just going to need to reopen it a minute later. I connect my phone to a Bluetooth speaker and start blasting music as loud as it will go. Then I sit down on my bed and just stare ahead of me. How did everything get so messed up?

Elena comes in and sits on her bed. If she has any problem with the music, which I suspect she does, she doesn't mention it. This whole thing would be easier if I could just blame her for everything that was happening, but I know it isn't her fault. At least it's not entirely her fault.

I lie back. More than anything right now, I want to talk to Marisol so I pick up my phone and text them, but they don't answer. I wonder if when big things happened to my mom she used to immediately want to talk to my dad about it. I wonder when she stopped wanting that.

I realize that I need to know when they started to fall out of love because I don't believe it was when Elena moved here. That would be too fast. You can't go from loving someone to just … not, in only a few months, can you? I decide the answer is no, but I suppose I don't really know for sure. Maybe I don't really know anything about love after all.

30

Nothing Ventured, Nothing Gained

I'm putting the finishing touches on my Secret Santa gift for Ollie. I was so glad Elena asked to trade with me when I drew Zeke's name from the hat. I wouldn't have known at all what to give Zeke, but apparently, Elena had "the perfect idea." I don't know what she got him, but she managed to fit it in an envelope, so I'm not sure how great it could possibly be.

I remembered how excited Ollie had gotten by the tartlets I made at Friendsgiving. He said they looked like tiny pies, so I decided to make him one big pie for Christmas, along with five vouchers for a dessert of his choosing that he could cash in whenever he wanted. I hope he likes it. I'm pretty sure he will because Elena assures me that the way to Ollie's heart is through his stomach.

My mom drives us over to Brooke and Zeke's house. They offered to host because they were the only ones who hadn't been busy celebrating Christmas with their families the past couple of days. Also, their house is huge. Despite being Jewish, they still decorated the room Christmas-style, even with a small faux Christmas tree. That's a nice touch, in my opinion. Brooke gives everyone an assorted box of homemade cookies when they come in, including me, which is cool because it feels like I'm actually becoming part of the group, instead of just being Elena's plus-one.

I appreciate the different levels of festive attire everyone in attendance has chosen to wear. Brooke is wearing a red dress that's nicer than anything anyone else is wearing. It's possibly nicer than anything I own. It makes the simple red and white dress that I wore look like garbage. Zeke is in his usual clothes. Violet is wearing a reindeer Christmas sweater, with an antler headband to match. Ollie is dressed in a full-on Santa Claus costume (minus the beard). Elena just wore a red sweater and called it a day.

Marisol isn't here yet and I feel a mixture of nervousness and excitement about seeing them. I have to apologize for the way I acted at the cast party.

I'm sure Marisol saw through my thinly veiled lie to get out of there, so the least I can do is explain that I just got scared. But I'm not scared anymore and that's the most important thing. I'm ready to tell Marisol how I really feel, although I suspect they already know.

The doorbell rings again and I feel my heart flutter as Brooke gets up to answer it. When Marisol walks in, I'm almost taken aback by how stunning they look. Their black hair is streaked with green and they're wearing a black and red Christmas sweater. When I look closer, I realize that instead of traditional Christmas shapes, it's covered in skulls and bats. I stand up to greet them as they enter, but they walk right past me and take a seat next to Violet. They don't even say hello to me.

"Should we get started with gifts?" Brooke suggests. I can't tell if she's more excited to receive her present or to show off what she bought for someone else. "Who wants to go first?"

Ollie jumps at the opportunity and slides a giant box over to Violet. It's almost the same size as she is and takes a while for her to open. I get bored pretty quickly and stop paying attention. I keep trying to telepathically make Marisol look at me, but they won't.

After a few minutes, it's my turn to give my gift. I hand the pie box over to Ollie and his face lights up when he opens it. He gets even more excited when I explain the vouchers that are taped to the lid. He hugs me tight.

"It can be Piesgiving every day!" he squeals.

"It can be Piesgiving for five days," I correct him, laughing.

Marisol gets up and walks out of the room. I think that this might be my only chance to talk to them privately, so I follow them into the kitchen.

"Hey," I say, as casually as I can. "How was your Christmas?"

"Fine."

I nod. "That's good." Why do I sound like such an idiot? I try to shake off my nerves. "I wanted to apologize for disappearing at the cast party like that."

"Whatever," they say coldly, "you can do what you want."

"Well, I just didn't want you to think it was because you did anything wrong."

"I know I didn't do anything wrong," Marisol snaps. "You're the one who flaunted your date in front of me like ten seconds after we almost kissed."

"I just got freaked out," I explain, "but there's nothing between me and Tyler. I like *you*."

"You don't act like it," they continue. "I invited you to see me perform and you couldn't even stay through the whole song."

"I'm sorry about that too," I stammer. "Look, I know I was acting weird, but that's done now."

"Oh, is it?"

"Yeah. I want to be with you."

"Do you really? Or are you gonna run to Tyler every time you get scared?"

"That isn't fair."

"I can't date someone who's ashamed of me."

"I'm not ashamed of you."

"Then maybe you're ashamed of yourself and I'm definitely not interested in *that*." They shake their head and for a split second I think they might cry, but they don't. I might. "It would be one thing if you just weren't ready to come out of the closet, but it really hurt seeing you rub Tyler in my face like that. I can't just forget what happened because *now* you decide you want to be with me."

They walk out of the kitchen and I wait a few minutes as I blink my eyes, trying to stop the tears. When I finally do go back into the other room, Marisol isn't there. I sit down, visibly confused.

"Marisol left," Elena explains. "They said they had to go." I get the feeling that everyone knows I had something to do with why.

"They told us to give you this." Brooke passes me a box. "Marisol was your Secret Santa."

I awkwardly open the box as everyone stares at me silently. It's a heart-shaped locket, just like the one I had admired at the murder mystery party.

Suddenly, I feel like I can't breathe.

♫

Ollie has to leave early to help his moms with some charity thing, so he gives me a ride home. I wasn't feeling very social after Marisol left. He doesn't really say much to me in the car and I am grateful for that because I don't feel like talking right now.

He gives me a little pity wave as I exit the car. "Thanks again for the pie."

I nod gently and go inside.

"You're home early. How was the party?" my mom asks as I walk in.

I intend to give a one-word answer and then run up to my room to hide for as long as I need, but when I open my mouth, no words come out. Instead, I burst into tears.

My mom jumps up to hug me. I sob into her neck.

"Baby, what's wrong?" she whispers. "What happened?"

"I ruined everything," I cry.

"Honey, I'm sure it feels like that right now, but it'll be alright."

"No! I ruined everything and now Marisol hates me."

"I'm sure your friend doesn't hate you."

I sniffle, trying to wipe my tears away faster than they're falling. "They're not just a friend, Mom." I pull away from her but keep my head lowered so I can't see her face. "Or at least, I didn't want them to be just a friend. I like Marisol. I mean, I *like* like them."

"Oh. Does Marisol like you too?" She's staring at me with almost no reaction. She's concerned for me, not angry, not disappointed, just concerned.

"I thought so," I say, "or at least they did at one point. I really messed up, Mom. I don't know what to do."

"Why don't you tell me exactly what happened?" She sits down on the couch and I curl up next to her. She looks at me with her therapist face on, but for once I don't really mind.

31

Shoot For The Moon

"Jo, would you just come?" Elena urges me for the billionth time. "It'll be fun. I promise."

"I don't want to," I call from under my covers, where I spend most of my time nowadays.

"Why not? Don't you want to be there for Levi's first Dylan-free party? Even Ren is going this time." A lot has changed in only a few months. When Elena first came to Woodview, I was the one inviting her to tag along to parties. Now, she's the one getting invited to parties, and I'm the one with no real friends.

"I didn't bring anything to wear," I say with a shrug. I have the perfect excuse. It is the first weekend that I'm spending at my dad's new apartment, so I only have a small selection of clothes with me. Dad really didn't waste any time moving out after I revealed the secret about their separation at Christmas. It's only been a week. They must have been planning this for a while if he already had a place lined up. How long were they lying to us?

"Wear something of mine," Elena insists, tossing me a sweater.

I laugh but then realize she's serious. "That'll never fit me right."

"Sure it will."

"I just don't want to go."

She groans. "Why not?"

"I just don't."

She sits at the foot of my bed, even though I did not give her permission to do that. We have bunk beds at my dad's apartment and since she lived here for almost a week before my first visit, she claimed the top bunk. Rude, honestly.

"Does this have anything to do with Marisol?" she asks softly.

I glare at her. "How do you know that?"

"'Cause I have a brain." She rolls her eyes. "Something obviously happened between the two of you. I just don't actually know what."

"It doesn't matter now."

"If it's the reason you've been so mopey lately, then yeah, it matters."

I sit up cross-legged. "It's stupid really."

"Just talk to me, Jo."

I bite my lip and take a deep breath in. "Marisol and I kinda have been almost having a … thing," I say, well aware that I sound like an idiot, "a flirting thing."

Elena laughs. "Yeah, that part I know."

"Really? I thought we were being subtle."

She shakes her head. "You were not."

"Well, that would have been great to know a month ago," I mutter. "Why didn't you say anything?"

"I figured you'd tell me when you were ready."

"Thanks, I guess."

"Continue," she insists.

I avert my eyes. "Well, we almost kissed at the cast party and I kinda freaked out and left, which was bad, I know."

"Is that why you brought Tyler to the open mic?"

"Yeah, and that just made everything worse. When I tried to apologize to Marisol at Secret Santa, they acted like what I did was unforgivable."

"Really? What'd they say?"

"Something about not wanting to be with someone who was ashamed of them, which is stupid, because of course I'm not ashamed of them."

"Then why'd you wait until now to tell anyone?" Elena asks. "Why'd you bring a date to the first big event after your almost kiss? Why, even now, are you talking about liking them as though it's a horrible secret?"

"I'm not."

Elena shrugs. "I think Marisol just wants to know that you're all in. Can you show them that you are?"

"I don't know. How do I show that?"

She shrugs again. "Maybe the party is the perfect place to do that." She smiles slyly.

I scowl. This was all part of her plan, but I think she might be right.

♫

Levi's End of the Year party is doubling as an End of the Suspension party, so it is even bigger and louder than I expected. Normally I would like that, but today I'm still hesitant about being here at all, so the extra fuss isn't exactly making me feel better.

Elena and Ren promised not to leave my side tonight until I was ready. Elena immediately leads us to where Zeke and Ollie are hanging out. She and Zeke get wrapped up in conversation pretty quickly, leaving me to talk to Ollie and Ren.

"You look pretty," Ollie tells me.

"Thanks," I shout over the music, even though I know he's just saying that to be nice. I'm wearing Elena's shirt, which just looks awkward on me. I don't fill it out the same way that she does.

I look around. I notice Brooke and Tyler by the staircase making out. I'm glad to see he got over our failed date so quickly and she deserves a rebound with a nice guy after her horrible relationship with Dylan. They look a lot better together than he and I ever did. Is that racist? I hope that isn't racist. I didn't mean it *like that*.

Olivia and Parvati notice me from across the room and wave. I wave back sheepishly. They smile and return their attention to their friends. Levi is telling them all a very animated story, probably about when he punched Dylan, although it seems like he's embellishing a bit. Honestly, he's allowed. I look through the crowd at plenty more partygoers, some I recognize, some I don't; some who look like they're having fun, some who don't. And then I see Marisol.

They are leaning against the doorway, with Violet, who is talking to a boy I think might be a junior. Violet hangs on his every word. Marisol just looks amused.

"You should go talk to them," Ollie says. He pauses when he sees my surprised face. "Marisol."

I turn red. I know I'm being obvious if even Ollie can see right through me, but then I notice how he's smiling at me and I smile too. I think about my mom and Elena and I realize that the only one making a big deal of things is me. I nod at Ollie and set off in the other direction.

"Marisol," I call out, once I'm close enough that they can hear me.

They look over at me, causing Violet and the guy she's with to look in my direction too. I maneuver my way around other guests until I'm next to them.

"Marisol," I say again, "can we talk?"

They look toward the ground. "What for?"

"I want to apologize."

They sigh. "I'm not in the mood, Jo. Just leave it alone."

A small part of me thinks about backing down, but a bigger part of me knows that if I don't say this now, I might never say it at all. So I take a deep breath. "I like you, Marisol. I really, really like you."

"Okay, maybe we should go somewhere else," they suggest.

"No." I shock even myself. "We can stay here, because I don't care if everyone at this party knows that I like you."

"You don't have to do this, Jo." They take a step toward me. "I know why you did what you did. You were scared. I get that, but it doesn't erase how I felt watching you leave with Tyler during my performance." Their voice softens slightly. "It just hurt, because I thought we had ... something."

"We *do* have something," I insist, "or at least, I hope we still can. Because I want to be with you. And I know that you might not be ready to forgive me, but I'm willing to do what it takes to make it up to you. If you'll let me."

Marisol looks around. "Let's go somewhere else."

They lead me upstairs and we find an empty bedroom. It feels eerily like that day at the cast party and I wonder if maybe I'm getting a second chance. I know I'll do things right this time.

"Okay, let's talk," Marisol says.

I tap my fingers together. "I don't really know what else to say," I admit.

"Well, let's start with this." They take a step toward me. "I really like you too."

I smile. "That's a good place to start."

"But..." they continue. Ugh, there's always a *but*. "...I don't know if I can do this. I can't just turn my feelings on and off whenever you finally decide you're ready to like me."

I nod, taking in a gulp of air. I feel my heart sink. "Okay." I choke a little on the word.

"Look, I'm not mad." They smile. "But could we just go back to being friends?"

"Of course." I'm disappointed, but I'd rather be friends with them than nothing.

"Thanks, Jo." They hug me and honestly, it's a little bit like torture, but it's also nice. At least Marisol doesn't hate me. That's what matters. They eventually let go of the hug and I awkwardly stumble backward.

"You wanna go back downstairs?"

"Um, sure," I stammer. I'm lying, just slightly. I'd rather stay here alone with Marisol, but a party with them is good too, so we go downstairs.

After making peace with Marisol, the party is actually a lot of fun, although I'll probably deny that to Elena later. I hang out with Marisol most of the night and things feel good. I like being their friend.

32

Friends Are The Family You Choose Yourself

The house seems quieter now that my dad and Elena have officially moved out. I try to look on the bright side of the whole situation. I have my own room again, although it feels oddly empty without Elena now. She and I have barely spoken about my parents' separation and that's okay because I already think about it enough. In fact, my brain has basically been alternating back and forth between that and an equally terrible topic for days now. As hard as I try, I just can't stop thinking about Marisol.

My phone buzzes. It's a text from Rachel, the second one she has sent me in four days, since I never responded to the first. I've been too stressed out to answer her, but I guess I need to eventually. Not that I really care at all about what she has to say.

Please answer me.

Fine, I reply. *What do you want?*

I really need to talk to you. Can we meet up? Coffee maybe?

I groan. I don't really want to go anywhere, especially not for someone who has barely spoken to me in months, but it's probably a good idea to get out of the house. Anything to get my mind off Marisol. Plus, I could kind of go for a coffee.

♫

When I get to the coffee shop, Rachel is already there sitting at a table near the door with two lattes in front of her. She stands up when she sees me.

"Hey. I ordered your favorite. Hazelnut."

I nod.

"Thanks for coming," she continues, not quite meeting my gaze.

I sit down and take a tiny sip of my drink. It's so good. I haven't had one of these in forever.

"What are we doing here?" I ask.

Rachel takes her seat across from me. She taps her fingers on the table a few times before speaking. Finally, she says, "I'm sorry."

At first, I think I may have heard her wrong, but when I look at her, she's staring back at me with such sincerity in her eyes.

"For what?"

She hesitates and looks away. Then she speaks, barely above a whisper. "I know what happened with you and Casey. I know about the kiss."

I almost laugh. That feels like so long ago. I can't even remember the last time I thought about that kiss, or about Casey at all.

"Casey got super drunk last week and told me everything," Rachel explains. "She said some really mean things."

I tap my fingers together nervously but force myself to stop once I remember that Rachel's known me long enough to recognize all my tells.

"So what?" I sigh. "I don't care if people know anymore. I don't care what anyone thinks, even you, and especially Casey."

"So it all makes sense now," she continues. "That's why Casey posted that thing about you on WoodNews. It was because you kissed her."

I nod. "I guess I should've told you that in the first place, but I didn't know how you'd react."

"I don't care," she assures me. "You're my friend. It doesn't matter if you're gay, bi, straight, whatever."

I smile. "That's good to hear," I say, "because I'm not straight. I'm a lesbian."

"That's great," she chirps, which makes me laugh a little. "I'm sorry I believed Casey's story instead of yours."

I shrug. "It's okay. I probably would've believed Casey over me too."

"Can we be friends again? Please."

I chuckle. "Yeah, we can be friends again."

She starts to laugh too. "Good. Because I have so much to tell you."

"Me too!"

We both laugh a little more and before I know it, she's standing. She walks around the table and bends down to hug me.

"Let's never fight again."

"Never."

♫

"Good morning," I say quietly, as I enter the living room of my dad's new apartment. For some reason, I'm nervous.

He glares at me and then looks at his watch. "I don't know if you can still call this morning," he grumbles.

I roll my eyes and walk past him into the kitchen. The fridge is practically empty. "Don't you have any food around here?"

"Of course I do. There's um … there's … there should be some cereal in the cupboard." He looks through the cabinets, triumphantly pulling out a box and handing it to me.

"Do you have milk?"

He deflates. "Why don't we go out to eat?" he suggests. "Go wake up Elena and we'll get going."

"Dad, could I ask you something first?"

"Sure, honey, what's going on?"

I breathe in and out slowly, not sure what's come over me. "Do you think you and Mom are really done?" He hesitates, so I backtrack. "Never mind, you don't have to answer that."

"To be honest, I don't know," he admits. "I'm sorry. I'm sure that's not the answer you want to hear."

I shrug. "I just want the truth."

"Things haven't been right between me and your mom for a while now," he admits. "That's the truth."

I'm not sure if I want to ask this next question because I'm not sure if I want to know the answer, but part of me thinks that not knowing is a million times worse. "How long?"

"Excuse me?"

"How long have you been having problems?" I clarify. "Has it just been since Elena moved here? Or has it been longer than that?"

He leans against the counter. "Why are you asking this?"

My lip quivers. "I don't know. I just … wanna know."

He crosses his arms and sighs. "You shouldn't be worrying about things like this."

"Why not?" I press him. "It affects me, doesn't it? You and Mom always act like I'm some dumb kid, but I'm almost sixteen. I understand real issues. You don't have to shield me from your problems all the time."

My dad's entire expression suddenly changes. "Elena! Good morning!"

I turn around to see her standing behind me, groggily rubbing the sleep out of her eyes. I guess this conversation is over. Damn it, Elena.

♫

I push my food around with my fork and don't really pay attention to my dad and Elena's conversation until she suddenly nudges me.

"What's going on with you?" she asks. "You never shut up for this long."

"I'm tired," I say. It's not technically a lie.

"You want a refill on that coffee?" Dad offers.

I shrug. "I guess." I wish he hadn't taken the easy way out with our conversation earlier. I'm sure there's something he isn't telling me.

I've been thinking a lot about the past. My parents always seemed happy, but that doesn't necessarily mean that they were. Maybe they didn't care enough to have any disagreements because maybe they didn't really care about each other at all. Maybe they knew that no matter what they did, it still wasn't what they wanted.

Elena leaves to use the restroom and I realize that this is my chance. It is just me and my dad and I can ask him anything I want, but it surprises even me what I actually ask.

"What was she like?"

He looks up from his food. "Who?"

"Elena's mom."

"Why the sudden interest?"

"Did you love her?"

He places his fork down on the table. "Jo, what has gotten into you?"

"Did you love her more than Mom?"

"Joanne, I don't want to talk about this right now."

"Because it's true?" I accuse. "Because you loved her more than Mom?"

"Why do you even want to know about this?"

"Why won't you answer the question?"

"Because what difference does it make?" He lowers his head and shakes it. "What does it matter? What does any of this matter?" He practically shouts it and I suddenly feel like I might cry. I blink my eyes repeatedly, trying to stop any tears from falling. Maybe he's right. Maybe I shouldn't be thinking about any of this, but I just can't help it.

"It matters to me."

He takes a deep sigh. Then he gets up and walks away.

Elena returns about a minute later. "Where's Kevin?" she asks, sliding into the booth next to me.

Before I can answer, I start to cry.

33

Give It Time

School is better now that Rachel and I are speaking again. The first day back after the break, she sits in her old seat next to me like absolutely nothing had happened.

"Does this mean you two are friends again?" Tyler asks. "Thank God." We all laugh together like old times until our teacher makes us stop.

Rachel starts to sit with me and all my new friends at lunch because she doesn't want to sit with Casey anymore. They are all very welcoming to her, of course. Well, all except for Brooke, but she wasn't very welcoming to me at first either. Sometimes Nico even joins us too, but he doesn't seem to really click with them … at least not yet.

I officially told the group that I was a lesbian and it felt great. They didn't care. They pretty much knew already.

When I told them, Zeke clutched his chest. "Oh. My gosh. I am so surprised. I had *no* idea." Brooke shoved him. Marisol smiled and gave me a knowing look.

Ollie said, "Oh, that's cool, Jo. One of my moms is a lesbian."

"Both of your moms are lesbians," Violet pointed out. "That's how lesbians work."

"No, one of my moms is bisexual."

"Oh. Right."

"Bi-erasure is not okay, you guys," Ollie stressed with a serious look on his face.

Zeke laughed. "Damn, Ollie just schooled you."

I should have known that everyone in that group would be cool about it. Telling them was really just practice for the person I was dreading telling the most … my dad. I haven't told him yet, but I will soon. I'm planning on telling him the next time I spend a weekend at his apartment. Of course, I also said that the last time I stayed at his apartment, so we'll see.

I've slowly gotten used to being alone in the house with just my mom. She's been trying extra hard to do fun things with me. I think she's trying to show me that she and I are enough and we don't need anyone else, but it feels kind of forced. All I really want is some closure on this whole thing. I want to know exactly when my parents' marriage fell apart … and why.

I have a lot more free time now that the color guard season is over, but rehearsals for the next play have already started so the whole group is still really busy. That means I've been hanging out with my old friend group a lot more recently, minus Casey, obviously. I had been a little worried about how Nico would react to me being a lesbian. I know he's not exactly the most politically correct when it comes to stuff like that. His parents are a lot more conservative than mine. But he doesn't say anything bad about it. He doesn't say anything about it at all.

One day, I meet them at the pizza place after school. I sit next to Tyler while Rachel and Nico sit across from us, cuddled up together, as usual. We must have gotten there at the perfect time because the place is suddenly now packed. When Parvati and Olivia walk in, they look around for a few seconds, knowing there's no possible way they can find an open table. When our eyes meet, I wave them over.

"Hey!" Parvati greets us.

"Hi," I reply. "It just got super crowded. Do you want to sit with us?"

"Really?" Olivia asks. "That's so nice. Thank you."

They squeeze in where they can and introduce themselves to Tyler and Nico. Rachel looks terrified. It almost makes me laugh, but then I think about how nervous I was that day at practice when they first spoke to me. Nevertheless, it feels cool that I'm the one with senior friends to introduce to others. I've never really had other friends before.

"Hey, I kind of overheard some stuff about you and Marisol Castillo," Parvati says slyly. "Are you two a thing?"

"Oh yeah," Olivia chimes in. "I saw you together at Levi's New Year's Party."

I shake my head. "We're just friends."

Parvati chuckles, but I'm not sure what's funny. "Give it time. I bet that'll change."

I don't know how I feel about that. Of course, I would love it if Marisol came around and wanted to be more than friends, but I am trying not to hold out hope. Later, when the four of us walk home, we one-by-one split off in the directions of our individual houses until it is just me and Nico. We walk in silence for a while. I never really know what to say to him when Rachel's not there.

Somewhere toward the end of middle school, it became abundantly clear to me that Nico was my friend only because our moms were friends and not because he actually liked hanging out with me. Had it not been for Rachel, we probably would've drifted apart entirely by now. It is pretty obvious that we don't have very much in common anymore.

"So you're … gay now?" he asks at one point, finally breaking our silence.

"Uh, yeah," I reply, not really sure how else to answer a question like that.

"And people are, like, cool with it?" he asks. "I mean, not Casey, obviously, but … most people? Like the color guard and those girls at the pizza place and … your parents?"

"Yeah." This is a weird conversation. "I haven't officially told my dad yet, but my mom is fine."

"And other people at school? Like, nobody cares?"

"I don't know, dude." I shrug. "Some people probably care, but I'm not paying attention to those people. The ones who matter don't care."

"Right." He stares at his shoes as we walk and I roll my eyes. Nico's a strange guy. Why would he care about any of this?

My mom's still at work when I get home, so I have the place to myself. Normally I'd like that, but, for some reason, today it makes me feel lonely. I sit in the empty living room and try to watch TV, but I can't seem to force myself to care about anything that's on, so I turn it off. Now it's quiet. Too quiet.

I slide off of the couch and onto the floor, pressing my knees to my chest. I should start doing my homework, but I don't want to. I want to sit here and pretend that everything's fine and that my family isn't broken, but it's getting harder and harder to pretend.

I call Marisol. I know I probably shouldn't. I should give them space, but friends call each other when they need help, right? Friends are there for each other when they need help. And Marisol and I are friends. And right now, they're the only person I want to talk to.

"Hey, Jo. What's up?"

It hits me that I have no idea what to actually say. Why am I calling again? Because I feel depressed knowing that my parents' marriage is probably over and there's nothing I can do about it?

"Hey, are you busy right now?"

"No."

"Do you … want to come over?" The words shock me. Did I really just ask that? Am I crazy?

"Sure," Marisol says, without any further questions. "I'll see you in a little bit." They hang up the phone and I'm left wondering what the hell just happened.

The doorbell rings a bit later and my heart skips a beat. When I answer the door, there's Marisol, looking far too incredible for a random weekday after a full day of school.

"You sounded kinda upset on the phone, so I brought cookies." Marisol takes a step inside and holds up a plastic bag with the name of our local bakery on it. "I got an assortment 'cause I wasn't sure what kind you liked best."

"Thanks." I am slightly taken aback. "That's so nice."

"No problem. That's what friends are for."

Friends. I'm surprised by how much the word stings hearing them say it. I like being Marisol's friend. Being Marisol's friend is great. I'm entirely fine just being Marisol's friend. Why can't I convince myself that that's true?

34

Some Things Don't Make Sense

"They're doing a promotion at the skating rink this weekend," Rachel says during English class. "Free skate rental. We should take advantage and go."

"That sounds fun. I'm in." I turn to face Rachel and cross my legs. "Should we go on Friday or Saturday?"

"Saturday," Rachel answers. "Nico has to babysit his brother on Friday. Tyler, you're coming, right?"

"Do you think I could invite Brooke?" Tyler asks, leaning forward across his desk. "You're cool with all that, right? I know she's kind of your friend."

"Of course I'm cool with that. I think she'd like to go ice skating." Then I sigh. "Ugh wait, I'm gonna be a fifth wheel then."

"Maybe Elena wants to come," Rachel suggests. "Or … Marisol?"

I glare at her.

"What?" She slaps her hands on her thighs. "You said you and Marisol were friends now."

"We are but…" I trail off. I guess there's no real reason why I couldn't invite Marisol. We *are* friends. That's what they wanted to be. And friends could certainly go ice skating together.

"Why don't you invite that whole crew?" Tyler suggests. "The more the merrier. And then Marisol can come without you feeling all weird about it."

Rachel laughs. "Tyler! When did you become smart?"

"I've always been smart. You just underestimated me."

♫

Elena doesn't really like spending time at our dad's apartment, so we hang out together a lot more now after school.

"I thought divorced parents were supposed to be extra nice to their kids," she complains as she absentmindedly pokes at her basket of fries.

"They're not divorced," I correct her.

"Just wait until one of them starts dating," Ren says, completely ignoring my comment. "When my mom first started dating, her boyfriend would do *anything* to get my approval. Not that she even cared. I assume the same would be true if my dad got a girlfriend, but I don't think he's even dated anyone since the divorce."

"I always used to wonder what it would be like to have a dad. I guess it's just not what I expected."

"Dads often suck," Zeke adds. "The sooner you accept that, the sooner you can stop being disappointed by them."

"What are you talking about?" Elena asks. "Your dad's great."

"My stepdad's great. My dad sucks."

"Well, my dad doesn't even seem to want me at this point," Elena continues. "It's like he's blaming me for his failed marriage."

"No one blames you," I say, unconvincingly.

Elena shakes her head. "Sorry, Jo, I shouldn't be talking about this with you."

"It's fine." I shrug. "To be honest, he hasn't been so great to me either lately."

Zeke chuckles slightly. "Sometimes I think Ollie is lucky to have two moms."

♫

My mom has been overly cheerful since my dad moved out. It is almost as if she thinks that if she acts like everything is fine, it magically will be. I wish I could share her optimism. It makes me a little angry sometimes. I want her to just snap already. I want her to yell or cry or show any emotion really. She doesn't seem to care about anything that's happened.

When we sit down for dinner, she smiles and she asks me how school was, as if everything's perfectly normal.

"Fine," I reply. "I'm going ice skating with some friends this weekend."

"That sounds nice. Do you need any money?"

"What's wrong with you?" I don't even register the words until I've already said them and I see my mom's smile turn into a confused frown.

"I just thought you might want a little extra cash," she replies, slowly. She clearly has no idea what I'm referring to and that just makes me even more furious.

"Why don't you care that Dad's gone?" I explode. Now that the floodgates have opened, I can't stop. Everything I've been thinking just comes pouring out. "Do you even want to try to work things out? Do you even miss him?"

"Of course I do, Jo," she assures me, but I'm not convinced. "It's just a complicated situation."

"Well, explain it to me," I insist, "because I don't really understand at all."

She looks down at her plate, likely trying to figure a way out of this conversation, but I think she knows that I'm not going to let this go any time soon. She takes a deep breath. "Okay. You can ask me anything."

I hesitate. I didn't really think I'd get this far. There's so much I want to ask, stuff that I don't even have the words for. There's one particular question that's been on my mind for so long and seems like as good a place to start as any.

I look up to meet her eyes and ask in the coldest tone I can muster, "Did you know about Elena?"

She almost laughs. "What are you talking about? Of course not."

I shake my head, unconvinced. "You didn't care at all when we found out. Any normal person would've been pissed. Your husband has another secret daughter. He cheated on you! But you didn't even seem surprised. It was … it was like you expected it."

She shakes her head, no longer meeting my gaze. "That's ridiculous."

"Is it?"

"I had no idea about Elena," she continues. "I promise you."

I lean back in my chair. Something still feels off. I'm sure of it. I steady my eyes on the table and let out a breath I didn't know I was holding in.

"Mom, I know you're lying to me about something. You and Dad both are. So if it's not that, what is it?"

"There's nothing more to tell, Jo. I'm sorry."

"Stop!" I say it louder than I mean to, so I pull back, just a little. "I'm not crazy. Can't you please just be honest with me?"

She lets out an exasperated sigh and lowers her forehead onto her palms. For a second, I feel bad. Maybe this is all in my head. Maybe I'm making a big deal out of nothing. My mom is going through a hard time too. Maybe I shouldn't be pestering her with all this.

Finally, she speaks. "I didn't know about Elena. That part is true." She hesitates before continuing and doesn't look at me. I just keep my eyes focused on her until she's ready. "But I did know about her mother. Or at least, I had my suspicions."

I don't say anything at first. There's this shame in her voice that I've never heard before and part of me feels like the worst daughter in the world for bringing this up, but I can't stop now. I'm finally getting the answers I've wanted this whole time.

"You knew he cheated?"

She nods. "I always knew." Her voice is soft and broken and I know I should back off, but before I can let her off the hook, she continues, "Because he didn't cheat *on* me. He cheated *with* me."

I stare at her, but she stares at the wall beside us. "I don't understand."

She gets up from the table and takes her plate into the kitchen. I follow her because there's no way I'm letting the conversation end there.

"I don't understand. What does that mean?"

"Enough!" She slams her plate into the sink and spins around to face me.

"No!" I shout. "You can't just say something like that and expect me to just go on with my day. What does that mean?"

"What do you think?" she lashes out, fiercely. "You're a smart girl. I'm sure you can figure it out."

This is exactly the kind of breakdown I've been waiting for her to have, but now that it's here, it scares me. I've never seen my mom like this. My face is burning and I feel the tears forming behind my eyes. This is all too much. This is all way, way too much. I shake my head, clinging to the stories I've been told and the stories I'd made up in my head, the stories I now know are lies. Suddenly I can't remember why I wanted the truth so badly in the first place, but there's one more question I need to ask.

"Why did you even get married?" I want to believe it's because they found their way back to each other against all odds. I want to believe that the stars aligned and true love prevailed. I want to believe that my dad left everything behind to be with my mom for no other reason than he wanted to. But deep down I know that's not the truth and I need to hear someone else say it.

She is quiet for so long, just looking out our kitchen window in the direction of Ren Hayashi's house. I wish she would just answer me because I can't hold these tears back much longer.

She finally says it, the answer I was dreading but already knew. "We got married for you."

I ruined my parents' lives. And Elena's and her mom's. All this time, I've been blaming Elena for blowing up my family, but I'm the one who shouldn't be here. The tears come pouring out and I want to scream. No, I want to disappear. I want everything in my life to just stop.

"That's such bullshit!" I shout. "You realize that, right?" I ball my hands into fists around large chunks of my hair and pull. "So your whole marriage was a sham? My entire life you've been lying to me? God, did you even love each other at all?"

She doesn't answer. It's the loudest silence of my goddamn life, and it tells me all I need to know.

"No wonder I'm so bad at love," I mutter. "Look at who I had to learn from."

"Jo, can you please calm down?" she begs.

"No!" My voice cracks. "No, I can't."

I start to leave. I'm already past the kitchen doorway when I turn around and walk back in. "Why now?"

She sighs. "What?"

"Why now?" I ask again. "If this whole thing has been fake from the start, then why are you calling it quits *now*? Is the charade really suddenly so much to handle?"

"I don't know."

"Oh, come on."

"I don't know!" she repeats, louder this time. "I don't know because it wasn't my idea."

I let out a short laugh. "What are you talking about?"

"It was your dad who suggested the separation," she confesses. "I didn't disagree, but it was his idea. He said he thought we needed time apart. I don't know why he finally chose it now." She sucks in a sharp breath of air, practically shaking at this point. "And that's the truth."

I stare at her. Absolutely nothing makes sense.

35

Live Every Day Like It's Your Last

I don't want to go ice skating. I don't really want to go anywhere, actually. I feel safe in the comfort of my own bed and don't want to face the outside world. But everyone else is going, so I have to pull myself together and at least pretend to have fun.

I wait on my porch for Rachel's mom to pick me up. It's too cold to be sitting outside, but my mom is inside, and I can't really face her after our last conversation. Although I still feel pretty angry that my parents lied to me, now that I've had time to calm down, I feel guilty for making my mom talk about it at all.

I see the dark blue minivan turn onto our street so I stand up and walk down the steps, timing it almost perfectly to when she pulls up in front of our house. Nico's already in the backseat so I have to sit beside him. In all honesty, I've felt awkward around him ever since that weird conversation we had on our walk home. Luckily, Rachel doesn't notice that anything is wrong and she talks enough for the three of us during the whole ride.

We are the last to arrive at the skating rink. At first, I think we're still waiting for Tyler and Brooke, but apparently, they decided to leave to go "take a walk" together. None of us are expecting to see them again any time soon.

We head over to a table where everyone else is sitting and drinking hot chocolate. Rachel takes the empty seat next to Marisol, probably so I don't have to.

"You guys ready to get your skate on?" she asks enthusiastically. I think she's the only one who genuinely likes ice skating and isn't just here to be social.

When we get on the ice, I manage to hold my own pretty well. Rachel has dragged me out here every winter, so I've become a fairly decent skater over the years. Still, she flies ahead of me. Surprisingly, Ollie is able to keep up with her. I didn't know he could skate so well. Is there any sport he's not good at?

Everyone else is having a harder time, some more than others. I've already watched Elena and Zeke fall over each other at least four times, but they definitely look like they're having fun. Violet's actually pretty good, but she slows down whenever Ren starts to slip in order to help hold him up. Nico opts not to skate, like always. He thinks he's too cool for fun.

Just when muscle memory is starting to kick in and I think I'm really getting the hang of it, Marisol appears beside me, almost causing me to topple over.

"Careful there," they say in the most nonchalant tone possible. My cheeks blush red. Hopefully, they think that's just because of the cold.

"We can't all be as good as Rachel," I joke. "You know, when we were younger, she used to insist she'd make it to the Olympics someday."

"She probably could have if she tried." We watch Rachel show off with some fancy spin. "I just wanna know how Ollie got so good. That guy is full of surprises. Who knew he had so many secret talents?"

"He's a man of mystery." It makes them laugh, which makes me smile.

Unfortunately, I'm distracted enough that when some kid knocks into me, it completely throws me off guard. I instantly lose my balance and fall toward the ground. My head hits the railing on the way down and I go flying backwards, landing flat on the ice.

"Oh shit!" Marisol exclaims. They bend over me so all I can see is their face. Their beautiful, blurry face. "Are you alright?"

I try to nod, but that just makes my head hurt.

"God, you're bleeding."

I lift my hand to my head and pull it back. Sure enough, there's blood all over my fingers. I didn't even realize I'd cut myself.

"C'mon, let's get you out of here." They fling my arm over their shoulder and lift me off the ground with a surprising amount of ease. They're much stronger than they look.

They lead me to the exit and I carefully step onto the carpeted floor of the lobby. My head throbs and I feel like I might puke from the pain. Marisol kneels in front of me, trying to brush my hair away from my wound.

"This looks serious," they say, looking around. They try to wave over one of the workers, but he doesn't see us. "Are you gonna be okay if I leave you for a minute?"

I nod slowly, feeling too dizzy to move my head too much. Marisol waves down Elena and Zeke, so they hobble toward me, struggling to walk in their skates.

"What happened?" Elena asks.

I open my mouth to speak but feel too sick to say anything.

"Keep your head up," Zeke directs me, placing his hand on the side of my head and pushing it back upright. I hadn't even realized I was starting to tilt.

Marisol comes back with one of the workers, who takes one look at me and declares he's calling an ambulance.

"We're required to call 9-1-1 when anything like this happens," he explains. "It's a liability thing."

I don't nod this time. Someone else can handle the nodding.

Elena and Marisol sit on either side of me, which is good because I realize I'm starting to tilt again. My head slowly falls onto Marisol's shoulder, causing me to cringe, but I can't lift it. They put their hand in mine and I think that's their way of telling me it's alright.

Their other hand cups my face, straightening my head again. We're so close and I stare into those beautiful, dark brown eyes.

"Stay awake," they whisper.

♫

The doctor tells me and my family that I have a concussion. It's a minor one though, so I'll be fine. My parents stand next to each other and I glance at Elena, sitting in a chair beside me. She looks back at me and I can tell she's thinking the same thing I am. Who knew that a head injury was all it would take to get my parents back in the same room?

The doctor leaves and my parents begin speaking over each other, both going a mile a minute. I don't think I can process a single word either of them says. When they're done, Elena summarizes in words I can actually understand. I only need a few stitches, but they're keeping me overnight for observation. I'm allowed to sleep, but someone needs to wake me up every few hours to make sure I'm not gonna die or whatever. That part sucks because all I really want to do right now is sleep for days.

My parents let my friends come into the room. They think it will help cheer me up. It works for a while until most of them have to go home. Honestly, I'm not sure why they came to the hospital at all. This really isn't a big deal. Eventually, the only people left in the room are me, my parents, Elena, and Marisol.

"You can go home," I insist. "I'm fine."

Marisol stands close to the bed, closer than anyone else. I kind of wish they wouldn't.

"My mom's working here anyway," they explain. "I might as well stay until her shift ends. It just makes sense."

I realize that I didn't know what Marisol's mom did. I never asked. I guess I don't really know very much about Marisol's life outside of school. Maybe I haven't been the greatest friend after all.

"Why don't I go get us something to drink?" My mom eyes my dad. "Can you come help me, Kevin?"

For a split second, I think my parents are trying to find an excuse to be alone together, but from their body language, it's clear that they're not doing this for their own sake.

"Someone's calling me," Elena lies. I look over at her and she quickly hides her phone screen. "I better take this." She hops up from her chair and runs out, not at all subtle.

Marisol laughs, which relieves me a little. I'm glad they aren't annoyed by my family's ridiculous ploy to get us alone. There isn't really any reason for them to even want to be alone with me.

"I'm glad you're okay," Marisol says, so quietly that I can barely even hear them.

"I mean, me too." I laugh, trying as hard as I can to break the tension in the room.

"I'm serious." Their voice is slow and steady. "That was really scary."

Our eyes meet and I get lost in them, but I force myself to look away. I'm torturing myself by acting like there's any chance of having something more with Marisol. I squandered that opportunity and I just have to live with it.

"I miss hanging out with you," Marisol says after an elongated silence. Their voice squeaks slightly.

"What do you mean?" I ask, letting out a tiny chuckle. "We hang out all the time. We were literally just hanging out at the ice rink together, remember?"

Their eyes are planted on the ground, so I have to crane my neck to see their face. "You know what I mean."

I don't. I really, really don't. I want to say something so badly. The silence between us is deafening, but I have no idea what I could possibly say.

"I have to go," Marisol blurts out, their voice even higher than before. They head to the door without giving me a chance to reply.

"But where...?" I try my best to form a sentence, but the words just don't come. And then Marisol is gone.

36

Live, Laugh, Love

Yesterday, we learned that, despite so many girls coming forward with stories similar to Elena's, the police have officially decided not to go any further with their investigation into Dylan. We all kind of expected this, but now it's final. Elena's been acting like she doesn't care, but I can tell she's upset. She's extra quiet at school today and it feels like there's a brooding cloud hanging over us. Needless to say, this isn't the best Valentine's Day.

But that's perfectly fine with me. It's been a few days since I cracked my head open at the ice skating rink and things are still weird between me and Marisol. We haven't really talked at all since the hospital. And since there's no one else I'm interested in spending Valentine's Day with, I'm okay with completely ignoring it this year.

The only problem is that for the rest of the world, Valentine's Day still goes on. I'm stuck watching all the happy couples walk around school, shoving their stupid happiness in my face. Brooke arrives at the lunch table holding a huge stuffed bear. It's so big, she has to give it its own chair. Straight people are so extra. I can finally admit that, now that I'm no longer pretending to be one of them.

"Is that from Tyler?" Violet asks.

Brooke blushes and nods. "He's literally the sweetest."

Tyler's a good guy, but he's definitely not "literally the sweetest." I think she just means that he's better than Dylan, which is a low bar. Nevertheless, I suppose I'm happy for her.

"I heard you got a valentine too," Brooke pries, eyeing Violet.

She averts her gaze. "It's just a rose," she says. "I don't even know who it's from."

"Mysterious," Zeke teases, raising an eyebrow. He pulls the rose out of Violet's backpack. It's a little crushed now.

"Why's it black?" I wonder.

"'Cause red roses are basic," Zeke says. He pauses to think. "Actually, all roses are kind of basic. Your secret valentine should've brought you a violet. Duh."

"I feel sorry for your future girlfriend." Brooke rolls her eyes.

"Excuse you, I am a true romantic," he insists. "Apparently a better one than Violet's secret admirer, that's for sure."

"I like the black rose," Violet says, but I don't think most of the table hears her.

Just then, Ollie appears with a big red bag, like an off-season Santa Claus. He reaches into the bag and gives each of us a handful of heart-shaped chocolates.

"Happy Valentine's Day! I love you guys!"

"We love you too, Ollie," Brooke professes. "I do *not* feel sorry for Ollie's future girlfriend. He's the best."

"Future girlfriend?" Ollie asks, puzzled. "I don't even have a date for Valentine's Day."

"Ollie, do you not know how many girls in our grade have a crush on you?" Zeke stares at him incredulously. "You could have a date every day of the week if you wanted to."

"Wait, what?" Ollie gasps.

Everyone starts to laugh.

"You didn't know?" Elena asks.

"No."

"Seriously, I don't even know that many girls in your grade and I still knew that!" I tell him.

"I barely know anyone at Woodview at all, and even I knew this," Elena says, grinning. It's the first time I've seen her smile all day.

"Why didn't anyone tell me?"

"We thought you knew!" Violet exclaims and everyone laughs even harder.

♫

"Jo." The sound of Marisol's voice startles me. I close my locker, turn around, and lean against it.

"Hi," I sputter, somewhat out of breath. We haven't actually spoken since the hospital and I feel kind of scared of what they might say. I was honestly a little relieved that they had spent the lunch period at a peer tutoring session. Seeing them today is just a big reminder that Marisol is not and will never be my valentine.

"I need to tell you something before I lose the nerve." Their speech is more rapid than normal.

"Okay." My voice barely makes a sound. Did I do something wrong? They ran out of the hospital room so quickly and seemed so upset. What if they're angry at me? What if they never want to see me again?

"I really like you," Marisol tells me.

"You do?"

"Don't act surprised."

"I wasn't sure anymore."

"I'm just scared, Jo..." They look down and whisper, "...of getting hurt."

"I never wanted to hurt you. I'm so, so sorry. I swear, if I could go back in time I would do everything differently."

"It's okay. I'm just scared that you're going to change your mind again. I know you liked me, but as soon as we got close to being together, you freaked out. What if you realize you don't like me enough for this to all be worth it?"

"I won't. I promise."

"But—"

"I didn't freak out because I didn't like you enough. It was me that I didn't like. I didn't like myself enough. I like you so much. And I like me better when I'm with you."

"Are you sure? I don't want to, like, force you out of the closet or anything. It's okay if you're not ready for the whole school to know or if this isn't what you want. I just—"

I grab Marisol's face and kiss them. Unlike the kiss with Tyler, which felt weird and unnatural, this feels right.

"I'm ready," I say. "I'm ready and I'm all in. I like you and I want to be with you. If you're not sure that you want to be with me, that's fine. But don't let it be because you're afraid that I don't know what I want. I know exactly what I want and what I want ... is you."

Marisol smiles and I kiss them again. And for a moment, it feels like the whole world stops, and the only thing that matters is me and Marisol.

♫

When I get home, I hear a crash come from the next room almost as soon as Marisol and I walk through the door.

We enter the kitchen to see my mom and our next-door neighbor standing beside a broken glass.

"Mr. Hayashi?" I tilt my head in confusion.

"Hi, girls," my mom replies cheerfully. "Or, sorry, um, I mean..." She pauses. "Hi, Marisol!"

"Hi," Marisol says, clearly trying to hold back a smile.

"What were you guys doing in here?" I ask.

"Oh, um," he stammers, "I just came over because I needed to borrow, um—"

"Eggs," my mom blurts out. "He needed some eggs. I'll go get those." She walks to the fridge as Marisol attempts to stifle a laugh.

"Yeah, I'm, uh, cooking ... eggs."

My mom returns and hands him an entire carton of eggs. He awkwardly accepts them. I guess we're having cereal for breakfast tomorrow.

"Thank you! Now that I have..." he pauses and looks down at his hands, "...all these eggs, I'll just be going. Since there's no other reason for me to be here."

He awkwardly stands there for a moment before nodding and heading toward the door. Marisol and I look at each other before I return my gaze to my mom. She smiles as if there was nothing weird about that entire situation. Normally, I would call her out on it, but right now, I really couldn't care less.

"We'll be upstairs." I grab Marisol's hand and pull them out of the kitchen. We dash to my room, and before the door is even fully closed, their lips are on mine.

I can't believe I spent so long fighting this feeling because, right now, with Marisol here with me, everything feels perfect.

♫

I'm just about to head to bed when I hear the doorbell ring. I let my mom answer it, but then I hear the voices from downstairs. I head to the top of the stairs and peer my head around the wall.

My mom leads Elena into our living room and sits her down on the sofa. She's soaking wet from the rain, so I don't notice the tears running down her cheeks at first.

"Sweetheart, what happened?" she asks, wrapping a throw blanket around her.

Elena sniffles. "It's, um…"

I race down the stairs to join her and my mom on the sofa.

"I'm sorry," she stammers. "It's stupid, I just … I don't know."

I place my hand on her arm and my mom asks her, "Elena, what do you need?"

Her lip quivers and the tears begin to fall again. "Do you think I could stay here tonight?"

Three Months Later

Jo

37

It's All So Bittersweet

This is a disaster. My dress is way too big. It's terrible! Okay, it's not *terrible*, but it's not good either. It isn't hanging on me the way it should be, especially considering that I got it tailored to my exact size. Or, I guess, to the exact size I used to be? How did this even happen? I was so worried that I might gain too much weight; I hadn't even considered that losing too much weight could be a possibility. Any other day, I'd be kind of happy to realize I had lost a few pounds. I'd be thrilled, really. But today? Today, it's horrible, awful news. Today is my sweet sixteen. It's supposed to be an absolutely perfect day, but the party hasn't even started yet and everything is already going all wrong.

"No one's even gonna notice," Elena lies, attempting to calm me down. "If it's bothering you that much, I can add a few stitches to tighten the bust a bit, but I really don't think it's necessary."

Elena does not appreciate how important a girl's sweet sixteen is, not even after my parents decided that this party would honor her as well. I understand why they did that. When we first started planning it, they didn't know they would have a second daughter turning sixteen in the same year. It was too late (and probably too expensive) to pull together a second event only a few months later. She probably wouldn't have even wanted her own party anyway. She definitely doesn't want to be involved in this one, but my mom insisted that she be included. So my sweet sixteen became *our* sweet sixteen.

I'd be lying if I said sharing this with her didn't bother me a little bit. It bothers me a lot. It's not like we're twins. It's *my* birthday. Her birthday isn't for another two months. Why should we have to celebrate together?

"Do you think you could?" I ask. "I don't want it to look like we had to have it altered."

"You already did have it altered, by the tailor," she points out. I hate when she uses logic against me.

"Yes, but he was a professional. Do you even know how to sew?"

"Would I have offered to fix your dress if I didn't know how to sew?" She laughs.

I don't see how this is funny, but I force myself to half-heartedly join in anyway. I guess it wouldn't hurt to lighten up a little bit. One issue is not going to ruin the entire day. Or at least that's what I'm going to keep telling myself. If I say it enough times, maybe I'll start to believe it. I really want it to be true.

"I'm just going to do a tiny alteration, just a few stitches." Elena walks over to me and pulls at the side of my dress until it is perfectly snug. "No one will even see it."

I sigh. "You better be right."

Just then, there's a knock at the door and before either of us can even say "come in," it opens. I spin around as my mom walks in with my cousin Kate in tow. Kate excitedly runs to me, wrapping me in a big hug and almost knocking Elena over in the process.

"Happy birthday!" she squeals. Technically, it's not actually my birthday for two more weeks and Kate knows that, but she'll be back in Chicago before then, so we'll both pretend that it's really today. "You look amazing!"

Elena poorly suppresses a chuckle and I know exactly what she's thinking. Maybe now that Kate has said it, I'll actually believe it. And she's somewhat right. Kate telling me I look good holds a lot more weight than Elena telling me does, because Kate and I are much more similar than Elena and I are. Elena doesn't care about appearances the way I do, because, unlike me, she's effortlessly pretty.

Her long, wavy, dark brown hair always does what she wants it to. It even looks perfect when she's just woken up. Meanwhile, my blonde hair always falls flat and limp. She's curvy, but in the right places, unlike me. Being half Puerto Rican, it's like she has a year-round tan, while I'm pale and always burn in the sun. And although she doesn't usually wear a lot of makeup (because she doesn't need to), today my mom insisted that she get her hair and makeup done, so now she looks even more beautiful than usual, which is so unfair.

On the other hand, Kate is just like me. We have the same blonde hair and the same pale skin. We look a lot more like sisters than Elena and I do. So if Kate thinks I look great, then maybe I actually do look somewhat okay.

"Thank you." I smile. I decide I will still have Elena fix the dress, but I don't tell Kate that.

"Is Marisol here yet?" Kate asks. "I'm so excited to meet her!"

"Them," I correct her. "Marisol is nonbinary, remember?"

"Okay, whatever, sorry," Kate says, rolling her eyes ever so slightly. "Are they here or not?"

"No, but they'll be here later for the party. You can meet them then."

Kate looks confused. "Shouldn't they be here early to prepare for the entrance? Aren't they going to escort you?"

I shake my head. "Actually, my friend Nico's gonna do that," I explain. "You remember Nico, right?"

She nods slowly.

I asked Nico to be my escort a long time ago, before he even started dating Rachel. Even though we aren't as close as we used to be, he's still one of my oldest friends and my only long-term guy friend. Our mothers have been best friends since they were in high school, so we've practically known each other since birth. It just made sense to ask him. At least, it made sense at the time.

Once I started dating Marisol, I considered asking them to take Nico's place and do it instead. I know Nico wouldn't have minded, but my dad didn't think it was a good idea. He said he didn't want to cause any drama with my grandparents on my "special night," but I think he just doesn't want to admit that Marisol makes him uncomfortable. Or not Marisol specifically, so much as the idea of me dating anyone who isn't a guy. After some convincing, my mom decided that he had a good point about keeping the night drama-free. Once they outnumbered me, I didn't have a chance.

My parents haven't agreed on much lately, but somehow they managed to agree on that.

Aside from Kate, I haven't told any of my extended family that I'm a lesbian. Dad thought it was best to wait. The news will probably go over a lot better if I don't do a surprise reveal during my sweet sixteen entrance. Although I think he secretly wishes that I'll wait forever.

Kate shrugs. "I just assumed you'd be telling people by now."

"Oh, uh … no, not yet." I smile and force a slight laugh, trying to act like this is no big deal, but suddenly I feel uncomfortable.

"Your dad's here too, by the way," my mom interjects, taking advantage of the sudden lull in conversation. I'd forgotten she was even here. "I just thought you both should know in case you want to go downstairs to see him." She smiles weakly. It's clear that she's not really thinking about me right now.

It's been months since Elena showed up on our doorstep in tears and asked if she could stay the night. Ever since then, she's been living at our house, instead of at our dad's apartment like she's supposed to be. I guess whatever happened between them must've been really serious, but she hasn't wanted to talk about it.

Whatever their problem is, they better not let it ruin the party.

Elena

38

Every Silver Lining Has A Cloud

Today really should have just been about Jo. I already take up so many of her spaces. We share a bedroom, a school... She shouldn't need to lose half of her sweet sixteen to me as well.

It's not like this party has anything to do with me anyway. It's just the title. Anyone can tell that Jo obviously chose everything.

She said pink is her signature color, so she is wearing a pink dress. She decided that I would wear silver, so we'd match the pink and silver decorations, which, of course, she also chose. She even chose the signature cocktails. Yes, that's cocktails, plural. This sweet sixteen has three signature cocktails (and of course, mocktails, because the majority of the guests aren't even old enough to drink alcohol). There's the Sweet Sixteeni, the Jojito, and the Ellini which are basically just a watermelon martini, a strawberry mojito, and a raspberry bellini. All three are pink, including the one named after me, because Jo even chose *my* signature cocktail. And I let her because I don't care what drinks are served at this party because it's *her* party. It's ridiculous that we're pretending it's anything other than that.

The only thing I tried to give a little bit of input on was the music. I don't care if the whole room looks like someone vomited pink and silver glitter all over it (and it does). I don't care if my dress is ridiculous (and it is). But I do care about the music. If I have to be at this party, there might as well be a few songs playing that I like. She accepted about a third of my suggestions, which is way more than I expected, to be honest. I don't have a problem taking a backseat to Jo on all this. It's her big day. It's like this is Jo's wedding and I'm her least favorite bridesmaid.

I tried to explain that I didn't need a sweet sixteen, and I certainly didn't need to co-opt Jo's, but Meg wouldn't take no for an answer. She always does her best to treat me the same way she treats Jo, as if I am her actual daughter who has always been part of her family instead of the surprise stepdaughter she met less than a year ago.

I appreciate it. Really, I do. But sometimes, I wish there was less for me to appreciate. I don't deserve to be treated this well after upending her life. She's not my mom. She's not even really my stepmom anymore because she and my father are separated. She shouldn't have to do all this for me.

Looking back, I wish I hadn't gone to their house the night my father and I had our big fight. I said I didn't know where else to go, which felt true at the time, but in hindsight, there were plenty of other places I could have gone. Ren and his dad definitely would have let me stay over. I probably could've gone to any of my friends' houses. Even Levi would have let me in, although that might have felt too weird. The last (and first and only) time I slept at his house was the night that he stopped Dylan from doing the unthinkable. He helped me then; I know he would've helped me again. Although his help probably would have made me feel as guilty as Meg's help does. My friendship with Levi is weird. I'm not sure if it could ever feel completely normal.

But I didn't go to him or any of my other friends. I went to Meg. Now she is stuck taking care of me because my father won't.

"Are you excited?" Ren asks, snapping me back to reality.

"I guess so."

As we stand in the back room waiting for the grand entrance, all I can think is that I shouldn't even be here.

"Come on Elena, you know this is pretty cool." I think Ren is just excited to be at a sweet sixteen. He didn't have a lot of friends before I moved here and the friends he did have won't be turning sixteen for another year. "Although I guess you'd probably rather be here with someone else." He looks down at his shoes.

"You're my best friend," I reassure him. "There's no one I'd rather be here with. I just don't really want to be here at all."

He gives his signature sad smile. The one he gives when he's trying to make everyone think he's happy instead of upset about something he'll never, ever talk about. I don't know what's upsetting him today, but even if I ask, he probably won't tell me.

I think that's what makes our friendship work. We can tell each other anything, but we don't. Or at least we don't have to. He hasn't pressured me to talk about the fight I had with my father so I haven't pressured him to talk about ... whatever it is that he's avoiding talking about.

"I'm so happy you're here," I say as I give his hand a little squeeze.

He smiles. "Me too."

Jo

39

Sugar And Spice And Everything Nice

I can hear our guests filling the banquet hall, and suddenly, I feel like I can barely breathe. I glance over at Elena. She looks perfectly calm, talking and laughing with Ren. I wish I could be more like her. She's going to have a great time at this party—*my* party—and I'll probably be too stressed out to enjoy it.

Sometimes I wonder if Elena is afraid of anything. She never seems to get nervous, even in extreme situations, which we both know she's been through her fair share of. She would never panic about a silly party.

I feel a hand on my shoulder, so I turn around.

"You okay?" Nico asks.

I nod, but he doesn't buy it for a second. We've known each other long enough that he can tell when I'm completely full of shit.

"What's wrong?" he continues. "Tonight's gonna be awesome. You know that, right?"

"Yeah, I guess." I take a seat on a nearby bench and look down at the floor so he won't see that I'm still lying.

He sits down next to me. "You don't have to be so nervous."

"I'm not nervous."

"Sure you're not," he says sarcastically. At first, I think he's mocking me, but when I glance back at him, I see that he's looking at me with genuine concern, like he actually cares about whatever it is that I'm going through right now.

Nico and I aren't particularly close. In fact, we aren't close at all. Not anymore. The only reason we ever hung out as kids was because our moms were best friends. Now, whenever I see him, it's usually just because he's my friend's boyfriend, not because he's my friend. Even when I asked him to be my escort, it was really more like my mom asked his mom, and she probably guilt-tripped him into agreeing. I highly doubt he would have agreed if he had a choice. I think he just considers me an acquaintance he's forced to be around sometimes.

I sigh. "It just feels like today isn't going how it's supposed to."

"What do you mean?"

I shrug, although I know exactly what I mean. When my family and I started planning this party, everything was so different. My parents weren't separated. Casey was still my best friend. I didn't know I had a half-sister. No one knew I was a lesbian, not even me really. I mean, I guess I always knew, but I wasn't ready to admit it to myself, let alone anyone else.

When we first started planning this party, life still felt easy.

"Is this about Marisol?" he asks. "I know you'd probably rather have her—sorry, *them*—here instead of me."

I shake my head. "That wouldn't have been a good idea."

"Why not? I thought your parents were cool with it and everything."

"They are," I assure him. "It's just that the rest of my family doesn't know yet and my dad thinks I should wait a bit longer to tell them. I mean, his parents are very traditional. I'm not sure what they'd say. It could ruin the whole night."

"Oh." His demeanor changes suddenly. He somehow looks smaller. "I didn't realize you still had problems like that. I'm sorry."

"It's fine. Marisol probably wouldn't have wanted to do it anyway."

That gets Nico to smile. "Yeah, they don't exactly seem like the type to be into this kind of thing. You guys are pretty … different."

Before I have a chance to really think about what he just said, someone comes around to inform us that it is time to line up for our entrances. Nico stands and extends his hand to me like I'm a princess getting out of a carriage to go to a ball. It feels like an odd allusion to an alternate universe where my life went the way I thought it would. As a little kid, when I pictured my sweet sixteen, I figured I'd have a boyfriend, some amazing lifelong friends, and a happy family, but that just wasn't in the cards for me. I guess not everything can go according to plan.

40

No Man Is An Island

I might not be good at many things, but I like to think of myself as someone who is good with words. But there are no words I could use to fully describe just how much Elena Mariana Flores does not want to be here tonight.

One would have to completely lack observational skills and situational awareness not to notice that Elena is miserable. If she could will the floor to crack open and swallow her up whole, she would. I have to keep reminding myself that she is unhappy, not because she doesn't want to be here with me, but because she just doesn't want to be here at all. Although, if I'm being honest, she probably wouldn't mind being here with someone else. I don't say that to be down on myself, even though I am usually pretty down on myself. I say that because I know she couldn't exactly ask her secret boyfriend to be her escort, even if he's not very secret at all. I think the only people who still believe their relationship is a secret … are them.

"Try to enjoy it," I tell her, knowing that nothing I say right now will have any effect on her mood in any way whatsoever.

It's times like these that I wonder if I'm not a good enough friend to her. A good friend would be able to make her feel better, but I can't do that. I'm useless when it comes to things like that. It is one of the many things I am not good at.

Maybe I'm just out of practice at being a good friend because I haven't had anyone to be a good friend to in so long. Elena is the first real friend I've had since I was in seventh grade.

I glance over at Nico without realizing I'm doing it. Luckily, he's too busy talking to Jo to notice me. Maybe I was naïve for thinking that Nico and I would always be friends. I'm not that naive anymore. It would be nice to believe that Elena and I could be friends forever, but eventually, I'll do something to ruin it, just like I ruined everything with Nico. It's hard to believe I haven't ruined it already.

I thought, for sure, that I had when I kissed her a few months ago. I don't even like her like that. Why do I do such foolish things? Through some incredible stroke of luck, I didn't scare her off, and we are still friends. Now, I am determined to be as great of a friend as possible for as long as possible. I never want her to start hating me the way Nico does.

"Earth to Ren." Elena snaps me out of my dramatic internal monologue. "We have to line up now."

"Oh, right." I get up and stand behind Jo and Nico. I wonder if there was any discussion about who would enter first. Jo probably didn't give Elena a say in the matter, but Elena doesn't seem to care that she's second because Elena doesn't seem to care about any of this.

"Are you ready?" I ask, putting on a smile.

"No," she replies instantly, but then a sense of realization hits her face, and she tries to cover. "I mean, yeah. I'm ready. Let's do this!"

I would find her crazy overcorrection somewhat comical if I didn't know that she is putting on this facade to hide how sad she really is. I want to ask her about it, but I always fear pushing her away. She has a tendency to run and hide when she feels cornered. Sometimes metaphorically, sometimes literally.

"I can tell that you're kind of stressed." I try to choose my words carefully, but nothing ever comes out of my mouth quite as eloquently as it is in my head. "Are you just stressed about the party or are you stressed about..." I hesitate, unsure how I should end this question, "...something else?"

"It's just the party," she lies, looking down at the floor.

Obviously, I know she's lying. And she knows that I know she's lying. But I don't know if she wants me to pretend I don't know she's lying or if she wants me to press her to tell the truth.

She hasn't spoken to me at all about her dad and the fight they had, even though it occurred months ago. I feel like I should continue to try to find out what happened, but I already tried that with no success. Eventually, I stopped trying. I don't want to push her to talk about it before she's ready. At least, that's the main reason I haven't pried deeper. There's also a second reason, a more selfish reason. I'm afraid if I push her to talk about her dad, she will, in turn, push me to talk about my disastrous family life.

So, instead, I pretend that I don't know she's lying. Does that make me a bad friend? I want to be a good friend, but I'm not sure if I even know how.

41

Pretty In Pink

Sweet sixteens are actually kind of stupid if you think about it. Why should this birthday be any more special than any other birthday? It's not even a round number. And why is it called a *sweet* sixteen? There's nothing that sweet about being sixteen. Sixteen is a terrible age. You still can't drink alcohol, or smoke cigarettes, or buy a lottery ticket, or vote. In some places, you can get your driver's license, but not here. So that really doesn't seem like a good enough reason to throw a giant party like this. It's excessive.

I know that tonight is important to Jo. I'm trying to play the role of a supportive partner, but I just don't understand her at all sometimes.

I impatiently tap my fingers on the table I'm seated at with the rest of our friends, as we wait for Jo and Elena to make their grand entrance. What kind of party needs a grand entrance anyway? It's as if they're being presented to society as part of some twisted debutante ball. Of course, they're both being escorted by guys in some bullshit display of heteronormative tradition. Elena is being escorted by Ren Hayashi, who she isn't even dating. One, because he's gay. Two, because we all know who Elena actually likes. Or at least I know. She's not as good at keeping a secret as she thinks.

Jo is being escorted by Nico Roma, a guy who isn't even that nice to her and is dating someone else. And Jo is also dating someone else. Me! Fifty percent of the people up there are gay, but they're walking down the aisle together like they're about to get married. It's actually kind of gross when you think about it.

"Are you okay?" Ollie asks. I must be making a face if even he can see right through me.

"Of course I am," I lie. "Isn't this great?" I don't know if he is actually convinced or just humoring me, but either way, he shrugs his giant shoulders and smiles, turning back to his plate which is piled high with tiny hot dogs and mini quiches.

No one could really blame me for being irritated by all of this, right? These kinds of parties are ridiculous. It's not my scene at all. Everything is pink and sparkly, even Jo herself.

I watch her and Nico walk through the banquet hall, holding hands. She gives me a little wave as she passes our table. I wave back, putting on a fake smile.

Jo is dressed in a light pink, glittery, poofy dress like a pretty pretty princess. Her normally straight blonde hair has been curled into golden ringlets around her shoulders, and she's wearing a bit too much makeup, which I guess you're supposed to do at an event like this.

She looks beautiful, of course. She always looks beautiful. Still, I feel like she's completely overdone it. This is a birthday party, not a coronation. Who does she think she is? I can't believe I am actually dating someone who would be into something like this.

Elena is wearing a very similar dress, which I'm sure was Jo's doing. I can't imagine she'd pick out anything like that herself. I doubt Elena wanted to match the decorations.

She looks like she doesn't really want to be here either. It *is* kind of weird. For one, her actual birthday isn't for months. And it's got to be awkward sharing a sweet sixteen with someone you didn't even know existed a year ago. Plus, Elena hates to be the center of attention and things have been weird with her family since … well, since she learned they were her family in the first place. But they've been extra weird the last few months. She hasn't told us much about what is going on, but it clearly isn't good.

Honestly, I'm surprised they're even having a sweet sixteen, considering all the drama they've been through together. But then again, I can't understand why anyone would want to have a sweet sixteen in the first place. I didn't have one. Zeke didn't have one. Ollie didn't have one. Even Violet isn't having one and her mom did everything she possibly could to convince her. Her mom is a lot like Jo in that way. She loves all this girly shit, but Violet doesn't. She's more like me in that way.

Jo and Elena finish making their rounds and join us at the table.

"Hey, birthday girls," Zeke says in a sing-song voice. "Time to dance!" He grabs Elena's hand with one hand and Jo's with the other and pulls them both toward the dance floor. I reluctantly follow. I don't want to ruin the night for everyone else, but it's really hard for me to pretend that this whole thing isn't idiotic.

"You look beautiful," I tell Jo. She blushes. I notice she's wearing the gold heart-shaped locket I gave her for Christmas, even though it doesn't quite match the pink and silver theme. Now I feel kind of guilty. She deserves to feel special tonight.

"What did you think of the entrance?" Jo asks in a small but hopeful voice.

"Oh, it was great! Everything was perfect. What an awesome party."

I hope I sound convincing.

Kevin

42

Good Old Family Values

When Joanne told me that she was a lesbian, I didn't know how to react. I have nothing against gay people. I just never imagined that my daughter was one of them. I'm trying my best to be supportive, but I'm not sure if I know how. My parents are very traditional and they raised me to be that way too. I don't want Joanne to be unnecessarily embarrassed in front of everyone, especially not on a day like today.

They're still recovering from the news that I have an illegitimate daughter from a past relationship. I love Elena of course, but my family doesn't believe in premarital sex and they *really* don't believe that children should be born out of wedlock. That's why

Meg and I got married when we learned she was pregnant with Joanne. Because I'd always been told that that's what you're supposed to do. I didn't know that Maria was already pregnant with Elena. I couldn't have ever predicted that would happen.

But now she's here and my private business is public. Elena and I can't escape the prying and judgmental eyes of the Reillys, but Joanne still has a chance to keep her private business *private*. I don't want her to throw away that option on a whim.

That's why I told her not to ask her girlfriend to be her escort. Not because I don't approve of the relationship, but because I know my parents wouldn't. What would they say? What would everyone think? I just didn't want her to cause a scene.

This night is supposed to be all about Joanne—I mean Joanne and Elena. I didn't want the party to be ruined by my mother and father saying something that offended her. They're not bad people. They're just old-fashioned. They're traditional. They're set in their ways. They're not going to understand something like two girls dating. They're certainly not going to understand the whole non-binary thing. I still don't even understand it. Keeping it all a secret is the best way to protect Joanne.

"What a lovely entrance," my mother leans in and says to me. "Joanne looks beautiful."

"For the price of those dresses, they better look great." I chuckle.

"Of course, Elena looks good." She gestures toward her own dress. "Some of us need to pick our clothing more carefully to go with our skin tones. But you know those people look good in any color."

I flinch as she calls Elena "those people." This is her granddaughter she's talking about.

"You look great, Mom."

"Is Joanne dating that handsome young man?"

"I don't think so, Mom."

"Oh well, it's probably for the best. He doesn't look Irish. Probably Italian."

"Yes, he's Italian, Mom. You've met him a few times. That's Sal and Angela's son," I remind her. "You remember Angela, Meg's best friend from high school."

"Oh, I can't be expected to keep track of everyone you and that Meg knew in high school."

"You've met her dozens of times. She was the maid of honor at our wedding."

"That was such a rushed wedding. Who could even remember anything?" She crosses her arms. "And look how it all turned out."

I need a break from her, so I get up and head over to the bar.

"Scotch, rocks."

"I'm so sorry, sir, we don't have any scotch tonight," says the bartender, who barely looks older than Joanne and Elena.

"Do you have *any* kind of whiskey?"

"No, unfortunately, we don't. Would you like to try the Jojito? Or the Ellini?"

I sigh. "Vodka tonic?"

"Coming right up, sir."

This is going to be a long night.

Elena

43

Of Course I'm Not Happy

I think I might actually be having a good time. I have barely left the dance floor since the grand entrance. It's a great way to avoid thinking about your problems. I highly recommend it. The only downside is that I'm starting to feel absolutely exhausted. But I can't leave the safety zone where I'm surrounded by my friends. If I do, I'll have to deal with Meg trying to force me into a conversation with my father. Or worse, I'll have to talk to any member of his extended family. It's definitely a lot better to stay here listening to a pop song I sort of know and watching my friends jump around like idiots. Eventually, the music shifts to something softer, and the deejay announces that it's time to line up for the buffet, so everyone begins to exit the dance floor. I guess that means I also have to.

I stick close to my friends, using them as human shields. None of them quite know why I'm avoiding my father, but they know enough to be down to help me do it, no questions asked.

"Are you having fun?" Ollie smiles a big, goofy grin as he shovels pasta onto his plate.

I smile genuinely. "Yeah. Yeah, I think I am."

"You *think*?" Ren teases.

I nudge him with my elbow. "Shut up. I'm having fun. I am."

"Good," Brooke says, putting her arm around me and pulling me into a hug. I'm glad she and I have become such great friends, finally, considering how rocky our relationship used to be. She's a really good person to be around, always there to comfort everyone, make us laugh, and cheer us up. Her friendship is one I'd really like to keep.

I realize how truly lucky I am to have each of these people in my life. I didn't think I would find a group of friends as great as my one back home in Miami, but I did. Meg had suggested I invite some of my old friends to come to the party, but I didn't want anyone to feel pressured to spend the money on a flight to New York. Maybe I can visit them this summer instead. I also didn't want them to see how toxic things are with my father. At least my friends here pretend not to notice, even if I know they do. I could not have gotten through the past few months without them.

I look down at my plate, which is loaded up with a bunch of different foods that Jo picked out. I miss my mother's cooking. The lights begin to dim and I realize that the slideshow Meg has prepared is starting. She'd asked me for photos from my childhood a while ago, and I'd given her some, but I still expected it to mainly focus on Jo. I should've known that, with Meg in charge, that wouldn't be the case.

It opens with side-by-side baby pictures of each of us, which fade into a photo of us together from this past Christmas Eve. Various transition effects take us through dozens of photos from over the years. Most of the pictures of me were taken since I moved here (which makes sense because I didn't really give Meg much to work with) but there are also some of me with my Miami friends and some of me as a little kid. I notice that there are even more than just the ones I gave her. I think she must have reached out to my friends for help. There are a few photos of me with my mom, which makes me tear up a bit. I wish she was here. Or really, I wish neither of us was here, and we were both somewhere else entirely, together.

There are a lot more childhood photos of Jo, from holiday gatherings, dance recitals, family vacations, and so much more. I feel a lump forming in my throat when yet another photo of young Jo smiling in our dad's arms appears on the screen. It seems like he was a really good dad to her.

Growing up, I never really cared that I didn't have a father. My mom was amazing, so why would I have ever needed anything more? But sitting here watching a montage of Jo growing up with our dad and me growing up without one, I think about how unfair this all is. I deserved to have that. I deserved a dad who came to all of my piano recitals, and took me trick-or-treating, and brought me on family vacations. I deserved all of that. And now that I'm here, now that there is finally a chance for me to have that, he still won't be the dad I deserve.

The song playing in the video is fairly quiet, so it draws the attention of everyone on our side of the banquet hall when I abruptly slide my chair out and stand up, but I don't even care. I run out of the room as fast as I can. I just need to be anywhere else but here.

I don't realize that I'm being followed until the door doesn't slam behind me. I turn around to find that all of my friends ran out to the lobby as well, even Jo. They all came after me.

Jo pushes her way to the front of the group and wraps me in a tight hug.

"I'm sorry," I say. "This is stupid. Go back inside. I don't want to ruin your party."

"*Our* party," Jo corrects me. "I'm not going back in until I know you're okay." I stare at her incredulously. There's no way she's willing to miss her party for me.

"I'm fine."

"You're obviously not fine," Ren says, coming closer to me.

"Is this about your mom?" Brooke asks.

"It's not about her," I whisper.

"Then what is it?"

Zeke walks forward and holds my hand. I look up into his eyes and then back at everyone else. They're all standing there worried about me. They left the party just to make sure I was okay. And they actually care. So why have I been keeping this all bottled up inside?

"A few months ago, my father and I got into this really big fight. The whole time I've lived here, I've felt like there was this wall between us. I thought it was all in my head, but one night I just snapped. I wanted to know why he kept pushing me away." The tears start falling uncontrollably. "We argued for a while. He claimed that wasn't what he was doing, but I insisted that it was. I said it didn't feel like he even wanted to be my dad." My voice breaks as the story becomes nearly impossible to continue. "And then he finally admitted it. He doesn't. He doesn't want to be my dad at all."

Jo looks like she's about to cry, too. "Elena, that can't be true."

"It is," I insist. "He said it. He tried to take it back afterward, but he said it."

I remember the night perfectly. His words are burnt into my mind. So is the way his face looked when he said it. It might've been the first truly honest thing I'd ever heard him say.

"There's too much pain here!" he'd shouted. "Every time I look at you, all I feel is pain. It's torture! How can you expect me to pretend like nothing is wrong and I'm happy you're here? Of course I'm not happy you're here!"

His words hung in the air, but his face softened immediately. I saw the regret in his eyes. "Elena, that came out wrong," he claimed. "I didn't mean it like that."

But he did. I know he did. Now, the truth is out there, and it can't be unsaid. I can't even blame him for how he feels. At least now I know there's no point hoping for him ever to be the dad I need. He won't. He doesn't even want to.

Meg

44

We Are The Choices We Make

I glare at Kevin, anger seething through me. I storm across the room and grab onto his arm. "Outside. Now."

He gives me an odd look. "What's going on?"

"We need to talk," I insist. "Come with me."

He doesn't move, so I take matters into my own hands and pull his arm until he's forced to follow me out.

"Jesus, what's gotten into you?"

"You have to get it together. Now."

He sighs. "I'm doing my best here, Meg. Same as you."

I shake my head. "No, you're not." I scoff. "I don't think you're trying at all anymore. Do you know what Jo just told me? Elena was just out here crying!"

"She was?" he asks. "What happened?"

"You happened!" I shout. "You hurt her, Kevin. Can't you see that? The things you said to her are eating her up inside. But you wouldn't know that because you haven't been there!" I turn away. I can't even stand to look at him anymore.

"Hey!" He puts his hand on my shoulder and forces me to turn to face him again. "We both agreed that her staying with you and Joanne was best for her."

"I thought you meant for a few days, just to give you some space away from each other so you could both cool off," I explain. "But Kevin, it's been months. She needs her father back."

He sits down on a bench near the wall and drops his head. He's quiet for a long time, but I won't back down. I just stand there, staring at him, until he dares to speak again.

"I don't know how to be her dad." His voice is so quiet I can barely hear it.

"Well, figure it out."

He looks up at me, clapping his hands together. "Why? She doesn't need me. She's better off without me."

"Why would you think that?" I sit down next to him.

"I'm not her father," he says, closing his eyes. "Not really. Not in any way that matters."

"Don't do that. Don't do that self-pitying bullshit."

"It's true," he insists. "I was never there for her. How am I supposed to just pick up and start now? All I can think about when I'm with her is all the things I did wrong … all the things I missed."

"If you're so worried about that, why do you continue to do the wrong things and miss even more?"

"That's not fair."

"You can't change the past, Kevin." I place my hand on his knee. "But you can try to make up for it. And you've got to start somewhere."

He takes a deep breath and turns his head away from me. "It's just so hard." He turns back to look at me again and I see that there are tears in his eyes. "It's so hard to look at her when all I see is Maria looking back at me."

"I know it's hard for you," I admit, "but I'll bet anything that what she's going through is harder. You need to be the adult in the situation and be there for her, even when it's hard."

"I know," he says. "I know." We sit in silence next to each other for a while before he speaks again. "Does it ever feel like no matter what we do, it's the wrong thing?"

I chuckle. "Yeah. I feel like that most of the time."

"Why do we keep torturing ourselves?"

I blink, waiting for him to continue, but he never does. "What do you mean?"

"Our separation. We're trying so hard to make things work between us, but doesn't it feel wrong? We've never really worked, have we?"

I bring my hands to my temples, not believing what I'm hearing. "If you've always felt that way, why did we get married in the first place?" He opens his mouth to speak, but I cut him off before he can. "Don't try to say you loved me. I know that's a lie."

He sighs and takes a seat on the bench. "I wanted to do right by you. To do what was best for Jo."

I shake my head. "You were worried about what people would think."

"That's not—"

"Please don't try to rewrite history. You didn't do it for Jo. Or for me. You did it for you." I take a deep breath. "But I agreed. All this time I've done what you wanted. I've played the part of the dutiful wife and co-parent. I did everything you asked of me."

He hesitates, but I don't remove my stare until he finally speaks. "I'm not so sure if we did the right thing. I mean, don't you ever regret it?"

"Of course I do, sometimes, but it is what it is."

"There was someone else, right?"

His question takes me by surprise. In all these years, he's never asked me that.

"I have never been unfaithful to you."

"No, I know that. I mean … before. There was someone else? Someone better? Someone … right?" By the look on his face, I can tell that he already knows the answer. Maybe he's always known.

"Of course there was," I admit, at a lower volume than I even knew was possible.

He smiles softly. "Who was he?"

"What does that matter?"

"Do you still think about him?"

I almost laugh, just out of sheer confusion. How is this conversation even happening? "Sure. Sometimes."

He closes his eyes and takes a deep breath in. "I've thought about Maria every single day for the past sixteen years."

I blink. "I didn't keep you from her," I remind him. "In fact, if I'd have known, I would've told you to go back to her. The only one stopping you was you."

"I know."

"*You* were the one who insisted we get married. I never pressured you. I said we didn't have to. I said I'd be fine, Jo would be fine, but you said we *had* to get married."

"I know!"

I look at him and my expression softens. He knows he's the only one to blame. And that blame is killing him.

"Kevin—"

"I did what I thought was right. I made my decision and never went back." He looks down for a moment but quickly looks back up to meet my gaze. "I'll never see her again. And that's my fault. We built a pretty good life together, but we both know we made the wrong choice."

I put my hand on his arm and quietly ask him, "What was she like?"

"She was incredible." He smiles. It's a bittersweet smile, but it's a smile nonetheless. "I mean, she was the kindest person I'd ever met. She cared about everyone. Really, truly cared. And she loved to laugh. She loved to make me laugh. She just never wanted to take anything too seriously. She looked at the world and somehow managed to see through all the bad. She noticed things. Amazing little things." His voice begins to crack. "And she was beautiful. She was so, so beautiful."

"She sounds like a wonderful woman."

"She was." He shakes out his body, collecting himself. "What about him?"

I shake my head. "It doesn't matter."

"Did you love him?"

"What difference does it make?"

He shrugs. "I just want to know. Isn't it time we finally talk about this stuff?"

I guess it is time we both start telling the truth. I lean back against the wall and just listen to the thumping of the music coming from the next room.

"Yes." I turn my head to look at Kevin. "I loved him, but that was a long time ago."

"What happened?"

I sigh, debating how much to reveal. "He had to move away and we didn't think the whole long-distance thing was going to work out. We agreed that whenever he came back, if it was meant to be, it would be. And for a while, I did believe that it was meant to be. But I guess it wasn't."

"You should tell him."

I laugh. "What?"

"You still love him. I can tell. Maybe he feels the same way. Maybe it *is* meant to be."

"Kev, this all happened ages ago. It's been twenty years. It's ancient history. You keep talking about how you made your choices. Well, I made mine."

"But there's still time to fix your mistakes. You can change your mind." He grabs onto one of my hands and looks deep into my eyes. "Meg, it's too late for me. But for you, maybe it doesn't have to be. Maybe you can make a different choice now. The right choice."

I don't say anything.

"I was never the one for you, but he might be." He smiles, and it's a true smile. "Why not give it a chance?"

I take a deep breath in and out. "Does this mean it's really over? Are we giving up on the trial separation and officially getting divorced?"

"Don't you think we will both be happier if we do?"

I pause to think about it, but I already know the truth. I've always known what would actually make me happy. "Yeah. We probably both will."

"Then yes," he says. "It's really over. We can tell the girls tomorrow."

We smile at each other. And everything feels lighter.

Kevin

45

It Is Always Darkest Before The Dawn

"Elena." I put my hand on her shoulder. "Could we talk? Please?"

She turns around to face me. Her friends glare at me. "What is there to talk about?"

"I want to apologize," I say softly. She doesn't respond, so I address the table instead. "Could I steal my daughter away for a few minutes?"

A few of the kids look to Elena for guidance. Some of them just keep glaring at me.

"It's fine, guys." Elena nods. "I'll be right back."

She begrudgingly follows me out of the banquet hall and into the lobby. Elena crosses her arms and avoids eye contact. God, she looks so much like her mother.

"Do you want to sit?" I ask.

She shrugs but heads over and sits down on a nearby bench, so I do as well.

"It's true," I start. "I'm not happy that you're suddenly here after years of me not even knowing about you."

She scoffs. "Great apology."

"I'm not finished," I assure her. "I'm not happy about the circumstances because, frankly, they're bad circumstances."

"Are you going somewhere with this?"

"I'm overjoyed to finally know you and have you here." I choose my next words carefully. I know I have to say this just right. "But the reason you're here is awful. I loved your mother. I can't believe she's gone." I take a deep breath, almost losing track of my point. "Every time I look at you, all I can think about is what could've been. It breaks my heart that I wasn't there for you both for the first fifteen years of your life." I notice that her eye makeup is smudged around the edges, likely from tears she cried earlier, and I hate myself because I know it was because of me. "It's hard to be your father. Not because I don't want to be, but because I don't know how to make up for all the time that I missed."

"So you decided not to even try at all?" Her voice is a little strained.

"I'm still figuring out how to do this."

"But there's nothing for you to figure out," she insists. "I saw all those pictures of you and Jo. You were a good dad to her. Just be one to me, too."

I sigh. "You're right."

"I wish you'd been there," she admits. "You weren't, and I've made my peace with that, but you're here now. *I'm* here now."

"I know. I've been selfish. I was so caught up in my own grief that I didn't think about how much harder this all must be for you. I should've been helping you through it, not making it worse. I can never apologize enough for what I've done and what I've said." I start to tear up a little myself. "I can never make it up to you. But you're right that I haven't even been trying. And if it's not too late, I'd like to finally start."

I put my hand on her shoulder again, as some sort of test, I guess, to see if she'll let me. She looks at me, and she still doesn't smile, but she looks just a little bit less sad, and that's enough for now.

"I guess it's not too late."

I let out a sigh of relief and force myself to choke back any tears that had been threatening to fall. "Well, uh…" I'm unsure if I should push my luck, but I think about what Meg said. I'm the parent. I have to go the extra mile and extend the olive branch because it isn't Elena's responsibility to fix everything broken between us. It's mine. "What do you think about maybe moving back into my apartment ... if that's what you want ... if you're ready?"

She fiddles with her thumbs, and I think I've gone too far, asked for too much, too soon. But then she speaks, without looking at me, and so quietly that I can barely hear her.

"I think that's a good place to start."

Zeke

46

Sixteen Candles

Elena doesn't notice me when I come out to the lobby, so I don't say anything at first. She looks peaceful, more so than I've seen her look in a while. I touch her shoulder gently. She turns around and smiles at me.

"Hey, I just wanted to make sure you were okay."

She lets out a deep breath. "I'm okay." She often doesn't mean it when she says that, but this time, I believe that it's the truth.

I smile. "Good." I glance around, not quite sure where I should look.

"Do you want to sit?" she offers. "Unless you want to get back to the party, which you probably do, so don't worry about it, forget I asked." She looks away from me. I can't tell if she's blushing or if it's just her makeup.

I sit down and place my hand on hers, slowly intertwining our fingers. "It's not much of a party without you anyway."

She looks down and I know exactly what she's thinking. We're supposed to be friends, but I'm not acting like a friend right now. Because I don't want to be her friend.

"You look beautiful."

She's still not looking at me, but I think I see her roll her eyes. Then she smiles gently.

"Thanks."

I wonder if I shouldn't have said that. She doesn't really look like herself with her hair all done up and wearing so much makeup. She definitely didn't pick out that dress. Still, even under all that, she looks amazing. She always looks amazing.

I shift a little bit closer to her even though I know I shouldn't. She doesn't move away from me. I use the hand that isn't holding hers to brush a small piece of hair out of her face. We look deep into each other's eyes and against my better judgment, I begin to lean in closer.

"Don't."

I quickly retreat, shifting away from her. "I'm sorry." I'm an idiot. What was I thinking?

"We can't keep doing this," she whispers. "I said that last time. We really can't, okay?"

I clasp my hands together and put my elbows on my knees. "Okay." I have to respect what she wants, no matter how badly I want something else. She's already been through so much; I don't want to be the cause of any more pain in her life.

I look at her, hoping it's not too obvious how sad I am. Before I can say anything else, she leans forward and grabs my face, pressing our lips together. At first, I'm too stunned to think. Then I pull her closer, and for a minute, nothing else exists. But then my thoughts return, and reality hits, so I pull away.

I catch my breath and whisper, "You *just* said we can't keep doing this."

She leans back and covers her face with her hands. "I know."

"Why *can't* we? Would it actually be such a problem if we were together?" I ask. "I really don't think Brooke will care."

She smirks. "Have you met Brooke?"

"Okay, you're right. She'll flip out," I admit, "but then she'll get over it. Eventually."

She shakes her head. "I feel like she and I have finally gotten past everything that happened with Dylan," she explains. "If I start dating her brother, I'll mess that all up again."

I put my arm around her and she rests her head on my shoulder. "I understand. It's not your fault my sister is such a drama queen."

She jabs me lightly in the side and I chuckle softly. I can't see her face, but I can feel that she's smiling. We sit like this for a while. I'm not sure how long. It feels like forever, but at the same time, it doesn't feel nearly long enough.

Levi

47

Timing Is Everything

I sit back down at my table with the rest of my friends.

"That was quick," Parvati says to me. "What happened? Is she okay?"

About a minute ago, I got up and went out to the lobby to check on Elena. I almost followed her when she first ran out during the slideshow, but her entire table got up after her, and I felt like I shouldn't intrude. Then after she eventually came back inside, she left again with her father. I definitely didn't want to intrude then. But after a while, her dad came back in, and she didn't, so I went out to the lobby to check on her. I didn't know she wasn't alone.

"Yeah, I think she's okay," I say. "She's, uh, talking to a friend. I didn't want to interrupt."

Parvati raises her eyebrows, silently waiting for me to continue, but there's nothing else I want to share. She gives up on getting any more information out of me, for now at least. I'm sure she'll force the rest out of me later, when there's less of a crowd. She's always been good at that.

"Poor girl," says Olivia. "I can't imagine not having my mom at my sweet sixteen."

"Oh my God, your sweet sixteen was so much fun," Danielle giggles. She has definitely been sneaking real Jojitos instead of the mocktail version. I give Parvati a look. We've been friends for so long that we can communicate without words. She understands me completely and offers Danielle a glass of water and a dinner roll.

I haven't really hung out with Elena that much since everything that went down with Dylan. It feels like whenever I try to do the right thing, I end up doing something wrong. Even now, I stupidly went to check on her, and she was kissing another guy. She obviously doesn't need my help at all. It was dumb of me to think she would.

I'm not jealous, of course. We're just friends. Elena is great. She's smart and beautiful, but we're just friends. Nothing ever actually happened between us. I mean, she did kiss me once, and I kind of wanted to let her, but I shut it down. She was in no state to be kissing anyone and I didn't want to take advantage of her when she was so vulnerable. After that, I never really got another shot. She's been through a hell of a year.

It's probably for the best, though. Even though we're only two years apart, that gap just feels like a lot when you're in high school. I'm leaving for college in a few months anyway. It would be stupid to try to start anything up at this point. One of us would end up getting hurt, and the last thing I'd ever want to do is hurt her. I want her to be happy. I hope that Zack guy makes her happy. She deserves it.

Parvati seems to sense that I need a distraction because she immediately stands up and announces to the table, matter-of-factly, "I think we need to dance."

Jo

48

Dance Like No One's Watching

"Hey." I sit down next to Marisol, who is pushing food around their plate absentmindedly.

"Hey," they reply without looking up.

"You alright?"

"Yeah."

I can tell they're lying, so I shift my chair to better face them. "No, you're not. What's going on?"

They shrug. "Nothing."

"You can't lie to me on my birthday." I hope they'll smile, but they don't.

"It's not actually your birthday yet."

I roll my eyes overdramatically. "That's a technicality." They still don't seem amused. "But it's my birthday *party*, so you're not allowed to be sad without telling me why."

Marisol tugs at a loose thread on the sleeve of their black suit jacket before finally looking up at me. "It's not important."

"I'll be the judge of that," I insist. "Now talk to me."

Marisol looks away, lets out a deep sigh, and then looks back. "Why didn't you ask me to be your escort?"

I almost laugh. "What?"

"You're my girlfriend. Shouldn't it have been me up there?"

I blink repeatedly, a little surprised. "I didn't think you'd care," I sputter. "I didn't think you'd even want to."

"Of course I wanted to," they say. "Or at least I wanted you to want me to. This whole thing is important to you. And if it's important to you, it's important to me. Why didn't you ask me?"

I hesitate, unsure if I should be honest, but my silence only seems to annoy Marisol even more.

"We've barely spent any time together tonight," they continue. "Sometimes I feel like we're not on the same page … like you don't really want me to be part of your whole world. Like maybe somewhere deep down you still want to pretend you're straight, to pretend you can still have that life."

I shake my head. "That isn't what I want." I don't even register the words until I've already said them. Wasn't I just thinking about this earlier? Wasn't I just wishing that I could have the easy life that I always thought I was supposed to want? Suddenly, everything feels different. Everything seems so clear. That isn't what I want. It truly isn't. I want *this*. I want Marisol.

"I haven't told the rest of my family yet," I explain. "My grandparents, aunts, and uncles, none of them know about us … about me."

Marisol's entire demeanor changes. They unstiffen and all animosity fades away in an instant. "I didn't know that."

"I should have told you. I'm sorry. I didn't want you to think it had anything to do with you. It's just my dad. He said I should wait. He didn't want there to be drama at the party." My breathing shortens slightly, but this time it's not because I'm nervous. Somehow, I feel calmer than I've ever felt. "But I can't blame him entirely. I didn't argue. I should have, but I didn't. I'm so sorry."

"I get it," Marisol assures me. "I mean, you think my lola[15] knows about me?" They almost laugh, but not really. "I guess I just thought it would be different for you. Easier. When you told your mom, she understood immediately. Mine is still … getting there. I

---

[15] "Lola" is the Filipino word for grandmother.

didn't think you had to worry about your family. But I shouldn't have assumed that. I'm sorry."

"I didn't realize you had problems with your mom."

Marisol shrugs. "It's whatever."

I never really thought about how lucky I am to have my mom. I know she will love me no matter what. Even if nothing in my life ever goes as planned, she'll still always be there for me. Not everyone can be who they are, but I can. Some people may never accept me, but the only people who actually matter already do. Anyone who doesn't accept me isn't worth worrying about. So why am I still hiding?

The deejay puts on a slow song and I know what I have to do. I stand up and extend my hand toward my incredible partner.

"Marisol Castillo, may I have this dance?"

They smile. "It's okay, Jo. You don't have to do this."

"I know," I say. "I want to. It would be an honor and a privilege to dance with you tonight."

They blush and bite their lip, averting their glance. When they look back at me, I'm still standing in the same position, looking at them in the same way, waiting for their answer.

Marisol takes my hand, and stands up, smiling just a little bit wider now. I lead them out into the middle of the dance floor, holding them tight as we look into each other's eyes and let the music guide us. I don't know if my family sees us because I don't care. All I care about right now is Marisol.

Younger me thought she knew exactly how her life would play out, but she was wrong. It is so much better than she could've ever imagined. I don't need a boyfriend to be happy. And I definitely don't need a so-called best friend who won't accept me. I have better friends now. And I have Marisol. And that makes me happier than ever.

Maybe my life can be alright, even if it's not the picture-perfect one I thought I should have. Maybe it doesn't matter that my dress didn't fit at my sweet sixteen, or that I had to share my party, or that my sister ran out crying in the middle of dinner because this day was still amazing, even with the bumps along the way.

So maybe it'll also be fine that my family is changing, because sometimes what we plan isn't actually what we need. If my parents decide to stay together, it'll be great. But if they don't, I think maybe it could still be okay.

Nico

49

Dancing In The Wings

When I see Jo and Marisol together on the dance floor, at first I think my eyes must be playing tricks on me. Didn't she tell me she couldn't come out to her entire family? If she's trying to keep it a secret, slow dancing is a pretty risky move.

But then I notice her face and realize that she knows exactly what she's doing. She's ... being herself. She's not worrying about what other people think. I feel stunned. She's not that kind of person. She is the kind of person who always cares what other people think. I know because I'm the same kind of person. That's one thing Jo and I have always had in common.

I was a little surprised when Jo asked me to be her escort. I figured she had plenty of better options, so why did she choose me? Was I her backup plan? We've known each other since we were babies, but we aren't really friends.

We were really close when we were younger, but at some point in elementary school, we learned that boys and girls couldn't be friends anymore, so that was that. I don't think either of us understood why that was the unwritten rule on the playground, but neither of us would ever go against the status quo. We just weren't like that. We cared what other people thought.

Somewhere in the back of my mind, I always kind of thought she and I might end up together. Our parents had been joking about it for years. Even when I was a little kid, they used to call her my girlfriend. When we started high school, I even attempted to flirt with her, but she didn't seem to be interested. So I took the hint and asked out her friend Rachel instead.

I guess now we know why she wasn't interested. And now she doesn't care what other people think. I still do.

I look around the room and try to gauge the reaction from Jo's extended family as they all slowly notice what's happening on the dance floor. Some look surprised. Some seem confused. Some of them are clearly trying very hard (but unsuccessfully) to hide their negative thoughts. A few aren't even trying to hide them at all. Her grandmother looks downright furious. But through it all, Jo doesn't seem to care. She is completely focused on Marisol.

Rachel returns from the ladies room and taps me on the shoulder. "Hey," she says sweetly, "I love this song. Can we dance?"

"Sure babe, whatever you want." I stand up and take her by the hand, leading her to the dance floor, still watching Marisol and Jo.

Maybe after tonight, Jo will think about the consequences of what she's done. Maybe she'll wish she hadn't done it. Maybe she'll go right back to worrying about what other people think. Or maybe she won't regret it all. Either way, right now, she's being braver than I'll ever be. She's doing something I'll never be able to do.

Meg

50

Take A Leap Of Faith

He's right there. He's standing by his car, checking his phone as he waits for his son to finish saying goodbye to his friends. The man I should never have let go of is *right there.*

Kevin lost the one he loved, but the man I love—the man I've always loved—is standing only a few feet away from me. So why am I still standing over here?

"Harry!" I call out.

He looks up from his phone as I run toward him.

"Hi, Meg."

I look into his eyes and take a deep breath. I can't remember the last time my heart was beating this fast, but I can't stop. All those years living right next door to the man I love, knowing we both married the wrong people, unable to do anything about it. I need to do this. Now.

"It's over," I announce.

He checks the time on his phone. "Ren said it didn't end for another ten minutes."

"Kevin and me," I say. "It's over. Officially. We're done. For good."

His lip twitches as he tries his best not to smile. "Really?"

I nod. "He's never been the one for me. You should know that better than anybody."

"I should?"

"You're the one for me. It's always been you. Please tell me it's not too late."

He lets himself smile fully. "Better late than never. So ... now what?"

I shrug. "Whatever we want." I smile. I'm sure I'm blushing, but I don't care.

Harry's eyes scan the rest of the parking lot to see who else is around, but to me, it doesn't really matter anymore. I can't wait any longer. We've already waited long enough. I grab his shirt and pull him closer.

We kiss like we should've been doing all along.

51

Cheers To The Nights We Won't Forget

The remaining party guests have pretty much cleared out by now, meaning it's time to start packing up everything and head home. Jo and I are supposed to be helping, but instead we're picking at the leftover cupcakes. With everything that happened, I sort of missed most of the dinner.

"You know what," Jo says, "I'm actually really glad we got to do this together."

"What? No you're not." I laugh as I lick a dot of bright pink frosting off of my finger.

"Okay, you're right, I'm not." Jo smiles. "But I had fun anyway."

"I actually did too."

"Really? You liked it?"

"Yeah, I did."

"Elena! Jo!" We both turn around to see Ren sprinting toward us. His momentum makes him slide even after he's tried to stop.

Jo and I instinctively move out of his way, but that just sends him flying into the table behind us.

"What's going on?" I ask, helping him regain his balance.

"I saw…" He pauses in an attempt to catch his breath. "They…"

"Use your words." I tell him.

"I…" He breathes heavily.

"Spit it out," Jo snaps, impatiently.

He looks at her and takes one more deep breath. "I just saw my dad kissing your mom."

Jo blinks. She looks at me, but I have nothing helpful to offer. We both look back to Ren for any sort of follow-up information, but he's silent with wide eyes. He looks toward me, then back at Jo, all of us too stunned to say anything else. Finally, Jo breaks the silence.

"What the fuck?"

Acknowledgments

I would like to thank my family for their unwavering love and support, especially my mother, without whom there would not be a book. Thank you to Scott Stein, Kathleen Volk Miller, Cassandra Hirsch, and Harriet Levin Millan from Drexel University. I had stopped writing for a while, but you all helped to reignite this spark in me. *Muchas gracias* to Dr. Jessica Nicholas for making sure that Nico sounded stupid in Spanish, but Elena did not. I also want to acknowledge my friends, my brothers from Phi Sigma Pi, and my neighbors for making my life richer in many ways. In particular, I want to thank the Hewlett-Woodmere community for serving as a loose inspiration for Woodview (although all characters, businesses, places, events, and incidents in the book are fictitious). An extra thanks goes out to anyone who ever invited me to their sweet sixteen, bar or bat mitzvah, or massive house party. Thank you to my beta readers. And finally, I also could not have finished this book if not for the love and cuddles I received from my sweet dog Lily. You're a good girl.

About the Author

Ian Rose Castro (he/they) is a queer Latine author who grew up on Long Island. He was an avid reader as a child, but as he grew older, he often wished he could see more characters like him and his friends in the books he read. He had always loved creative writing, so he decided to try writing his own.

Ian graduated from Drexel University magna cum laude with a B.S. in Music Industry, dual minors in Communication and Business Administration, and a Certificate in Creative Writing and Publishing. He loves to listen to music, binge trashy TV, and cuddle with his dog.